THE AGE OF MIGRATION

THE AGE OF MIGRATION

a novella and stories

KAI MARISTED

wtaw press
Ann Arbor, MI

Cover Art: Evening Light #1448 (2020) by Vicky Colombet. Pigment, oil, alkyd on canvas. Photograph by Christian Koopmans. Courtesy of the artist. © Vicky Colombet

Edited by Peg Alford Pursell
Designed by Jasper Nighthawk
Author portrait © Tom Dodge

ISBN: 979-8-9923690-5-2 (paperback)
ISBN: 979-8-9923690-6-9 (ebook)

Published by WTAW Press

WTAW Press
PO Box 130025
Ann Arbor, MI 48113
www.wtawpress.org

WTAW Press, a not-for-profit literary book publishing press. This publication is made possible by the generous contributions from individual donors, public arts organizations, and private foundations.

For André Dubus II, who lives here still.
And for Chris, always.

Contents

In der Liebe suchen die meisten ewige Heimat.
Andere, sehr wenige aber, das ewige Reise.

In love, most people seek an eternal home.
Others, very few however, the never-ending journey.

—Walter Benjamin, *Einbahnstraße*

The Age of Migration

Charley swipes a sponge over the dinner dishes—hers and Karim's, the girl's, The Goat's—then slots them into the rack to drip. She's not looking at the washing-up, but straight ahead, through her night reflection in the window, vaguely toward the distant crystal-bright heart of Paris. Despite the heat, unnatural for late October, she keeps the windows latched against police sirens and Maghrebi rap and air pollution, level orange. But there's no defense against the soccer match blaring from the next room where Karim and his pal are smoking cigarettes and slurping mint tea.

"Are you trying to wake up the kids?" she says, passing through the smoke-thick salon toward the bedroom. "Could you turn it down, please?"

Karim flashes her his hundred-watt smile, teeth made even whiter by the frame of a luxuriant new black beard, eyes crinkling with sympathy. Otherwise, he doesn't budge. Probably he didn't hear her.

In the bedroom Charley navigates by city glow, the aura of traffic lights and illumination from identical high-rises that surround theirs.

Bracing her arms on either side of the crib she leans down to inhale the warm bread-and-oil scent of Sami's head. Her mouth parts to savor deeply, as cats do. Nothing in the world smells as wonderful as her ten-month-old son. *Here's how you'll grow up in this ghetto of Seine-Saint-Denis, little one.* It's an exhaled thought, an inverted benediction, less than a whisper. *You'll dump the useless school and learn to deal drugs. You'll prey on girls. You'll get hauled up in court and released the same day. You'll look at me with the same blank eyes as the dropouts who watch us down in the streets. You'll be out of my reach.*

On a floor mattress to the left of the parents' bed lies Rachida, Karim's six-year-old niece, curled into a question mark. Charley has tried to fill the empty mother-hole in Rachida's heart.

She holds her breath to hear the children's. Rachida, dreaming, emits snorts and starts, while the baby's sighs flow almost imperceptibly, like lapping waves.

MAÏWENN LIFTED CHARLEY'S hand in hers, peeled open the clenched fingers. Maïwenn's nails were manicured, Charley's jagged. She has never understood the sense of manicures.

"You're not an egotist, cherie. You are the opposite. You'll be rescuing them. It requires courage, okay. But afterward, there is the rest of your life, and theirs."

"But Rachida, she's not even my—"

"No. But Dennis promised to arrange for her! Didn't he?"

"Um." Charley looked away, past her baby carriage to the tree-studded cliffs of the Butte-Chaumont park. A miniature Alpine wilderness on the outskirts of the city, only a twenty-minute bus ride from her gray, steel, and concrete suburb. Hard to believe it had become the HQ of fundamentalist terrorists, but that's what everyone said.

Maïwenn clasped Charley's hand. "Dennis is an American. And an attorney. He is charming like Clooney, no? Okay, laugh! Little idiot, he would die for you! Doesn't the man realize he could have any chick in Paris? Maybe he's an idiot too. But if you don't believe *Dennis*—"

CHARLEY LIFTS THE scarf from the bureau and drapes it around her head as best she can, as The Goat himself insisted on teaching her, right after Karim brought it home. She fumbles with the pins and the slithery cloth, afraid of waking one of the children.

Shutting the bedroom door behind her she announces, "We're almost out of diapers. I have to go down. I'll be quick." Go down: fourteen stories to the Proxi market. If the elevator is working.

The Goat says, "Come here so I can fix that hijab. You actually look ridiculous."

The Goat is in his forties, green-eyed with a wispy, grizzled beard. He is only a self-proclaimed theologian, not a real imam. His visits began soon after Charley moved in with Karim, months before the baby's birth, and now like a blood relative he acts completely at ease touching Charley's long chestnut curls, while teaching her how to hide them.

Karim says, "Let her go, The Goat. What matters is, she's halal. Right? Good girl."

Take that, she thinks. *See? We're a couple.* Karim has always understood her, deep down. He glanced at her—checking her over before letting her enter the public space—but now his gaze has reverted to the Samsung wide-screen, where black and white men with muscular thighs are zigzagging around each other. She waits, pulse pounding in her throat, wanting him to turn and see her again. Really see her.

Wanting him not to turn.

"Need anything? Sure not? I'm off then." Her mouth is dry. She coughs words out like broken eggshells, while one hand pushes down the door latch.

"Wait!"

A bird of prey comes hurtling toward her. His obsidian eyes. His sandalwood perfume. "Here, silly habibi." Ten euros thrust into her hand. "You forgot to ask for money."

MAÏWENN IS INDEPENDENT in her life and in her mind. She has no obligations to anyone. Her adoption never took, she says; the sole moment of mutual joy was mother and daughter seeing the last of each other. Maïwenn attracts eyes everywhere, with her blond hair in cornrows (hell to braid, she says, but easier to keep clean where there's no water), Nefertiti neck, and large, mobile features ever so slightly flattened, as if the artist who drew her had wiped his sleeve over the page. She's a connoisseur of designer labels, foie gras, and champagne who lives on pennies. She teaches self-defense freelance and helps manage humanitarian missions all over the world. She could organize hell itself. Charley has never heard her complain. The darker things look, the more raucous Maïwenn's laughter.

Maïwenn at thirty-six is everything Charley would wish to be, while Charley, just twenty-three, has everything Maïwenn wants. Parents who give a damn. A Sorbonne degree. A man who doesn't cheat on her: *find me another one of those in Paris!* And a child.

Why then—only last week—did Maïwenn again insist on Charley leaving?

"Because I want something more for you, ma 'tite."

"Go on. You want more for me than for yourself?"

"Shit, when you put it that way . . ." A soft chuckle. "But absolutely *yes*! I do." Leaning into the pram that she insisted on pushing as if Charley were sick, "True, little cabbage?" And then, straightening up, "Besides, don't you see? Your relationship is not only going nowhere at this point. It's getting dangerous."

"Oh, please." But Charley's eyes were riveted on Maïwenn's perfectly lipsticked mouth, waiting for her friend's next words.

"It's not only Karim, cherie. Life as we know it is about to go kaboom. Daesch is getting its ass kicked in Syria—you think that's good news? Wait. The volunteer jihadi from France will come home. All trained up. Or—" she glanced around with a glinting grin. "They are here, already."

Charley reached to take back the carriage. "Paris isn't Aleppo. We have laws. And trained-up police."

SUMMONED FROM THE top floor, the elevator shudders out of its coma. A narrow cylinder, an upright fluorescent coffin she ducks into quickly, jabbing the ground floor button. The herky-jerky descent is agonizing. Through the glass door she sees a cluster of boys on the tenth-floor landing, dealing drugs or shaking down apartment dwellers or both. On the third, a family of clandestines huddles under bright filthy quilts despite the heat.

Appear, disappear.

In the still-intact sliver of elevator mirror she encounters a stranger. Framed by the hijab her face looks round as a peach, youthful. The lips full and pale, brows arched high over half-closed eyes, all serenely concealing the storm inside her. She tucks the scarf's folds tighter.

"Really? You brought me a present?"

Karim held out a white bag tied with a red bow, embossed with a logo she didn't recognize. The expression on his face wavered as if reflected in water. She'd seen that look on him once before, when he presented her with the Swarovski ring. The ring flashed now as she dug in the tissue paper to draw out, like a stage magician, a long piece of grainy yet slithery cloth.

"A scarf? It's—really fantastic. Thank you!" A hideous color. The beige of dead flesh. *Go on, kiss him.* "Thank you, my love."

"As I promised, habibi. Your first hijab. Silk jersey, the best. Here, let's see it on!" He studied her, then stroked her cheek. "Do this little thing I ask. Not for you, for me. Although soon, you won't want to be without it. Else you'll feel naked out on the street." He smiled, as if at a joke between them.

Later she would ask herself over and over: what is the difference between wearing a ring and wearing a hijab? A riddle that seemed trivial at first.

When she met Karim, he scoffed at what he called the third monotheism, which he blamed for turning the Arab civilization, after its glorious flowering of art and mathematics, into a repressive theocracy ripe for colonial takeover. Around his family he sang a different song, but would she have wanted him to disrespect his parents? And any twinges of misgiving Charley may have felt about putting on the ring were swept away by her own parents, old-time lefties over the moon at the prospect of an alliance between their daughter and a politically active son of the immigration.

Two years ago, as they walked arm in arm in the forest of Vincennes, Charley told Maïwenn, "My folks don't care that he's jobless. I swear they see me as their personal reparation for the Algerian War. Like the Catholics buying an indulgence for their sins? Shouldn't I feel angry? Instrumentalized? But you know what? I love to see them happy about me, even if—"

Maïwenn reached to tap Charley's head lightly. "You and your over-intellectualizing! Anyway, it's not like you two are getting married. It's only the civil contract. For your protection, so he can't just walk out. I mean, suppose you get pregnant?"

"Not a chance. He hasn't got a job."

"With his looks he'll soon find one. Besides, I think you're in love?"

Charley looked down at her rough nails. She felt the opposite of a blush: all the blood had drained from her face. That thing Karim and she made together, that fusion, a long explosion of light *like a star being born*—so they both agreed—so overwhelming that for days afterward she avoided even looking at him, not wanting to inadvertently arouse his desire. Because she hadn't yet been whole again.

In the lobby the lights are smashed out. Shards of glass sparkle everywhere, fallen stars. The blue rotors of a fleet of police cars bloom on the walls. She nearly goes flying when her foot rolls over a bottle on the ground.

The Proxi's narrow aisles overflow with canned goods, soft drinks, chips, soap, diapers, rotting plantains, all the necessities of ghetto life. She stumbles over the crates and pallets and hands the Tunisian a five-euro bill in exchange for the powder-blue suitcase stowed behind his counter.

Money is the least of her worries. There are two thousand euros in crisp fifties hidden in her Lancel purse. She used to keep all her stuff—books, snacks, makeup—in an old backpack, but in Maghrebi culture it's a man's honor to dress his woman well. She, Karim, Rachida, and the baby live in a three-room dump, but her dress and leggings come from the Galerie Lafayette.

WHEN DID THEIR life begin to change course? In little increments like degrees on a compass, and too gradually for Charley to put her finger on any starting point.

While she was pregnant, Karim started taking free Arabic lessons (her Sorbonne version was hopelessly academic, he said, incomprehensible to real people) and studying the Koran in translation, as well as philosophers such as Al-Farabi and Ibn Arabi. "Pure curiosity," he assured her. "They're amazing, the convergence of mysticism and rationality. *You* should read these guys! And by the way, how would you have me live day to day, habibi? Standing in line like a dumb statistic for a job that doesn't exist? Or expanding my mind?"

After Sami was born The Goat dropped by daily to take Karim down to the pubs, where women were considered haram, to smoke chichi. There was an androgynous quality about the theologian, with his long, striped robe and fluid movements. Perhaps that was the reason for his unflattering nickname: she'd heard older Arabs, who couldn't bother with their wife's name, refer to her generically as "The Goat."

KARIM'S CLOSENESS AND the reek of perfumed tobacco while he was jerking the fold of the beige cloth into place around her face had made her stomach churn. As he looped the generous swath of cloth over her chest, she realized that the purpose of the hijab was as much to conceal her cleavage, the pride of every Frenchwoman, as her hair.

"I feel like I'm in transformation," she joked apologetically to Dennis the first time he saw her wearing the scarf. "Someone who used to be one thing and isn't yet another. Wrapped like a pupa in this beige cocoon."

WHEELING THE SUITCASE to the next corner, out of sight of the Tunisian, hugging close to her building to stay invisible from high above. Scanning the flow of cars and vans and cycles. If her driver doesn't arrive soon, Karim and/or The Goat will come down to hunt for her, instantly bloody-minded, ready to set fire to the neighborhood if that's what it takes.

Nervousness can blind you. There's the black Opel, waiting patiently all along, its taillights blinking. The driver, nearly as shiny black as his car, leaps out as she steps forward.

"Abdul?"

"Caroline?" he responds, already reaching for the suitcase. She's reminded of the opening scene of Hamlet. *Stand, ho! Who's there?* Thank Uber for bringing intrigue back into the everyday world.

The car jolts into traffic, throwing Charley/Caroline back into its puffy leather embrace. She doesn't dare look up until they've crossed the frontier of the burb of Seine-Saint-Denis into Paris proper.

WHAT HAS SHE forgotten?

She ticks off in her mind:

cellphone
passport
cash

underwear
sweaters, jacket
clothes she was no longer allowed to wear
toothbrush, face cleanser, creams, tampons
contraceptives

What has she forgotten? What?

"DARLING. DARLING. *DARLING*." Dennis pulls her from the car into his arms. His lips graze lightly over her face, stippling kisses. Behind him rolls the indigo Seine. The air tastes fizzy-clean here in the seventh arrondissement, home to ministries, museums, and the extremely well-heeled.

He tugs at her scarf. "You can lose this now. Ugh. What a nightmare."

"I forgot." She stuffs it into her bag.

"And what's this?" Caressing her back pocket. "Oh Christ. Your cellphone, are you crazy? Sweetheart, give me that, they're probably already using it to find you—" He half turns, manipulating the phone's controls. "There. I killed the GPS. But just in case—" With a baseball player's spin he lobs her phone over the stone parapet into the river. "Hasta la vista! We'll buy you another one tomorrow."

"I don't care."

"My brave girl. You did it. You're here, safe!"

"You didn't trust me?"

"You, of course. But I was going nuts—you can ask your friend. I wasn't sure. Not until this moment. Come on, she's waiting up in my place."

He runs over the plan again as they walk. They leave for New York tomorrow. He will set gears in motion to gain asylum for her, and while those wheels grind away, he'll direct the French authorities to reunite mother and child. And why not try for the orphaned girl? After all, isn't she at risk of female mutilation, given the nest of fundamentalists holding her captive?

Rachida's future sounds less sure than Charley had thought. *Don't start thinking, idiot. Hug Maïwenn instead, inhale her cologne, twirl this glass of champagne. When is the last time you drank alcohol? Absorb this fabulous living room: the designer lighting, the rose satin sofa and chairs, the glass tables.*

She'd been there only twice before. The last time two months ago. Before or after The Goat started having her followed? Or following her himself.

"How do you expect me to convert? *Convert* means to turn from one thing to something else. I've never been anything."

"You are Catholic, of course. You're French."

She threw The Goat a look meant to wither. He shrugged.

Karim stretched his long limbs, rotated his head. It was high summer. He hadn't changed out of his polyester team soccer shorts and shirt, the shin pads, and cleats. "Listen, habibi," he said. "You don't have to convert. You don't have to believe anything. Faith doesn't enter by force, right?"

Charley wanted to cry out *hallelujah*, to throw herself on Karim's gleaming sweaty chest right in front of The Goat.

"All you need to do is behave like a good Muslim. Then we'll see what develops."

"Or not."

"How does that Beatles song go? *Smile and you'll feel happy*?"

"Wrong, my love. It's from Charlie Chaplin." Had he forgotten she was nicknamed after the silly little actor? "It goes, *Smile, even if your heart is aching . . .*"

"Dum, dum de dum da de dah," The Goat hummed the tune. Karim and Charley ignored him.

"To act the part?" she asked Karim. "That's really all you expect from me?"

"That's all."

The Goat fumed.

Charley grinned. "You know I won't set foot in a mosque. Not in a million years."

"No problem, habibi!"

Why not act the part, then? Like most French teenagers she'd grown up movie-struck and taken a few courses in acting before reality sunk in. Why not play the good Muslim woman, enjoy the fun in it? Learn to cook halal from Karim's suddenly affable mother, try out the novelty of wearing a skirt over long pants, go to the hammam to be scrubbed and oiled while enjoying the gossip of the other women. At last putting her Arab language study to practical use.

After that first shock, even the hijab became possible. All part of learning her role.

Is Maïwenn wearing more makeup than usual? No, it's her rising blood suffusing her cheeks like a rash. A spilled dash of champagne sizzles on the rug as she lifts her glass to Charley's "feminist backbone." She winks at Dennis. Her English is colloquial, if not always grammatical. "Learned in the field," she says with a wink, "not at the pillow." She launches into the details of how she will manage Karim, commiserate with him, insist on watching the children so he can do whatever he needs to do—thus she will flush out his plans. "Don't worry, you two. You'll win."

Charley nods, bowled over by Maïwenn's gift for reducing mountains to sandcastles. But this is someone who organizes shipments of tents, medicine, and even doctors to war zones. Protecting a pair of children will be, so to speak, child's play.

"Take it down a notch, Maïwenn," says Dennis. "We're infinitely grateful for your help. But this is not a game."

THE FIRST TIME Charley entered this apartment she knew she would sleep with its owner. They both knew, without saying a word. They had met a month earlier, when he belatedly joined the business French course she taught at AngloFrango. Dennis Altman irritated her: another foreign big shot above learning the basics, and it would be her responsibility to save him from flunking.

In the fabulous apartment she first checked for signs of a resident female. An empty space on a shelf where a photo had been removed, a lingering scent, or some overlooked bathroom article. Not out of jealousy—that would be absurd. She had no emotions for the American. It was only because she didn't want to raid another woman's life merely to satisfy an inexplicable drive. Which was what? Pure curiosity? Or awakened vanity?

Each time he invited her for coffee he slathered on compliments about her eyes, "brilliant as topaz," her slender hands, her underused intelligence, her wit. When for the first time she turned up wearing the hijab, his knobby face fell to pieces. "It's a crime," he said hoarsely. "A crime to cover your beautiful hair."

That first visit, she was drying her hands in his bathroom when he knocked. Through the closed door he offered to draw her a bath in the Jacuzzi. She laughed *yes*; this was so unexpected, and so welcome, after a day's teaching in hot July—the same week, she recalls now, as the gift of the hijab. He watched her as she lay in the bath letting the jets play on her like little hands. His close scrutiny was surprisingly arousing. She had just stopped breastfeeding and her breasts were still full. In his bedroom she came only moments after his pale sex entered her. Then he heaved over her like a sail in the wind. With his tears dropping on her neck, he lifted her hair in one hand and ran a lock through his open mouth.

Resting her head on Dennis Altman's shoulder, inhaling the vinegar smell of his older man's body, Charley dug deep inside herself for the backlash of guilt. For a paralyzing twinge of remorse. She found nothing. There had been a moment of physical release, forgettable, and for that reason unregrettable. It happened in a universe light-years from the one she and Karim made together.

NOW AS SHE sips and listens to the others, the apartment asks: was it betrayal you came looking for here?

Charley approaches the full-length, east-facing window. A lawn of lights twinkles to the horizon. Beyond, lies invisible Seine-Saint-Denis.

Maïwenn touches her cheek. "Whatever it is, you better get over it."

Dennis comes up on her left. Three reflections lined up in the window. "Darling. You know it's now or never. I'm an attorney, not a miracle-worker. With this clown in the White House, it's getting tougher week by week to bring noncitizens in. And with your set of relationships here? Ouch. Fingers crossed nobody digs too deep."

KARIM WAS GOING to the mosque every Friday. He unrolled his prayer mat five times a day in the bedroom. Three weeks ago, beaming, he told her their marriage party was scheduled for mid-November. The Goat, managing the details, constantly reminded Karim that the Prophet preached against long engagements.

"The Prophet is so irrelevant to us. Wait. Will there be an imam there?"

"Of course."

"An imam! Karim, no! I said *never.* And you promised—shit, you agreed!"

Karim put his hands on her shoulders. He ordered her down on her knees.

Charley found herself obeying, with a shiver of arousal that left her shaken.

"The Goat told me to beat you if you made a fuss. But I can't do that, habibi. I love you way too much."

Her forehead had rubbed the gritty floor. *Not now, but when?*

So The Goat had not told him her secret. Because he only had suspicions? Or in order to be able later to hold that much more power over her?

Maïwenn's phone plays "Je Veux" by Zaz. She squints at the screen. "Oh, the fuck. It's him."

"Karim? Calling you?" With a shaking hand Charley sets her champagne flute down to safety on a glass table. "Already?"

"Power that damn thing off!" Dennis reaches for Maïwenn's phone.

Maïwenn, who is a good six centimeters taller, holds it high overhead. "I did. And hands off! Don't you tell me what to do."

"If that madman turns up here now it will be your fault."

"So, leave!"

Charley sinks to her knees on the white tile. "Please. Don't argue, please!" A child begging her parents to reconcile. How pathetic. Her own parents, who never argued, who always seemed melted together like wax, would be devastated to see her in this fabulous apartment, having left her family, about to run away with a rich American. In silence she suddenly cries out to them, *It's your fault that I'm here. I need my freedom too!*

Maïwenn hauls her upright and hugs her close. Breasts crushing breasts. Charley wants Maïwenn's arms around her forever.

DENNIS AND CHARLEY taxi to the airport Hilton for what will remain of the night. Charley dozes, waking every hour or so with a sense of a trapdoor flying open beneath her. Can she do this? Must she? If it is about her freedom—and yes, that *is* the matter, not vanity, not lust, not boredom—couldn't there be another way?

She sees herself back in the park with Maïwenn. A week ago. A world ago. Rachida and Sami were happily grubbing in the sandbox, laughing at each other.

"Suppose," said Charley, fumbling for words. "Suppose Karim is simply being . . . honest. With me. Okay, right now he's asking me to help him lead a more traditional life. As an enlightened seeker. Why not? Islam doesn't equal radical Islamism. You'd be the first person to say so."

Maïwenn leaned very close, frowning. "One thing I detest is sentimentality. Believe me, Karim is heading down a one-way street. If you want to stay, stay! Follow him! But with eyes wide open either way. Because if once you trick him and leave and are ever stupid enough to come back—"

She broke off. No need for an ending.

Karim never suspected. Never smelled a thing, literally, because she showered every trace off her skin before going home. But somehow The Goat smelled her deception. After he began having her followed, she stopped meeting Dennis. From then on, they only communicated through Maïwenn. Like Romeo and Juliet, connecting through the friar. What would she have done without Maïwenn? She'd have been trapped forever.

But tonight, Karim is out looking for her. By now he will know of her crime. A crime in his view, in its classical outlines—this time around, Iago, aka The Goat, hadn't lied. And if Karim were to find her? What would he do, in his pain and fury?

The children are safe, she tells herself. No one hurts children. Soon the authorities will take custody of them. Dennis promised. I'll have Sami back in my arms before he takes his first step. If I've harmed anyone, it's Rachida. The girls lose. But Rachida's not mine.

THEY'RE FLYING BUSINESS class. The exclusive express line for passport control trots swiftly through the rat's maze of rope barriers, leaving no time to drag one's feet. Dennis gives her a firm squeeze as if to say, *Good girl, brave girl, you can do this*! The uniformed policeman behind his Plexiglas window rifles through her passport to bestow its first exit stamp. Bang! She is through, right behind Dennis.

If he weren't leading the way Charley would be lost. Broad corridors lead in all directions, gleaming bright. A sleek railway runs to the gate hub, the security check where she must strip off random bits of clothing. Then aisles of gold-bright shops: Hermes, Dior, Lancel. Groups of heavily made-up women wearing vanilla-colored hijab and long tunics scout for luxuries.

In Seine-Saint-Denis some wives defy the law by wearing the black, suffocating, face-concealing, mobile prison called a niqab. Charley didn't pity them. They scared her.

In France the face-covering veil was banned in 2011. She'd clung to that fact when Karim brought home a complicated dark garment for her to model. "Hush. It's only to try, habibi," he'd said. No one can be forced to wear the niqab! French women are the most educated and emancipated in the world. Thanks to the bloody battles of the Revolution. Thanks to heroes like Simone de Beauvoir and Simone Weil and, yes, her parents' generation, the old lefties . . . Her heart is near bursting. Is this some sort of schoolgirl patriotism? Maïwenn would laugh at her, for sure.

Or perhaps not.

"Where are you going?" Dennis catches the crook of her elbow.

"I don't know!" But like a dog straining against her leash, she rears back to where she came from.

In the plane a voice announces the doors have closed. They will be taking off shortly. Expected flight time is eight hours. The weather in New York is eleven degrees Celsius, fifty-two Fahrenheit. "An honest-to-God fall at last." Dennis sighs, buckling her in. "You will love Central Park in autumn."

Three things happen.

First, she remembers what it is that she forgot. The photographs. Because now that her phone is sunk deep in the Seine, she has no photos of Sami. Or Maïwenn. Or of anyone.

Next, her chin is nudged by Dennis to raise up for his kiss. It is not an amorous kiss, but a slow press against her lips like a seal on a document. When he pulls back, his face is transfigured. Tears magnify his blue eyes. "Never," he says. "Never in my life have I been truly happy. Until now."

Charley's heart twists. She is the opposite of free. She is responsible: the cause of this man's terrible happiness.

A flight attendant offers champagne from a tray.

Casually, as if she had dropped something, Charley reaches down into her purse to wrap her hand tightly into the hijab.

THEY ARE AIRBORNE! She scarcely felt it happen. *Like childbirth under anesthesia*, she thinks. Maïwenn would like that one. The flight attendant exchanges her empty glass for a menu decorated with a red ribbon. Flight attendants wear their hair rolled into chignons tight as Minerva's helmet. Charley must learn that hairdo. With her chestnut curls spilling over her shoulders, swinging when she moves, she feels half naked. As in one of those dreams where you're walking in a crowd in daylight wearing only panties, trying to put on a bold face.

"You look tired, darling. Mini siesta before dinner?" Dennis leans over Charley to demonstrate the controls: the movies, the book light, buttons for moving one's self upright, halfway, or flat. He tucks a quilt over her legs. She realizes that she's been shivering in the air-conditioning.

Business class is a strange concept: each passenger is enclosed on three sides by a personal plastic cage. Once her bed is lowered, she and Dennis can barely see each other over the edges of their individual shells.

She pulls the scarf out of her purse and drapes it across her eyes as a shield against the light. Yes, to cut the light, that's all. She doesn't weep into the cloth that smells of herself. Maïwenn would despise that. But every cell in her body is seeping microscopic tears, while in the dark world created by her scarf the jet engines pulse like a lullaby for the stars she imagines them flying up to meet . . .

"Oh, for Chrissake!"

Dennis's voice startles her awake.

"That damned headcloth again? I don't *believe* it. We'll give this rag"—he tugs the scarf up and away with a barking laugh—"a ritual burning in Central Park."

Dazzled by the overhead lights, Charley reaches blindly.

"Hold on, darling! Let me get your flight kit open. What you want is—" Sound of a tearing zipper. He circles her wrist, prods something into her hand. "Now won't this be better?"

Her fingers meet silky cloth, elastic bands.

"Your eye-mask! Like the color? We can change. They have blue, red . . ."

Charley struggles to sit upright. The seatbelt holds her awkwardly on the bed.

Dennis kisses her bone-white knuckles one by one.

"Relax, darling. Here, it's simple. Let me help you put it on."

The Toubaab

Malik N'Deye lies at ease on his back on a slab of stone, eyes wide open, silver-coated by starlight. The nearby swish and slap of the Seine muffles the roar of traffic from the opposite shore. Malik is tracing the curves of letters—or numbers beyond mortal grasp—etched into heaven. Arabesques on pages written in a language no one has ever been able to unlock, not even a Sorbonne professor or a blind, inner-sighted griot.

The moon, playing hide-and-seek, betrays her presence by a halo snagged on a cluster of chimney pots. Above her, the stars blinking between woolly brown clouds are a mere dispirited handful compared to the billions that lit up his nights when he was a small child.

Malik can never forget that billowing banner over the grassy heart of Senegal. Even after he was sold away from his village, the same moonlight and starlight pierced through the city's fumes and cook-fire smoke to guide his lurching steps. They accompanied him in his years of apprenticeship as a talibé, a holy beggar in the city, through the cutthroat alleys of Port Saint-Louis. Later still, when for one fateful moment his hunger and curiosity overcame fear and for a second time he followed a stranger into the unknown, the stars and moon witnessed. They saw Malik led away from the Daara, the holy school of the Marabout Ali, by the hairy hand of the foreign Toubaab.

They revealed the Toubaab: a lumpy European, outlandish in his paleness and alarming in his insistent attention, his soft often incomprehensible voice, his questions in weirdly-accented French. Boys in the alleys called this stranger Toubaab out of a mix of respect and derision. The Toubaab would shake his red-seaweed hair, insisting that he was no wise healer. Only a common sailor. And a fucked-up one at that—un marin foutu.

One day the marin foutu hoisted Malik into a battered, topless Jeep. Churning dust and mud, the Jeep bucked away from Saint-Louis—that ancient, rotting town of smugglers and peanut oil merchants and drug-dazed fishermen—southward through Thies and along the Cape Peninsula to the capital, where the dawn sky was the color of disease. From the quay at Dakar, the Toubaab pushed and shoved his stolen beggar boy, now folded like a bat into a splintered wood box, into the belly of a cargo ship.

At sea, during the brief night interludes when the Toubaab guided him up from the hold onto the deserted rust-scabbed deck, Malik recognized with a silent inner cry the stars of his infancy. They burned a diamond path on the wrinkled sea ahead of the freighter ferrying him from there to here, from then to now. Once that crossing is made, you can no more return to the old place than you can swim backward in time.

Not that the boy knew or cared about such things, in his timeless once-upon-a-time.

Back then, he was still a living, breathing Nothing, a bag-of-bones talibé astonished to wake up breathing in his nest in the hold, not dead or not even in any serious pain. A beggar boy so ignorant that he believed the rolling sea to be merely a wide part of the Senegal River. Who inwardly scoffed at the Toubaab's promise of a town where even orphans ate their bellies tight as melons every day, where school might mean something other than the vigorous daily beatings meted out in the Daara of Marabout Ali.

Then. Then, time began to begin. Then was when? Twenty-odd dark and dank French winters ago. But years become transparent in starlight, and it takes only the calm contemplation of a night sky to put Malik back on that rust-eaten freighter with its dangling tail of a torn and dirty Liberian flag. Under the night sky the present, visible world begins to swim and quiver, and the stones supporting his back rock slowly up and down on sea swells. The proofs of Paris around him—glinting waves and gleaming headlamps streaming past the fortress fronts of revetments and old prisons turned to luxury condominiums—all these fade away into a boy's unknown future.

HE IS THAT scrawny boy, back on the ship again. The hours move fast. Night is rinsing her face in the dawn, and young Malik is being led up from the baggage hold by the Toubaab, spiraling higher, threading the maze of metal gangways that in daytime twang like struck strings under sailors' boots. But the iron jungle keeps silent now under the Toubaab's thick socks and Malik's bare feet. The heat of engines strikes a rush of sweat from his face and arms; the stench of engine oil and bilge turns his stomach.

If speech were not forbidden, Malik would be apologizing for his own bad smell, the vomit clinging to him despite the cloth and salt water provided for washing in his makeshift lair below—for the Toubaab has done everything imaginable to provide Malik with comforts down in that boundless dark hold. There are bottles of sweet water and a metal box that protects bread from even the most devious rats. A plastic-bucket latrine with a snap-on lid, the same bucket that Malik now holds at arm's length to minimize its sway as they continue to climb.

Below decks, he nests in quilted blankets rubbed silky by age, the same kind as the fabrics wrapped around the trunks and crates that occasionally slip their tie-downs to slide around the vast hold and crash lazily into each other when the seas heave and tangle.

If in the Daara any talibé had ever boasted of such luxuries, Malik would have punched the guy for telling outrageous lies.

But despite the bliss of bread, despite blankets to cushion his healing sores, he has hardly slept for more than a few hours straight since the ship threw off her docking ropes. The hold is hotter than Port Saint-Louis at noon. Alone in the dark for endless hours, he sits rigid and straight-backed with fingers clamped around his shins. Listening for the soft slithering tread of the Toubaab, he anticipates the sailor's flashlight, its sweeping invitation to rise and head for the stairs and the fresh air above. He waits to learn the next turn of his life.

Surrounded by quarrelsome, scuttling rats, Malik is a boy-rat himself: pointing his ears, sifting animal squeaks and engine throbs for the threat of pounding steps of legitimate sailors who, if they find the stowaway, will give hullabaloo and corner him, and maybe crush him like a rat on the spot. Or else tie him in ropes head to toe to be sent back to Senegal, to Saint-Louis, to the alleys where he will be instantly recognized as the property of the Marabout Ali. Who will skin him alive, to teach an opportune lesson to any other talibé dreaming of escape.

But it's the Toubaab who has come again, and as Malik climbs eagerly toward tendrils of ocean air, he decides he would rather have his life end here on the ship—if that could be gotten over with quickly, without serious pain—than be returned to the fate assigned to him by Allah Al-Qadir, the All-Powerful.

But what kind of nonsense has invaded his head? No one wants to die. He has seen flogged donkeys stagger on to take one more step, until they can no longer rise up off bleeding knees. Even a wretch of a talibé, hustled out at dawn from the Daara with an encouraging blow of the Marabout's stick to his head and a begging bowl pressed into his hands, will return obediently in the evening, flies feasting on the oozing sores on his skin, to offer up to his Marabout the small coins of charity. For what? A fist-ball of rice. A space on the floor. Any life is better than not-life: that is the rule that keeps one creature doing the bidding of another. Has he caught the Toubaab's craziness, to think anything else?

Of course, Malik the boy didn't grasp what is long since obvious to Malik the man. The change that was working its way into the boy on the ship was not insanity. Not *quite* insanity. On the stone step, warmed earlier in the day by embracing lovers and weary tourists, Malik breathes out a long, sibilant word that creates a widening of the lips, a word-smile: *espoir.* Hope.

His smile vanishes. Dazzled by a barrage of electric beams brighter than the Eiffel Tower lit up at Christmas, Malik jerks from head to toe. Lifting chin to chest he sees a bateau-mouche that seems to be bearing straight down on him. Whenever one of these tourist barges rounds this corner of the Seine, it's as if a prison searchlight has been switched on. Malik imagines the helpless ire of millionaires whose Seine-view apartments are thus invaded all evening at ten-minute intervals. But it's late now; this boat must be a straggler. He sits up, rubbing his scalp through the cushion of dreadlocks, watching the bateau-mouche.

Why *mouche* anyway? The barge in no way resembles a fly. It is more like a giant water worm. The PA system blares incomprehensible noise. The boat could hold a hundred tourists easily, but only a few dozen figures are visible, clustered near the prow. A private party. A wedding, perhaps. But why no music?

The engines cut back. The guests on board are agitated, some running back and forth along the rail. Silhouetted against the pulsing light, a figure climbs up on the rail, balances with arms outstretched. A drunk attempting a party trick. His shirt flutters. The man arcs out over choppy black water. There is a crisp splash. A powerful searchlight hovers over an eddy in the water, illuminates an arm up-reaching, then lingers on the closed surface. On the bateau-mouche people are shouting and crying. Malik is on his feet, hopping, grabbing for his crutch. He is a poor swimmer who can barely keep his head above water, and yet he teeters at the edge of the escarpment, preparing to pitch himself, like the stranger, into the roiling river.

"Pull him out of there, you guys." A deep voice carries far in the night.

As the barge pulls closer to Malik, a figure emerges from the water, climbs a ladder. The dripping survivor is hauled up by those on deck.

"Shit! That's my last fucking take. Nine billion bacteria per square inch. My fucking suit's sprung a leak!"

"Nothing's leaking here except your brain, Nigel, you paranoid old diva . . ."

Accelerating engines drown out the voices. The bateau-mouche lifts its blunt nose, plows onward. Further up the embankment, truck-mounted strobes wink off one by one. That's Paris, Malik thinks. One big movie factory, especially in summer, when half the streets are taped off for camera crews. Tonight, even the river has been rented out. Malik settles back on his slab, gazing upward, waiting for his temporary blindness to pass.

The stars vibrate in their places like dancers in rehearsal, their positions perfect except, perhaps, in the eyes of the celestial Director.

The river slaps and clucks. Malik recalls the gold-haired, sinewy hand of the Toubaab drawing in a stained spiral notebook the River Senegal with its spirit-eyed boats, the exhausted coastal flats and, beyond, the true sea. Explaining that the waves shoving at their ship weren't the humors of a wide and salty river, this was the ocean, and Malik would soon see the shores of "la douce France."

Oh, that dumb beggar boy, dumb as a gum tree, who had neither family nor village nor even a single person who understood his own mother tongue, because who in Saint-Louis spoke his inland language, Pulaar? True, in the course of his rounds in Port Saint-Louis he began to siphon some meaning from the French chatter and Wolof shouts all around. But what use was any language, other than to squeeze a coin from one of the guilty faithful by yammering, in harsh approximate Arabic, a few lines of the laws of charity and threats of damnation drilled daily by the Marabout into his unworthy disciples?

Because they did receive an education, Allah be praised! An imam of his word, that Marabout Ali. An intrepid pilgrim and discerning collector of souls who would not dream of cheating the bumpkins who gave up their deformed offspring for a blessing and some tissue-thin bills so filthy one could hardly read the value. Ali's charitable Daara was a Mecca of education, to be sure. Every newly-minted orphan learned by heart the multiplication tables of fear, the biology of hunger, and the gymnastics of forgetting: the mind vaulting away from a village, a gentle luminous mother, a shadowy dark father, a heroic brother, and a mischievous little goat just outside the cloth door.

It would be the peculiar destiny of the beggar-boy Malik, who was certainly no prize to look at, to be snatched not once but twice, by two different traveling strangers. The first time, away from his birth home. The second time—turn and turnabout is only just—pilfered from the Marabout Ali by the Toubaab.

In the streets of Saint-Louis a whining talibé is everyday bad luck, to be ignored or bribed to disappear. But when the Toubaab first appeared in the shaded alley, he carried a duffle bag full of fruit and cakes. The children swarmed over him until the bag was a flat bladder; then they ran or crawled away. The next day he brought magic: colored pencils, paper, French picture books from Allah-knows-where.

Was it fascination or greed that spurred Malik one day to slide his hand into the Toubaab's sun-browned paw? Because yes, he had done that! Already an intrepid beggar! Looking back, he wonders just who, so long ago, first mesmerized whom. Certainly later, on the ship manned by sailors of all tongues and colors, it was the Toubaab's steady green gaze and the lessons by flashlight that scrambled Malik's mind to the point of believing that death would be better than a return to the old life. He was infected. He had only the protection of a sailor, who himself confessed that he had snatched Malik on impulse the way other foreigners might smuggle a charming parrot or a bright-patterned snake. This sailor's lunatic act, if discovered, would bring disaster on them both. And yet from that man he caught l'espoir.

"You there! Wake up! Show us your papers, if you please."

Malik is frozen, but not by surprise. The vibration of motorcycle engines reached him through stone even before their boots clattered down the narrow steps descending to his shelf beside the water.

"Bonsoir, Monsieur, I am speaking to you! You understand French? Hey, how much have you had to drink?"

Malik pushes himself up on one arm. The universe wheels: from stars in the sky to the legs of a pair of gendarmes. They are V-spread in military stance; the truncheons hang straight down against their thighs. They are clothed in the familiar uniform with flared trousers. Their silhouettes differ; the one on the right is a woman.

"Yes, Monsieur. Madame. I do understand French. Truly, I've had nothing to drink. I am regrettably sober." He smiles up at them, offering a pleasantry. The moon, edging out from her bunker, sends down light to illuminate his bared teeth.

"What's your name? What are you doing here? Papers, if you please!"

"My name is Malik N'Deye."

"Malik," the Toubaab had repeated. "Are you sure that's what your parents named you? Do you know what it means?"

"This crutch, it's yours?" A boot-toe topples the object in question. A clumsy accident, surely.

"King." *Malik* means king.

"Yes. Of course, it's my crutch." Malik speaks while rummaging in his backpack with its multiple compartments. He knows exactly which inside pocket holds the wallet, with its stamped lines of fake crocodile almost rubbed out by handling. The wallet contains forty-eight euros, pay for the morning's job cleaning a bistro kitchen. And his identification papers? His hand jabs into one cul-de-sac after another. His fingers jostle familiar shapes but never the wallet. The seconds fuse to minutes. The two gendarmes breathe heavily.

It would be a mistake to move too fast. He has never seen these two, they must be new on this patrol. He senses tension to match his own pouring from the man. Seated this way with his right leg out of sight, Malik is an imposing figure, made taller by his dreads wrapped in a knitted rasta tam. Nothing like a lifetime of crutch-work to build the upper body. And in any case, it is normal at night for strangers to be wary of each other.

"Voilà." He straightens with a cheerful note of relief, holding the wallet. "My papers. Bon lecture."

"We don't want to touch your money, Monsieur. Show the papers."

The woman plucks the documents from his hand. Her flashlight wobbles over them. Her partner retrieves the fallen crutch and examines it. It is the English style, with a grip for the hand and a cradle for the elbow and forearm. Malik reminds himself to breathe.

"It says here"—the woman's voice rises sharply as she taps his residency permit—"you are domiciled at 24 rue Deslarmes. In the Twentieth Arrondissement. That is your current address?"

"Absolutely." No sense going into details, explaining that Mamie-Mamie's rooming house is six men to a room, and so in passable weather one spends the nights outside.

"Then tell me, Monsieur N'Deye—"

"N'Deye?" interrupts the man. "Same as the singer?"

"The same patronymic. But we are not related."

"He's an amazing vocalist. Cool show. He should stay with his hip-hop instead of that folksy stuff—"

"Explain yourself!" the female gendarme interrupts sharply. "What brings you so far from the Twentieth? If you have a roof, why are you sleeping outdoors? On a quay in the Fourth?"

"I am not sleeping, Madame. I was not sleeping. I believe a citizen has the right to enjoy the public spaces. To admire the architecture of Paris on a fine summer night. Perhaps even to occupy a bench?" Malik's heart is reproaching him frantically, beating out a staticky alarm. He orders his stupid heart to calm down. Sometimes, calculated provocation sounds like innocence.

"Citizen." She bites her tongue, but it's clear what she is itching to retort. A ten-year residency permit does not make a citizen of France. She flaps the other document, the identity card of Malik N'Deye, issued by the Republic of Senegal. Both documents are forgeries. But so thoroughly used and inspected, each so venerably oiled by so many official hands that Malik feels they have absorbed a kind of retroactive legitimacy.

"N'Deye. I love that guy." The male gendarme hands the crutch back. "Excuse us for having disturbed you, Monsieur N'Deye."

The woman, taking care that their fingers don't meet, returns Malik's papers. "Stay out of trouble, you."

He nods, looking away, across the river. Listens to their diminishing steps. Another patrol may come along to interrogate him, to make sure that the night hasn't become too comfortable for a loitering African who is no tourist attraction on these quays in the shadow of Notre Dame. To make sure that the suspicious person in question is not plotting suicide nor so tanked that he might roll snoring into the river. Because any such incident, even concerning a mere SDF, a homeless, sans domicile fixe, would be a nasty blot on their files.

For now though, his prospects for a few hours of undisturbed peace are good. The papers fold up back in the wallet that goes into the pocket inside the zippered compartment. Malik N'Deye's backpack is a horn of plenty that answers all needs. A Vichy bottle filled with tap water. Hand sanitizer.

Bandages. Change of clothing. Reading glasses. *Le Parisien*, the gossipy socialist newspaper. Soap, razor, hand cream, free samples of cologne. Half a tablet of dark chocolate. Two oranges.

To be able to eat whenever you feel hungry: now that's a great pleasure in life. He slowly peels open an orange, catching drops of the juice in the callused palm of his hand. When the fruit is gone, he arranges the triangular peels in a little stack that resembles the temple pagoda in the Bois de Vincennes.

Paris is his home now. A village of two million or eleven million, depending on whether you count the mostly immigrant banlieue rim. He would never toss trash into the river of his village. The moon sends her reflection to play before him, sliding on black ripples.

THIS TIME THERE is no warning. He heard no steps. Not so much as a pebble scraped underfoot.

But there's a presence. The heat of a body inches from his. And now a pressure smooth as a feather traveling up his lip. A tangy odor of metal. The pressure increases across his right cheek with the silky elasticity of a blade stropped thin.

Fear can burst out like a fever-sweat inside the body. It floods down the bones, loosening ligaments and liquefying the intestines.

"Debout, toi!" The voice is fierce and intimate. Get up! The voice comes from just over his head.

He sits up very carefully. The blade moves upward on his cheek, sticking in the night's start of a beard, then continuing. Stops at the corner of his right eye.

"Open your sack, asshole. Everything out on the bench. Quick!"

This isn't supposed to happen. Not here, in the heavily policed Fourth Arrondissement, just beneath the shuttered apartments of movie stars and government ministers.

"Let's see your measly crap, asshole. Everything!" Malik claws his possessions out onto the damp cobblestones.

Bric-a-brac for a flea market. The moon shines down, aiding inventory. The blade follows every move of Malik's head, although not in perfect synchronization. He senses his cheek has been cut. With a very sharp blade there's often no pain at first. It's hard to be sure.

The blade juggler grabs Malik's wallet, shakes it open, pulls out the forty-eight euros. "Shit, shit!" Wallet, money, and papers scatter. "Where's the stash? Pockets!"

"That's all I have."

The free hand is irritable, scattering blindly through Malik's possessions. "You're not born yesterday. I can see that. Where's the dope, putain!"

"I don't have any." He has pissed himself, just a trickle. His thigh stings. His mind moves away from his body, closer to the stars.

"You're lying, crip!"

Malik can see that death has joined their little party and is lounging just beyond the two of them, close enough to reach out and touch. Malik registers warm blood flowing down his face just in front of his ear. Tickling. He resists a powerful desire to brush it away. One should not draw attention to a wound.

"You have drugs written on you like a billboard. Fork it! Now!"

The second cut, crossing the first one at an angle, is deeper. There's pain this time. Malik stands, sucks in air. His wasted leg buckles; he reaches out automatically for the crutch. The crutch seems to fly into his grip, that's how well-trained it is.

Malik takes one step back, pivoting on his good leg, fueling his crutch with the torque of motion like a discus thrower. Swung high and horizontal the tip of the crutch collides with the bum-roller's jaw, sending him staggering. Malik lets the motion carry him through into a second circle, a second strike that smashes into soft, giving lower ribs. Two more steps backward from the crutch take the man over the lip of the quay. It is a slight but irreversible drop. He flounders for traction on the embankment stones, but river slime and steep pitch make it impossible for him to do anything but slide downward. His arms windmill as he descends, not fast but steadily. Feet first into the black smacking water.

He is screaming for help, there can be no doubt about that. But his strong voice is almost immediately overcome by the PA announcements from yet another approaching bateau-mouche—surely this one is the last for the night? As the man thrashes in the fast-flowing river his face is lit by the boat's festive lights. From that distance he'll look to be a bit of flotsam, maybe a bottle bobbing on the stream. A screaming bottle.

Malik shoots a glance up at the barge. The handful of passengers are all craning upward, taking pictures of the square towers of Notre Dame. When he looks back at the water in front of him, there are only random twigs and trash bobbing in the current. He stares until his eyes burn. The boat twirls on, smaller and smaller, like a floating carousel.

Malik bends down for his wallet and papers and stows them deep in the backpack. His remaining possessions follow one by one. He feels light-headed. Nauseated. He scans the black water. The sparkling current flecked with fast-flowing debris. Is there a man still fighting for breath, for life, under that eddying surface? Malik gags. He's the one left standing, if only on one leg.

He stirs the Seine with his crutch, then inspects the tip end for any fresh marks or stains. The metal shines evenly, but he will wash it thoroughly later to be sure. His crutch is a custom job, just as the thief's blade was customized. Years ago, a fellow roomer at Mamie-Mamie's who worked in a motorcycle repair shop did him the favor of filling the tip with five hundred grams of lead, then resealing. "To help you balance things out, crip," he said, flashing a broad smile. Malik quickly got used to the extra bit of weight.

The mechanic has long since moved on. Impossible to thank him. But then, he might prefer not to know where his act of kindness led.

Malik wonders if from now on he will be changed. A different person. Different, or simply less? He has known men reputed to have killed. He realizes that he'd always assumed those people were somehow diminished, as if they had destroyed a piece of themselves. Their souls were damaged.

Damaged or not, he will have to get to know himself again. And accept himself. No choice there.

The philosopher-cook at the couscous restaurant where he works likes to say that a man's life is about how he meets and makes hard choices. Tonight, there's no doubt, Malik N'Deye met and made a hard choice. But when, exactly? It seemed like he acted in accordance with what he was given moment to moment, and that's all.

It's time to stop staring at the water. *Get your ass out of here, espece d'idiot! Bid your quick adieu to this bench.* This quay will be forever out of bounds. From now on the river herself is poison for Malik, who stands and hoists the backpack on one shoulder. To go where? The city parks are all fenced and locked at night. Will he stretch out on a sidewalk like a sozzled clochard? Or lie waiting for dawn in the airless crowded bunk room at Mamie-Mamie's?

Use your common sense, man. Just get moving! Those two young gendarmes, they saw you here, your name and address are written in their patrol book. If and when a body bumps up downstream, they will come looking for you.

But don't run crazy, Malik. Don't panic. Eleven million inhabitants. Haven't you already forgotten his face? Did you ever see it? Yes—permanently angry. Deep seams. White. A blurred impression. Between you and him, what possible connection can they make?

Malik limps toward the steep un-balustraded stone steps that lead upward from the quay. There he stops. He leans back against the wall in the deep shadow of the escarpment. The nausea is worse. His cheek is throbbing. He taps around the wound, cautiously. Still bleeding some. Good. He's not about to wash in the river. He read in *Le Parisien* about monster bacteria in the Seine invulnerable to antibiotics. His heart rate is slowing down with each deliberate breath.

The moon, suddenly in bold three-quarter profile, has swept forth into a wide sea of sky, obliterating the pallid stars. She beams on him without judgment, like a mother. They are mother and son.

The pages of stars written on the sky may turn and change from continent to continent and with the seasons, but there is only this single unchanging moon, she who poured milk-white light all around a small crooked twig of a boy in a village whose name he recalls only in dreams. By that light he played his lonesome night games in the dust outside his parent's hut.

Adult Malik has surely changed so much that his earth mother, if living still, would not recognize him. For that matter, would he recognize his dear Neené, even if—as he sometimes imagines—she were to trace him through the Senegalese immigrant grapevine to Mamie-Mamie's men's dorm on the Rue Deslarmes? But his second mother, the moon, has kept up with him all along his life's journey. She followed him from the northern inland village to the Daara on the colonial coast, out into the Atlantic Ocean and all the way to the port of Marseille.

It was there in Marseille, on the evening of their first wobbly stroll-around ashore, that the moon tsk-tsked when he dashed away from the Toubaab and toward a group of soccer-playing boys roughly his own color. He didn't heed her. The European black boys lost no time making him regret his impulse—they led him on, mocking, jeering, and tossing the ball over his head to make him hop higher and trip. But when he turned back to rejoin his protector, there was no one.

He had no idea where he was. Or which direction he'd come from. He ran unsteadily down one street after another, panting, in tears, afraid to call out. The hard pavement spanked his soft soles. Deeper and farther into the maze of the city. There was nothing the moon could do.

The Toubaab and Malik never crossed paths again. Malik the man always keeps an eye out for a knobby-faced, ginger-haired fellow, especially when water or ships are nearby.

The lost boy Malik, after turning circles in Marseilles, discovered that even for an illegal ship-jumper that city held infinitely more opportunity than Saint-Louis. He began by plying the trade he was trained to. Thanks to his stupefied expression and unfakably deformed leg, he earned enough money to get by. But he was constantly wary of being grabbed by the authorities, a nervousness that boiled over at any glimpse of a uniform or even the habits of the Daughters of Charity, who harass hard-working beggars with soup and prayers and questions.

After a few months he managed to move on to less harrowing work. Countrymen, often saviors and cheats in the same person, turned up from nowhere to show him the ropes. He found day jobs, unloading trucks for cash in hand at the end of the day. The rich French food he gobbled went straight to bone, to height. He saved up a hundred francs, enough to buy his first set of papers, papers promising employment security, but which in fact turned out to be of such ludicrously poor quality that he barely talked his way out of being turned in to the flics then and there the first time he showed them to a prospective boss.

That spooked him. He hit the highway with a couple of older fellows who were hitching north on the A7, heading for Paris. La capitale, everyone assured him, was full of patrons and beautiful, easy women and so many thousands of black bastards that the gendarmes couldn't tell one Galsen from another. In Paris, a guy could find plenty of work and live a practically invisible life.

That much was true.

Invisible. Invisible now. Leaving the quay for the bridge over to Rive Droite, limping in the night-shadows of massive buildings toward the rooming house where no one will ask about his wound, or perhaps even much notice, having scars new and old of their own.

In the moonlight outside the family hut, very small Malik digs lines on the ground with a stick. He tosses a rattling gourd ball over the lines and tries to run, hup-*hup* hup-*hup*, on his leg and a half to fetch it back. That's the name his father and brother call him by: Leg-and-a-half. Only his mother calls him Malik. He doesn't mind; at his age, what are words? Only the voices matter—are they soft and indulgent or abrasive and threatening? In the daytime, his mother's voice goes brittle as dry kindling with warnings: Do not do this, stay away from that, hush that noise, hush! Wait here until I come back. And above all: Do not show yourself outside. Never in daylight.

All his family suffered the shame of his existence. Even his mother's eyes gentled only when the two were alone, and she gave in with a hug or caress. He carried a curse, the mark of a devil's passing: a shriveled right leg. The first thing he learned about the world outside was that at the mere sight of him the neighbors might take fright. Or do worse.

But sometimes, when all the village was settled asleep, his mother would help him outside, to play to his heart's content in the fresh moonlight.

This was his first life. His second began when the Marabout Ali, on a talent-seeking circuit, stopped into the village, having heard rumors of a little Leg-and-a-half. This Marabout was a sage entrepreneur. He could discern value in things despised by other men.

His offer to Malik's parents caused an uproar of envy and incredulity among the bystanders: he would pay the bonus of a she-goat in addition to providing a religious education to the shriveled, bag-of-sticks child. A useless creature that would grow ever more repulsive. Uglier than sin, so the other talib in the Daara would soon inform him, with his skin yellowish as a tree frog's, uncured by the sun.

But by then he was already a twice-lucky boy, that Malik. Despite the lifeless leg, his father had not set him out as an infant on a moonless night in the bush to die. Moreover, at the moment of being taken away by the Marabout, he was given a coin of memory to keep him rich for all his days: when the Marabout Ali carried him blinking and wondrous out into the daylight, and as the gathered crowd parted to let them pass, he twisted backward to see his mother wearing bright jewels on her cheeks.

Malik had never seen her tears. He shouted to her: "Neené! Neené! Look, it's the sun! The people let me go outside now!"

She covered her face with slender-fingered hands, and dipped and bowed away, gracefully, as if inventing a new game between them.

The Philanthropist's Daughter

I TURNED TWELVE on the twelfth of March, with cake, lemonade, and noisy games in the backyard of our blue split-level. When the precociously warm sun gave way to a New England snow squall that drove us inside, one girl cried, "An omen!"

"Omen amen!" I whooped. Of what didn't matter, as long as I was singled out for some special destiny. You, I'm sure, understand. But I had no idea how quickly the door from childhood would swing shut and lock behind me.

In April I completed Preparation, a year of instruction crowned by a spiritual retreat with two hundred other fervent adolescents on the blooming campus of Boston College.

I knelt, starved for the Sacrament. The chrism traced on my forehead by Father Lacey's muscular thumb spread a golden warmth. "God our Father has marked you with his sign!" he thundered to the congregation. In my ear he whispered, "Mariel! Don't you dare go faint on me!"

My Confirmation gift was a Butler's *Lives of the Saints*, bound in white fake lambskin. I couldn't sleep without first devouring three or four of those succinct gory biographies. So many ways to sin, and then repent and be tortured to sainthood.

A week after Confirmation I got my first friend. My mother said tampons weren't for virgins, so I sat up in bed with Butler's *Lives*, trying to ignore the alien elastic straps around my skinny hips and the thick pad between my legs, the towel underneath for good measure. I managed, so I thought, to hide my marvelous blooming to womanhood from my brother Mark, who sprawled on his bed six feet away, reading a Hornblower novel, needling me. "Earth to Mariel, *hell-oo*? Those saints are sickies, El. Just don't get brainwashed, okay?"

I threw a teddy bear, secretly pleased that my brother risked damnation by insulting the Holy Spirit, proving he secretly cared about me.

Yes, we still shared a bedroom, even after our dad made his first million. A bookcase separated our territories. What did we know then about his Forbes-worthy rise from renting cheap apartments to building skyscrapers? He brushed our questions off. "Real estate's boring. Paying taxes and making repairs. You guys want excitement? Let's go watch the Sox lose!" Mom drove her Corolla to work as a pediatric PT. Dad had a vintage Ford 150. We lived in our first and only house they'd ever bought.

The third change came when our parents, galvanized by my hormonal surge, moved us into an enormous fake-looking Tudor in a neighborhood with not only gardens but gardeners. From then on, Mark and I woke up alone in the morning in separate rooms.

Irish twins: Mark being only ten months younger than me. That old joke about Catholic fertility. But at twelve, I believed they meant I looked like my brother, the fifth-grade heartthrob. We had the violet eyes and curly dark hair from our mother, a Cahill from County Sligo.

Our dad was Jewish. From a shtetl "east of the moon." If you've lived around Boston you've heard of Sidney Rostock.

I go out of my way to avoid Government Plaza, because who wants to see her father's jowls and baggy suit and battered briefcase frozen in bronze, frosted with pigeon crap? Alive, he never stopped moving. He hit the office at six in the morning and after work, there'd be a charity board or a soup kitchen. Some nights he didn't come home at all. "Marry a saint and you need the patience of a saint," said my mother, tucking me in bed. But when he did get home to the dinner table, she looked at him with wild, shining eyes.

That was marriage, I assumed: unspoken, endless adoration.

And weren't most adults like my parents? Opinionated, not perfect, but kind and trying to do the right thing.

"YO, SID! ROSIE? Kids! Anybody home?"

Arctic front-door breath blew into the pantry, where I, a high school senior, was prodding linen napkins into tarnished silver rings. Guests were rare, my parents' social life limited to fund-raisers. In her frumpy good dress my mother could be mistaken for one of the homeless women invited to make a plea to prospective donors.

I juggled a stack of plates into the dining room just as Franny Garofalo burst in, with his daughter Cilla and a new lady. Franny was Dad's partner from before I was born. He grabbed the plates and me in a bearhug. "Mari-*el*-ly, happy Christmas! *Niiice* tree!"

"Are the blue and white lights, like, about Hanukkah?" Cilla, a freshman at BU, did her mouth-breather gape. Amazing that she got the joke with our tree.

"Bingo." I wriggled free of Franny's cream cashmere embrace. "Mom's in the kitchen with the *Messiah* blasting. Dad's late."

"When's he gonna hire Rosie a cook, for Chrissake?"

"Is Mark home?" Cilla squinted around our chandeliered dining room as if my brother might pounce on her. She once told me Mark was a spoiled brat—she should know.

"He will be if he knows what's good for him." Mimicking my mother.

At the table, buzzed on watered Lambrusco, I appraised the new lady friend Pamela. Turquoise eyelids, bare shoulders, prominent teeth. Four years at a girls private school got me straight As in snobbery. She smelled of sex—whatever that smelled like. I pictured her arms wrapped around Franny, who looked like an older rock star with his hawk nose and slicked hair. Mark plopped down in his sweaty jersey and talked to Cilla through his food. I sat wedged between Franny and my dad, facing roast beast, latkes, brussels sprouts, salad, and strudel mit schlag. Pure heaven.

Only my mother spoke to the Pamela.

Franny rang his knife on crystal, his housewarming present. "Here's to a supersonic 2003 for F&S Holdings!" He gulped champagne. "Sid, we killed it. Deal's in the bag."

"Oh?" Dad's eyebrows rose. "And what deal is in this bag?"

"Inside track bid. Five acres waterfront in Charlestown. And no height limitations." Franny marked each advantage with a jab of his knife.

"How much up front?"

"All the cash we got, plus credit. We go fifty-fifty, like always. *Just the two of us, dum-de-dum, gonna make it big . . .*" The knife bounced like a bandleader's baton.

"Fran, I hate to rain on this parade, but."

"What, *but?*"

"I have commitments already. The home for low-income retireds. The clinic for kids who—"

"Seriously? What about *your* kids? Mariel here, smart as she is gorgeous. Mark—okay, kind of a nerd but my kind of nerd.

What about Rosie, the queen of Newton Heights? Sid, I gave our word! Listen: after this project you can build fifty homes and halfway houses! Hell, you can run for mayor!"

They sparred over my head. My dad looked down. His brown eyes were almond-shaped, forever young. "What do you think, Marielka?"

"You *should* be mayor!" The wine burned my cheeks. Everyone laughed and drank. Franny planted a kiss on my palm so lightly I'm still not sure it happened.

"Only if you will be my campaign manager, Schaetzle." My dad turned to Fran. "So, what now?"

"Only a couple signatures. Hey, kids! If it wasn't for your Uncle Francis, your pinko dad would've given the farm away two times over!"

"Fran Garafalo! Shame on you!" My mother lobbed a biscuit that he fielded in midair.

The Pamela pointed toward the window. "Look, you guys! Now everything's perfect! It's snowing."

My father knew Boston like the lining of his overcoat. Where the city held up and where it needed stitching. As kids we did the rounds, to Chinatown, Southie, Dorchester, Eastie, J.P., Roxbury. Each neighborhood a different country. He would check on his buildings but mainly stop in diners with steamed-up windows to talk baseball and hear kvetches. I gorged on moo shu shrimp, chicken and collards, gelato. On the drive home he'd be on the phone with city bureaucrats about trash barrels blowing down the streets. Glass in the playgrounds. Grit in the water. Rats. I didn't know that on frigid nights he'd been spotted strolling in the Combat Zone or the Commons. If he couldn't rouse someone lying on a bench or subway grate to take them to a shelter, he would tuck a Benjamin into the sleeper's pocket. "Covers a motel," he explained to a reporter. A shower and a meal. Twenty-four hours of decency. "Suppose they spend it all on drink, Mr. Rostock? Or drugs?" "Then that'll be probably what they need."

After he was gone, legends of his generosity swirled around that bronze statue. How much was true? He always hired union, I knew that. And in a notoriously corrupt business he refused bribes and shakedowns. He liked investing in projects with no return.

"You must be so proud!" people gushed after his death. I was. And also burning mad. But my anger had to hide.

I see him in the luncheonette, his full lips smiling, his eyes widening at some new injustice. What drives a person to give away so much—time, money, sympathy? What was it, I wondered as I grew older, that Sidney Rostock needed to prove?

When therefore thou doest alms, sound not a trumpet before thee, as the hypocrites do in the synagogues and in the streets, that they may have glory of men.

His life put Butler's showy saints to shame. Not to mention my own self-centered efforts to root out sin and replant my garden with virtue. Was I a free agent or a hypocrite? Or, as in the gospel according to Mark, a patsy of the most powerful gang in the world?

College saved me. I discovered irony and derision. Baby Mariel faded, cool Mare roared at dirty jokes and explored sex to the hilt. I titrated relationships (males and females) and drugs (coke, E, uppers, downers) to protect my complexion and A-minus average. I cheated on lovers and exams.

FRANNY GARAFALO HAD foreseen the future. Less than two years after his Christmas toast, the Charlestown project was completely pre-sold, and new investors were begging to throw money at F&S Holdings LLC. It reached the point that my dad fumed about having to push cash around like a croupier. Franny drove a red Maserati, took us fishing in his teak-lined Boston Whaler, bought Cilla an apartment on the Hill. His new Pamela—not her real name—had perfect teeth. Even my dad bought a new truck, once we could see pavement through the old Ford's floor. He cut ribbons for a clinic for street kids and for harbor-view settlements for oldsters who had previously been sucking up Alpo in a bus shelter.

We were, as Mark elegantly put it, "rolling in shit."

Which was often as bad as that sounds. Let me put it this way: fitting into wealth was like having to put on an incomprehensible dress, all silk and brocade. You tug at sashes, get it on backward, inside out. Finally, when you go out, people stare at your getup, and whisper things you can't hear.

My real uniform was jeans and Mark's old shirts. Even so, when anyone complimented my looks, I wondered: can you smell my wealth, the way dogs smell cocaine?

Not that Mark and I could touch the money. Yet. But it enveloped us like perfume. We had the newest flip phones. Franny heaped us with goodies, partly to tease my parents.

I started my second year at Brown, Mark his first at Brandeis. We came home for Sunday dinners. After a hard week of sex, drugs, and poetry slams I needed R&R. Dad proposed a family vacation. My mother side-eyed him. "I'll start packing when pigs fly." She had taken unpaid leave to mentor teenage mothers. We all floated in choices, lighter than air.

Out on the veranda Mark passed me his blunt. "We're free. We can be parasites, El! You study Sanskrit. I'll deconstruct baseball." He flashed his dimple. "Or just drop out."

I punched his chest, hard as teak from lifting weights. "Jerk. We can't do that."

Everything was coming at us so fast. On that, we agreed. If we had only known.

One September morning when I was sleeping over with a girlfriend in Allston, my phone woke me. I groped for it under the springy, unfamiliar bed. The girlfriend had left already. "Yeah? Who is this?"

A voice bubbled. Rain lashed the window. "Can't hear. Sorry."

"Mariel. S'me. Dad." There was a wheezing, a snapping sound. "Ho. Don't tell your . . . I was . . . Eight hours. Opera. They . . . opened up."

"Opened? *Operation*? Dad, where are you?"

"Tensive. IC. They let me . . . Finely. Call. No, no. Not now Miss . . ."

I guessed he was trying to fend someone off. I jammed the phone against my ear. "Dad. What happened."

"Anoorr . . . Anoorr . . ."

"An aneurism?"

"Yeah. Belly . . . slit. From guggle to. Me zatch."

I sob-laughed. If he could quote James Thurber, he must be okay. "Where, what hospital?"

"Maa, maa . . ."

"Mass General. Yes? I'm on my way!" I was hopping, yanking up my jeans while holding the phone.

"El. I heard. The doctors. Talking. Like I was un . . . un . . ."

"Under?"

"Said I oughta be dead. 'Heza lucky bastard.' El, I'm thinking. When I get. Out. Of here. Things to tell you. And Mark. Reason for life. God, I love you kids—"

"Daddy, shh. I'll be there in ten."

"An, an . . . Franny."

"I'll call him. Sure."

"But *first.*"

"What?" Buttoning my shirt wrong.

"Home. Rosie. Better from you. Don't want. Rosie. Scared."

"Okay, Daddy. Sure. I'll go tell Mama first. And then I'm coming over!"

LANES STALLED FROM Allston to Newton. A 'Nam vet holding his waterlogged sign. Red traffic lights smeared the windshield. Blood. An aneurism, out of nowhere? When did it happen? What were his chances?

Good chances. That's what he was telling me. Not luck, I thought. Every life is saved for a purpose.

Tears burned my eyes. Cars stuttered forward.

MY MOTHER WAS holding the phone at arm's length, like a snake she couldn't let go.

"Mariel! Perfect timing. Call the police. I don't trust my temper. Some teenager has been playing a prank. Pretending to be a doctor. Telling me that Sidney Rostock passed away half an hour ago at Mass General. What's wrong with kids these days? I keep hanging up but he—"

I took the phone from her hand just as it began to buzz again.

RABBI GAEL SAID, "We'll be honored. Maybe Sidney Rostock never set foot in my store except for bar and bat mitzvahs—he was a tzadik."

Franny sent the invitations, fact-checked obits in the *Globe* and the *Times*, ordered squadrons of lilies. Dad had been gone for three weeks. *Gone* was all I could say. He'd stayed away late before. He always came home.

The Bet Tikva Prayer Hall was a sauna in that warm, rainy October. The mourners all had notes sticking out of their pockets: life-changing moments, thanks to my father.

Mark went first. He told about Dad teaching him not to swing first. "But if someone clobbers you—like this—you give back better!" Mark had given Dad a black eye. Chuckle chuckle. People at funerals are always thirsty for a laugh.

I clutched the lectern next. Did I speak? I only remember Franny rushing up to the dais with long, swift steps, grabbing me and holding me on the long way back to my chair.

ONE WEEK LATER we three remaining Rostocks rode up to the thirty-first floor offices of Dozent and Frost. Suits ringed a long mahogany table reflective as a koi pool. Mark poked me, but I wasn't surprised to see Franny and Leo from the office. They were almost family, right?

My mother clasped my hand hard as the executor began to read.

The will was simple. All that Sidney Rostock owned went to his wife and, on her passing, to his children. Assets, bank accounts, etc., etc. My mother nodded, eyes closed. *Let's go. It's done.*

"There is one . . . issue," said the attorney. "Not a legal problem. However . . ."

I saw Franny swipe his hand down his face, gazing away at the white-speckled blue of Boston Harbor.

Mark leaned forward. "What kind of problem?"

"To be frank, these assets are of modest value. The checking account holds over one hundred thousand. There's that.

Also, a life insurance policy with Mrs. Rostock as beneficiary. Five hundred thousand dollars."

I said, "And the rest?"

"The other named assets are empty."

Mark slapped the table. "What the *hell?*"

The attorney took us on a tour of emptiness. Empty files, empty promises. Sidney the Good had plowed his profits into housing for the left-behinds and endowments to keep them going.

"He wasn't a miser, okay." Mark leaned forward. "But what about his half of F&S Holdings LLC?"

"As to the company—well. At the start of the partnership, Mr. Garafalo contributed the capital, while Mr. Rostock took on the day-by-day management. Garofalo *could* have demanded a lion's share of the equity and income from the start—quite customary."

Franny nodded emphatically to the window.

"Instead, documents were drawn up such that, in the event of Mr. Rostock's demise, his fifty percent of the company would transfer to Mr. Garafalo."

My mother said, "That's ridiculous."

My chair arms went slick with sweat.

Franny coughed. "Rosie. It was Sid's idea, to protect my stake! And then business took off and—in all the craziness who remembered details? I mean, who looks back? We were *growing*."

"Sidney always did sign whatever you wanted. He trusted you like a brother!"

"Rosie, he was a grown man! Anyway, I was floored, when Lou here showed me that old piece of paper. But legally speaking, it's—"

I lunged. "Let me see that." The yellow rule paper had been folded twice, making a brown cross. My father's signature.

That comma over the "I", meant to fool forgers. "You bastard! My dad wasn't stupid!" I started hammering on Franny's meaty shoulders, his back, his ribs. "You conned him!"

Franny turned his face away. I bit into his ear until it crunched. Mark caught my arms.

Franny took the napkin from under his coffee cup to blot the blood.

My mother said, "You—you—you could eat my food, sit at my table—"

Mark said, "The house, Ma! You still got that."

The attorney winced. "If you mean the Newton house, that was held in a trust, apparently for tax reasons. With F&S Holdings."

Mark let go of me. I shook.

My mother said, "The house was never ours?"

"Rosie, hey. Hold on. The house? Me and Leo can find a way to fix that. Hey, you know I've always been there for you and the kids! Anything you need, Rosie!"

"Is that how you see it from now on? I should beg from you?" My mother stood, reaching for her coat and purse and dignity. "No thanks, Francis Garafalo. Farewell."

A SPECIES ABLE to detect subatomic particles can always find a silver lining. So, how screwed up would Mark and I have turned out if millions had landed in our twenty-something-year-old laps? But that day I was beyond fury.

I hadn't yet witnessed the full harm money can do.

My mother got her old job back and found a small apartment near the hospital in an aluminum-sided triple-decker. Dad had to be rolling in his grave at the lousy construction. Her living room was so full of the past that you could hardly get to the john. She palled up with an AA divorcée from downstairs for movie dates. She only complained when dragged out in public to unveil another plaque or award another Rostock scholarship. Eventually I got it: she was like a cat drowsing on the windowsill, wishing only for nothing to happen.

Mark enlisted in the Marines. "Way to act out," I told him. "Go kill people." After some kind of secret training, he deployed to Anbar Province. No warning. Same way Dad used to leave us.

I couldn't even pray.

I needed rent, food, tuition money, or a job. I was in a frozen panic, until a Goth girl in my personal essay seminar read her paper aloud about getting through school by turning tricks. It was a blueprint. All I needed was Craigslist. What is the difference between hooking up and hooking? Roughly $300 an hour. And power. I dictated what was kosher, not some campus stud. I invested in luxury lamb Trojans and a year's supply of antibiotics and acyclovir. I wore cashmere and silk.

I forgot what an orgasm felt like. I always prepped with three shots of vodka, the booze they say can't be smelled. The wadded greenbacks left on top of my textbooks smelled like rotting lilies. I jammed cash into drawers, shoved wads into Jimmy Choos I never would wear.

Some nights I slid fifties into street people's pockets. Sid's little princess.

Prostitution had another benefit. Company. Nights in my room alone, I ached. I missed Mark. My dead father and comatose mother. I even caught myself missing Franny—his prosecco grin, his sinewy arm squeezing the breath out of me. You could say I missed *us.*

In August of 2006 Lance Corporal Mark Rostock was discharged with a Purple Heart and a spray of shrapnel in his right leg. He moved in with Mom, bivouacking on her couch. I chauffeured him to surgeries and rehab.

"Whence the beemer, sister mine?"

"Loan from a friend on her year abroad," I lied.

"You got generous friends. Anyway, you hear anything from Franny? Or Cilla?"

"Him yes, her no," I said. "But I trashed his letters unopened."

"Maybe it's eating away at him."

Mark slowly rubbed his leg bandages. He'd come back different, quieted down. "Maybe he deserves another chance. The thing I learned in Anbar is, holding onto grudges can kill you. Nobody's a saint. Well, maybe you are." I glanced over at his grin. "There are two kinds of people, Mariel. The ones who hold on, and the ones who can let go."

"Garbage. You hate the bastard as much as I do."

I clung to my anger like a shipwrecked sailor to a spar. Mark kept trying to unpeel my grip. Maybe Franny *had* forgotten the original deal. "Look. Can't you find space for—I won't say forgiveness. But understanding?"

Catholic situational ethics from Mark? Embrace the sinner? The grateful married men who paid me for sex wanted a chaste kiss I would never give. As we rattled over trolley tracks on Huntington, some lines bubbled up in my English major memory.

"O Opportunity! Thy guilt is great." I drove one-handed, gesticulating. "Tis thou that execut'st the traitor's treason! Thou set'st the wolf where he the lamb may get . . ."

"Exactly." Mark laughed. "Life's a fucking minefield. Shakespeare?"

"Just don't ask me which play."

AND SO BEGAN the Thaw. I agreed to drive Mark to a date with Cilla, who was majoring in public health so she could photo-op with lepers in tropical climes. In Starbucks dim light Mark's dimple flashed so hard you'd think he'd gone to charm school in Kabul.

In no time, Cilla took over the rehab driving gig. Be my guest, I thought. Her desire to atone for her father's sin might not go so far as drinking pus like Saint Catherine, but Mark's injuries were a start. Anyway, I needed to get back to work. My bank balance was flatlining.

Two months later Cilla was flashing a hideous rock. In mid-June at Our Lady, bump concealed under an empire waist gown, she promised to love and obey my brother till death did them part.

Which is how and where Franny Garafalo made his way back into my life.

The settlement had, visibly, been eating at him. At the wedding, Mom glowed thanks to Xanax, while Franny looked gaunt as the after of a juice fast. His cheekbones stood out like knives; his Zegna suit hung in folds.

This, he swore, was the second happiest day of his life.

He'd bought the newlyweds a flat in Harbor Towers. He whispered an offer to pick up the tab for my tuition. *Not a prayer.* But we couldn't duck a renewed stream of goodies. Wine, theater tickets, spa vouchers. Hard to say no, now that Mark was working for his father-in-law.

No way would I let go of my brother. I hung out with them and the baby. I was sure the symptoms of PTSD did not include diapering, praising bad cooking, or a two-beer limit. But obsessive behavior, maybe. Mark hit the office by six, just like Dad had; he studied until midnight for his broker's exam. He couldn't sleep, so why not? He blamed the Percocet—or rather, getting off it. While Cilla and I struggled to make conversation, a muscle bounced in his jaw.

Maybe this was the real Mark, revealed in the crucible of Afghanistan.

Often when I was there, Franny stopped by. We four sat on the rug munching pizza and watching the baby—Sydney, for cripes sake—lift her wobbly, bald head and wriggle forward, like it was the most fascinating show. Which it was. A strange feeling came sneaking up on me like a gun-shy animal. Happiness! I wanted my mother to see her grandkid. But only Sid could have talked her around.

I READ ONCE that people average three lies per ten minutes of talk. Lying is in our genome; it's the snake oil that lubricates daily life. And it turns out the more someone lies, the better their chances of success.

One night Franny came down with me from Mark's place to where I'd parked on India Row. "You tired, Mariel?"

I was on meds for the tail end, so to speak, of a yeast infection. I felt itchy and disgusting. "No, why?"

"Maybe we can walk a little?"

I shrugged. Stuck. We set out along the wet, reflecting wharf.

"Mariel, I want to tell you a secret. Thing nobody else knows. Va bene?" When had he started with the phony Italian? "And then you, cara mia, maybe you got a secret to share with me? To get off your heart."

I looked up. I saw myself in his eyes. I fell face forward, into his Burberry. To hide.

"You know," I blurted into the thick cloth.

"Oh yeah. Actually, for a while. Never mind how." His arms kept me from sliding to the cobblestones. "Hush. What's so terrible, Marielly? I mean, who've you been hurting?"

I ground my face deeper. *God please don't let him ask why.*

"Nobody, that's who." He stroked my hair. For a confused moment it felt like a client was holding and stroking me. "Nobody except you. Only, you're done with that stuff from now on, right? Or you need someone to talk to, Mariel? Therapy, that type of thing?"

I shook my head against his chest.

"No fucking shrink, okay. But maybe—whaddaya say, a priest? I know a real good guy. A mensch."

Which is when I remembered who gave me Butler's Lives. On the flyleaf: May you have All of God's Blessings. F.G. Where was that stained, dog-eared book now?

"No priest. No thanks." I straightened and took a shaky breath. I *was* done. I hadn't known until that moment.

He pressed his knuckles to my cheek. "Ah, don't cry, Marielly. Please."

"Did you tell anyone?"

"Don't talk crazy. Let Uncle Franny help you out some. Just a little while. For me?"

I nodded.

"Promise?" Like we were kids.

"Hey. It's your turn," I said.

"'Nother promise, though. You don't tell no one. Especially not your brother, 'cause he will blab to Cilla."

"I promise. Blab what?"

"I got that cancer. The guy cancer. The one guys get from fooling around. Pardon the expression, that stupid dick cancer."

The harbor lights swung. "But don't most men get prostate, sooner or later? It's totally curable!" I sounded optimistic as Franny on a Christmas. "You're having treatment, right?"

"Not radical. Let's not get into the details, okay? Hey. Mariel. Carina mia! I knew you wouldn't go all drama-mama on me. I knew that you could take it and—" He hugged me again, a long time, as if it was my turn to hold him up.

Fran had tossed his heavy secret to me. But to the others he announced he was going off radar, taking an October cruise around la patria, bella Sicilia, the cradle of civilization. Mark, with a bunch of POAs, Leo and the consiglieri, could keep F&S Holdings running fine. At last, a man can take a vacation, with a son-in-law like this!

I WASN'T SURE Italy was where he'd gone. But I had just started grad school in the exhilarating lightness of celibacy. I had only an occasional worried, grateful, still outraged-under-it-all thought for Franny, and less and less time for hanging out with the biomass, as Mark called himself and Cilla and Sydney and their yellow Lab puppy.

A week before Thanksgiving Mark called. Where the hell was I and did I know Franny was back? Checked into Dana Farber, for cripes sake?

"Oh good," I said. Despite Franny's fatalism on the wharf, as long as he was in the hands of specialists, we could expect a positive outcome. Growing up in a city with the world's best hospitals, you take miracles for granted.

"I CAN'T," MY mother said. "Quit nagging! I never want to see him again. Least of all in the shape he's in."

"He's dying, Ma. He asked for you. He wants us all. You know how Franny loves a party. Do it for Mark and me? Please?"

"How dare he! All right. Only for you, Mariel! A party, he wants? Go on, look if there's a bottle of wine in the fridge."

I'd sold my car. We called a cab. Ask me how the poor get poorer.

Stepping out of the brightly lit elevator into the dim eleventh floor ICU felt like entering a spaceship. Green LEDs glowed from the floor. Bed-pods radiated from a round central desk bristling with computer terminals. Machines bubbled and pinged.

This was a single-purpose ICU. For the patients, one-way.

Where pod-beds were empty, the curtains had been drawn back. I tried to imagine being wheeled in and hoisted onto a bed where someone had just died.

Without all the equipment, Franny's pod would have felt spacious. But there were bulky instruments bolted to the walls, two stands for drips, and the mother of all, the wheezing ventilator.

Franny lay cranked up in the bed. Tubes snaked under the sheets, more tubes were taped into the thin blotchy arms arranged on top of the sheet, two yellow tubes ran into his nostrils. A plastic ventilator mask covered his mouth. So much for the Prosecco I held.

His hair was white.

Cilla, Mark, a nurse, and a middle-aged couple who introduced themselves as Franny's cousins, ringed the bed. I never realized he had family outside of us. People lead multiple lives.

Cilla went out hunting for more chairs.

I flashed on a painting of the death bed of Louis XIV, with courtiers, children, and mistresses vying for a view. The propped-up monarch wheezing orders up to his last breath. Privacy was never the Sun King's priority.

Franny couldn't give any more orders. His lungs were soaked sponges. "Do you want to suffocate?" The nurse scolded every time he tried to pull the ventilator mask away with a shaking hand. "Drown yourself? Is that what you want, Mr. Garafalo?" The hand fell back. She moistened his cracked mouth with a gel swab before plunging the mask back in place.

One hour passed like three. Cilla pulled back the sheet to massage two swollen ivory balloons, her father's feet. Mark, with his warrior stillness, studied Franny's ravaged, still stubbornly handsome face as if memorizing every line. My mother watched us all as reflections in the window. The hour ticked on to two. Whenever Franny began to doze off, his eyes flew open in sudden terror and he flailed for our hands.

The nurse checked his signs and frowned at the blood oxygen reading. "If you want to say something to him, this might be the best opportunity."

The middle-aged cousin gave a loud sob. His wife hurried him out.

Cilla steadily rubbed the balloons. "I love you, Daddy, and baby Syd loves you, and Mark too, and we always will, and now, Daddy, you just rest and get better."

I had nothing to say. I took his hand and felt a slight pressure. I found myself smiling. I mouthed, *This sucks. I'm sorry.* Under the plastic he twitched a smile back. *Me too.*

My mother stepped forward. "Oh, Francis. I wish there were—" She made a sweeping gesture. Franny blinked three times. She ceded the bedside spot to my brother.

Mark leaned carefully over Franny and whispered in his ear. Their private moment. A long one. Suddenly Franny's face cramped. He grunted, reached for Mark's arm with one hand and raked at the plastic mask with the other. An IV line popped out. The nurse hustled us all out of the pod. "Until he calms himself. The stress . . ."

I nearly tripped, running after Mark as he trotted down the greenlit passageway. "Hey, bro! Where are you going?"

"Home. I'm done. It's over."

"No, it's not! Come back! Mark—what the hell did you say to him in there?"

He turned. "Are you sure you want to know?"

His expression chilled me. "Tell."

"Okay. I said, 'Listen up good, Fran, you sonofabitch. I clawed back every cent you stole from us. I have every cent of your money as well. All legally signed and delivered. You taught me the ropes. By the way, you raised one spoiled idiot of a daughter, who I am about to divorce. As for *my* little girl—I'm getting sole custody. How do you like that, Uncle Francis? We're even, now.'" Mark's smile skewed sideways, no dimple. "I did it, El. Took a long time. Wasn't easy. Patience—another thing I learned over there. Come on! Act proud of me!"

You either hold on, or you let go. Mark had held on. Mark, the only one left who I still completely trusted, had lied to me. Mine, theirs—lies everywhere. I wanted one more.

"Please." I pulled at him with both hands. "Come on back. Tell him you didn't mean it. Mark, what'll it cost you? One word. He's dying. Show mercy!"

Still wearing that sideways smile, my brother let me lead him. But when we reached the pod, Franny's wracked body already belonged to the staff who were crowding in and shooing us away. His soul was gone.

Mother Benedicta,

This ends my true and complete confession. I pray to God the Almighty, and petition you, Reverend Mother, to be received by the Order as a Novitiate, at such a time as you and the Sisters shall deem me worthy and prepared.

Yours in the love of Christ,

Mariel R. Rostock.

The Catamount

DEANNE AND I were heading out to the barn when the phone rang. "Don't," I said. "I'm not on call." Night wind and a few ice-flakes jitter-bugged into the kitchen.

"Too late." My wife reached me the phone. As it fell between us, clattering on the planks, a silvery sound came spiraling up. Even before I pressed the receiver to my ear that sound thrilled me, and even though I hadn't seen or heard from Claudia Francke in almost a quarter of a century, my legs went weak. Not until after we hung up did I notice that Deanne had gone ahead, to feed the critters.

I should have followed her immediately. True, the horses were her babies, not mine, but since the mastectomy she'd been told no heavy lifting, which would include dragging hay bales. I stepped closer to the woodstove. Numbed. Or suddenly alive. *Claudia.* That voice again, the wry twist to it, as if every word came with a grain of salt. That voice, despite a new film of accent, had catapulted me through the emotional rainbow of a seventeen-year-old—pride, joy, shyness, wild exultation.

She hadn't asked many questions. She seemed to know about me; after all, my number and address are public and my career path is charted by a slew of doctor-rating websites. She knew I was married, no children—except for the whole town's kids. She talked about her life and I was glad to listen. "I have one boy," she said. "He's grown up, my best friend now." On the other hand, she'd said quickly, she'd co-failed three marriages. "Are you shocked, Olen?"

"More like impressed." I mentally divided the years of love offered by the number of takers. I was not in that league. "And now, Claudy? Are you all right? Where are you calling from?"

She was here. Passing through, on her way north to Canada, stopping only for a short while. Short made sense: upper Minnesota is not a tourist mecca. "But—" She paused. "Olen, I don't want to intrude. But could we meet? Soon? I'd like to see you."

My heart slammed like an unlatched gate in a storm.

"Probably simpler," she said, "if you don't mention me being here to anyone, not yet." She was thinking of me. Two old friends getting together. Well, small-town people are never satisfied with the obvious.

My mind—no, my heart—raced so fast that I didn't think to ask why a person once hell-bent on getting out of this backwater region would return for even one day.

A SMALL-TOWN DOCTOR'S hours are unpredictable. In other words, even in a rural area where apparently everybody lives in everybody else's pocket I've had plenty of chances to fool around. I have colleagues so overwhelmed by opportunity that they seem compelled to take some exams of Ms. So-and-So to the extreme, without any starchy nurse standing nearby—

maybe a daytime house call, or in one of the motel cottages up by the lake. I never was tempted.

The following day, having rescheduled my afternoon, I drove out to meet Claudia by the lake. Hardly a soul goes there in February. Only a trio of ice fisherman had parked their Chevys out toward the middle of the ice sheet.

I parked in the lot. She was sitting on top of a picnic table, looking out at the frozen world. Claudia: a red coat on a brushed-off dark picnic table in the dense glitter of week-old snow.

When the crunch of my boots came close enough, she turned and jumped, agile as a child jumping off the examining table. "*Olen!*" She threw her arms around me and pressed into my jacket. She didn't want her face seen, wanted to put off crossing that border as long as possible. Perfume rose from the curled shoots of next year's plants, submerged all around us under a layer of skeletal leaves. Her narrow face pressed against my shoulder. Through our winter layers, the sharp bridge of her nose.

Looped around her red wool collar was a brown scarf. A shapeless fuzzy hat covered her hair. Salt-stained boots with lopsided worn heels. The boots worried me.

She pulled back. I had been leery of this close-up moment, too—not of how Claudia might judge my appearance, since I never rated much in that department, but afraid of seeing her face saddened by gravity, overlaid with that crackled-glass, sun-damage effect you notice at school reunions. Even worse, she might have gone under the knife, and I'd be running my professional gaze over ears, eyebrows, temples, examining the incision sites.

"Is something wrong?" she asked.

"Nothing." I stared longer, to reassure her. "You look exactly like you." Foxtail lashes. Irises spiked green. A song about kaleidoscope eyes was playing on every radio the year I was sixteen and she was fourteen. Now I saw only a softening around her jaw and lowered fold to the eyelid. Time had been gentle to Claudia Francke.

"I should hope so." She turned away a little, raising her chin from its nest in the scarf. I almost kissed her, for that vain innocence. "What is it?" she asked.

"I want to kiss you."

Evidently honesty still scored with Claudia. After our chaste, brief, infinitely reverberating kiss she seemed at ease, fists jammed in pockets, swishing her coat as we set out on the path around the lake. "I've been exploring Torwald," she said. "What a perfect little town! What a time-warp! I went into the lobby of the Cinotopia. Pure 1963. A real human to buy tickets from. And I walked around that little park behind Town Hall. Those cannons the kids climb on? Those plaques to the war dead? Even the Korean war. I can see why you decided to—Olen! You tell something. I'm babbling, aren't I?"

"By local standards." But I was grateful. My mind was swimming between the past and the future, diving deeper on each lap. "Say, are you cold?"

"Not a bit. The desk clerk at the motel—"

"The Lamplighter or the Piney Point?"

"Piney Point. He said a thaw like this is unusual for February. And isn't it dangerous for those fishermen out there? Aren't they afraid of falling in?"

"They've got two hundred years' experience between them. Retirees. This town is getting old. I'm a clearinghouse for geriatric referrals: hair transplants, knee replacements."

"And Viagra?"

Motels, Viagra. Now who was on thin ice?

"Not from my store. Wouldn't be surprised if the tobacco runners bring it across from Canada, though."

Claudia laughed. "When we were kids, I thought our Stevens Point was the back of beyond."

"You had yet to feast your eyes on Torwald."

I saw the limits of life out here—of my life—with a kind of shock. Why had I chosen this speck on a map? I remembered boycotting my own graduation from med school. My father had died that winter; the invitation I mailed to Claudia had boomeranged back to me stamped Recipient Unknown. There is an American tradition of the depressed and aggrieved burrowing deep into no-man's-land.

Claudia said, "It's perfect for children."

I was braced for that. "We can't have them. And Deanne was adopted herself. She didn't want to risk that lottery."

A thoughtful nod. "I don't blame her."

Not being a cheater doesn't imply superior moral fiber. I was simply your classic serial monogamist, immune to the virus of adultery. Two women during internship and residency, and then Deanne. And looking back over that particular day, I can't see where Claudia and I took one false step. But walking by the lake with her I felt the ice in me shifting.

It's possible to not have your cake, and not eat it, and yet to feel content, even happy. There is a kind of freedom to be found in the company of a person you have been in love with nearly as far back as memory reaches—but who won't ever, cannot, feel anything but friendship for you. You're free to be abject, or cynically brilliant. To clown, rave, or tell forbidden truths. You let yourself be seen through, as if made transparent by the pure futility of this attraction. Self-respect is meaningless. What's left to be stripped off you? She witnesses your longing, in friendship. Hopelessness is an acquired taste. With Claudia, I became a connoisseur.

The path narrowed. Claudia forged ahead, turning sideways to send her voice. She was talking about this son of hers, Noel, who had served a humanitarian stint in Nigeria until the increasingly brutal warfare closed his chapter down. With no warning he'd turned up on his mother's doorstep, broke, no job, but with a bad case of drug-resistant malaria. That he had a wife, too, Claudia only learned a few days later. All this had happened last year in London, where Claudia was living after her third divorce.

Across the lake, bare tree branches cradled the flame-disk of setting sun. I wanted us to press on and complete the loop, even though we'd be navigating by moonlight by the time we reached our cars. I pictured my Jeep and her rented Toyota, huddled side by side in the picnic parking lot like a pair of loyal companion animals.

She was describing her rowhouse in Kensington: three of the narrowest stories imaginable, one front and one back room per floor. Steep steps, iron grilles on the windows, a wooden WC with a chain flusher, and heating pipes that rumbled like elephant guts through the night. Claudia, having thrown out every object connected with the ex-husband, had pulled the small house around her like a brick blanket. Her words.

I wondered if she'd rather turn back the way we'd come, but hated to interrupt. Claudia seemed indifferent to the fading light.

"Of course I took them in. Him and Mandy too, once she arrived from Lagos. It was kismet, do you see? For me, I mean! Whatever bug Noel had picked up—no one knew exactly—went into remission. And he was a practical genius after two years in the bush. He went through my house, cellar to roof, like a detective, fixing everything. Whenever I'd hear the rat-a-tat hammering, or the buzz of a drill, I felt so secure. Knowing my son was there, putting all those things ship-shape around me.

"He was starved for music, theater, just the bustle in a pub. And I had been living like a hermit. People shun the newly divorced, you know, as if their own marriages might get contaminated. We started going out together. Noel and I, that is, because Mandy, the new wife, was too tired to 'dress up' for dinner or a show.

"We'd come back late, tiptoeing in—and then hear the TV snap off. The times she did join our outings, they bored her. I got the impression she looked down on fun.

"Oh no, she wasn't Africa-African! Hah, if only. Mandy grew up in Connecticut. A 'Daughter of the Mayflower.' Big girl. Square shoulders, broad hands. Mandy Dodge. A runaway debutante at daggers with her family. Her eloping with Noel can hardly have helped. I told them I didn't care about having not been told, they were here now. And then she announced she was pregnant."

We had reached the three-quarter point around the lake. I knew the landmarks—I'd had a dog. Under our feet the snow was freezing up for the night. Claudia, whose worn boots had slipped a number of times, took another stumble. She reached for my arm. "Is all this stuff boring you?"

"Don't be silly." But we walked in silence for a while, under branches cracking in the cold, Claudia's weight on me.

"Ice and snow," she said. "The default state of the planet." Her voice was calmer, more contemplative. "Living in the north, summer feels like a mirage. Did I mention I lived in Toronto for four years? After my second divorce. Before London. Everyone loves Toronto! Not me. Way too much architecture. Whenever I could, I escaped. Noel and I went cross-country skiing. He was co-captain of his high school team. For endurance training he liked to cut fresh trail in the forest, so on weekends I drove him out to Algonquin. I skied along behind in the tracks he'd made. We'd be skiing in twilight, then by snowlight—like this, now. We looked for animal traces: prints from deer, wild turkey. Bear scat. Feathers.

"One afternoon Noel stopped to study prints he said were from a wildcat. 'More likely a big dog,' I said. But he pointed out the lack of claw dents. Only cats have retractable claws.

"After another ten minutes on the trail we saw the same prints again. 'Too big for a bobcat,' Noel said. 'More like a mountain lion.'"

"What we used to call a catamount. But they're practically extinct," I said. "Certainly around here."

"That's why Noel was so excited. He tapped my sleeve with his pole and pointed. A shadow in the shadows. Something moving a little behind us, to the right. I felt—you know that feeling, when your limbs are flooded by ice? But I went back to Noel's rhythm: pole, kick, glide, pole."

"We talked over what to do, if. Shout? Wave our poles like crazy? Or hold still and keep silent?"

Claudia went quiet. I asked, "And so?"

"We were just getting our stride back when the animal appeared. Her whole long tan body. Bounding closer. Clearing low bushes, making snow streamers. Coming straight at us. Noel grabbed for ice chunks. I did the same. We threw hard but the chunks fell short, knocking more snow off the branches. We yelled, 'Shoo, scat, go to hell, damn cat!' Lobbing ice chunks into the woods, we pushed for the road. I was dripping sweat. Then our voices gave out. Like in a dream."

Claudia bent down to scrape the top crust of snow. She compressed a fistful in her glove, then put it in her mouth, and crunched the ice. "Thirsty." Her teeth shone in a smile. "Talking so much."

We walked on. "Don't leave me hanging, Claudy!"

"We saw two gleaming yellow eyes. Huge. Just ahead. I thought, oh, this is it. She's here. I could smell something rank and hot mixed with the fresh pine and snow. But then my fear switched direction. It was for Noel. I wasn't afraid for myself, I was set to leap in front of him and—" Claudia snorted. "Believe me. I was going to go at that cat. *I was ready.* Nothing could have stopped me. But then, no need. The yellow eyes turned out to be the headlamps of a car. We'd reached the road."

"You were lucky." I felt let down, of course. "So, no catamounts after all."

"Weren't you listening? We saw her."

"Right. Bet you never skied there again."

"Did so. Packed cans of mace, a rifle, and a camera. But no sighting. No luck."

Claudia and I were nearly at the lake road. Headlamps, had there been any, would have spooked me too.

I ARRIVED HOME a little after six. Light spilled from the barn. I heard the swish-swosh of pitchfork through straw. Deanne was in the third stall, mucking out. I sidestepped a flying load of manure aimed at the wheelbarrow.

"Anything you need me for?" I shoved away the pygmy goat chewing my jacket hem.

"All under control," she called back.

I filled and hung up the rubber water buckets. Five months after a double mastectomy isn't long. Deanne was pushing too far too fast, her way of putting cancer in its place. She'd said, "Good that it's a double, this way the reconstructions will match."

My colleague had done clean surgery. All he left for me was to change her dressings. Check the drainage tubes.

For nineteen years we've told each other everything about our days. I mentioned that a childhood friend had looked me up.

"Great, let's invite him out here."

I replied, "She's probably not here long enough."

"In case you're wondering," said Deanne, "I'm bringing the critters in every night from now on. You read about the wildcat?"

"Say again?"

"You didn't read the paper today? A snow-shoer was mauled. Eighty-eight stitches. Imagine. A hunter heard the commotion and shot at the animal so it fled. She—the human—nearly bled to death. They don't know if she'll make it."

WHEN CLAUDIA AND I had said goodbye in the parking lot, there was no mention of a second meeting. I'd long ago learned not to push her to no.

Next morning I went to the clinic in a mental fog. Around ten, my nurse interrupted me doing a strep check to say that a Ms. Lessard—"She's not in your file, Doctor"—was on the phone. I handed her the swab to finish up and hurried, receiver in hand out to the empty corridor to take the call.

IT WAS EASIER, this time. "Let's start a tradition," I proposed. We had a place to go.

"So, how many times have you saved my life?" We were circling the lake clockwise, in the breeze of the thaw. Claudia's red coat billowed behind her, unbuttoned.

It was a good question. We started with the summer when Claudia would only go barefoot. One day her leg buckled and she fell in the grass. While she lay laughing, I checked the culprit leg and saw a long red vein beneath the tan. Haemosepsis from a puncture through the callused sole. In the ER, she lay prone on the gurney while a nurse held her foot in the air. "One more day and this girl'd have lost her foot," said the doctor, slicing in. Was that when I pictured myself wearing a white coat?

"On the night of the school prom I didn't go to, did I save your life?" First-stage alcohol poisoning. She'd managed to toss pebbles at my bedroom window, and I went down and walked her, held her head while she vomited.

"For certain."

"What about your sicko stalker? When you were sunbathing topless in your yard. If I hadn't come by—"

"Not the first time you just barged over, without asking."

"I missed you!"

Her hand squeezed my arm.

"I saw that man standing over you. Wearing a suit. In that heat. You had your eyes closed. No radar."

"You scared him off. But maybe he was harmless."

"Then I've got a pineapple farm in Alaska to sell you."

It was a mellow day: dark melted pools crossed the lake like prints left by a giant. Normally I brown-bag lunch to the office. This spring-like outing felt like a vacation. "Lessard. Is that your name now?"

"From Noel's dad. I was tired of the name-changing. You have to get a new passport, new driver's license—"

"It's his name also? Noel Lessard?"

"Yes. Not that his father—" she broke off. "Olen? Aren't you curious why I asked that question? About saving me?"

"Nope. I figure you'll get there." Today she wore sunglasses. Seen from the side, her eyes were fixed wide open behind the dark lenses. "You're in some kind of trouble? How can

I help?" I aimed for an ironic tone, but the idea knifed through me. Was this what I had been anticipating, since her first call?

"Maybe. Not exactly. Not *me.*" Running her hands up and down her sleeves, as if she was cold after all.

We had reached an ice-fringed stream and had to concentrate on crossing it. Her boots slithered on the rocks. I gripped her elbow. Let her take the time to find words. I had never promised Claudia anything more earthshaking than to change a tire or explain osmosis. Because it wasn't necessary: she knew, and I knew she knew, that if she ever was in real need . . . Now she'd found me. I guessed that the request was somehow hard for her to express. Money? Yes, money would be hard for Claudia to ask for. But what would justify coming all the way here?

I felt poised, hyper-alert. Claudia spoke in a voice so low that it took a moment to pierce my thoughts. She'd shifted the topic back to London. "Five months," she said. "She was already five months pregnant, secretly throwing up."

"Your son's wife?" I'd forgotten the name. "Hyperemesis gravidarum is no joke. No wonder she didn't want to go dancing. How did Noel react?"

"Thrilled! But right then the malaria blew up. He'd had the first attack just before he left Nigeria. I liked to think he came to London because of me, but he came mainly for the Hospital for Tropical Diseases. They put him on experimental drugs. He was officially disabled."

"No job, no home of their own, and a baby coming. Tough spot," I said. I suddenly thought about our kiss, receding like a Cheshire cat in the tangled trees.

"He had his second attack the day after she announced the pregnancy. Have you ever seen malaria in action? How fast it comes on? One minute he's talking normally, the next minute Mandy and I are piling on all the blankets we can find, trying to hold him down so the shaking doesn't throw him again clear off the couch onto the floor. That went on all night. His fever spiked 104. We couldn't reach a doctor that late. Nor get a taxi to the hospital—"

"Ambulance?"

She flapped her mittened hand. "They told us to get a taxi. Mandy went out to the pub for a bucketful of ice, which we wrapped in towels. The sweat pouring out of him melted it in minutes. A fever smell I will never forget.

"A week later, he was himself again. Thin but cheerful. Who wouldn't be after that kind of near miss? He went back to the tropical medicine wallah who said the parasite was under control now. They had its number."

"So, everything was fine!"

"Wait. From the moment Noel got better, Mandy's mood changed. It was her third transformation. She had started out distant and sullen. Then, credit where it's due, she became a real, caring nurse when Noel was sick. But once he recovered, she turned shrill. Coming home, I would hear her voice sawing up and down before she heard my key in the lock.

"I felt bad for Noel. It hurt me to hear her cut him down, reproach him for—what? Not being able to work! Going out with his own mother! Worse was not to hear him defend himself. I began to worry about the baby. The child in her womb was drinking these black moods of hers—trapped in the poison liquid of her emotions. All the chemicals of anger and malice and jealousy! You're a doctor, Olen, you understand what I'm saying. I decided to move out."

"Out of your own house? Where to?"

She waved again, just as she'd brushed off the ambulance. "My presence was doing no good. It was dividing them, no matter how much privacy I tried to give. See, Noel and I were—well, when one of us had a thought, the other would answer it out loud. And she had to witness that close connection every day. I understood. I have *some* friends, and it wasn't for forever, only three months or so. Until the baby was born."

"Not many people would be so generous."

She blew me a mittened kiss. "Olen, you know me. I had my selfish reason, right? It was for the baby. Noel's baby. For its healthy start in life."

I was paying full attention. "Where is the family now? Back up in Canada?" Which would help explain her coming here.

She turned to me. "I'm getting to that." Her look was unreadable behind the sunglasses.

"Mandy was set on a home birth. That's fine by the National Health, cheaper than Hospital, but it wasn't fine by me. She lectured me on how in Africa she had seen women go through natural labor alone in the bush. I said, 'We in the first world, pardon the expression, are different, believe me.' Noel kept out of it. When we met for lunch he talked about his idea for a book, a memoir of the bush war. We hardly touched on Mandy or, for that matter, his health.

"She went into labor three weeks early. Her contractions went on and on, too weak. A doctor was rushed in and it ended up a forceps delivery in an ambulance below in the street. Luckily, despite all that, the baby came through with flying colors. Harold. Harry the Hobo, I call him." She smiled.

"After your father." I remembered a tall man with scoliosis who had been an engineer back in Dresden but in Stevens Point fixed clocks and watches for a living.

Claudia nodded. "Once the dents healed, Harry was one gorgeous infant. Twenty-seven inches at birth! Rosy skin like a peach. I started him on pureed carrots at two weeks, to give him a tan. One of those mother's secrets."

"You moved back into your house? Right after the baby was born?"

She cocked her head. "It hardly felt like my house, all rearranged. The top floor bedroom was still mine, but Noel had his things in my study. Mandy occupied the guest bedroom and pretty much full-time the parlor as well. Nothing had improved between them. She accused Noel of making her so miserable she'd lose her milk. But she had milk: the parlor stank of poor Harry's spit-up, and of her hormonal changes, and God knows what. Everyone tiptoed around her. When he wasn't actually at the breast, Harry tried to fish-flop out of her arms. The newborn's first week should have been bliss. It was hell. I tried bringing Mandy treats to sweeten her with—fruit, candies, books, anything. It was like paying tribute to some implacable goddess.

"Then I learned that while I was away Noel had suffered another malaria episode. I was scared. Furious. She might have called me! And now what? We all gnawed on the question. Would we stay locked in that house together for years, the years of Harry's growing up, honing our grudges and slicing bits out of one another's hides?"

"Shh, Claudia." I looked around, into the woods, where the snow was pocked by ice-fall.

"Sorry, Olen. But how in this day and age can there be a disease with no known cure or treatment or even prognosis? I mean, malaria isn't new like AIDS or Ebola. It's ancient, older than the pyramids."

Too quickly, we had arrived back in the picnic area. We gravitated to the table she'd cleared the day before and sat down facing the lake, hip against hip.

"More and more, I found myself caring for Harry. Soothing him, changing him, feeding him formula—which I'm against, in principle, but when it's all the baby can keep down? Meanwhile Mandy napped, cried, and waved us—her baby and me—away."

"Classic post-partum depression."

"I thought so. Enough depressed that she should see someone. But while I tried to convince them, Noel's malaria came back. The first time hadn't been a nightmare, only the rehearsal. This was the full-dress. Mandy blubbering, Noel shaking as if possessed, raving, teeth clacking like castanets. In the midst of it all, there was Harry to look after. Once when there was a lull I took him up to my room, put him in his bassinet, and closed the door, and went back down to Noel.

"He'd fallen asleep in his nest in my study. He looked so peaceful. I prayed the fever had broken. From the ground floor, Mandy's territory, came no sound at all. It was three-thirty in the morning. I went back up to check the baby, and lay down, hoping to get some rest. As soon as morning came, I meant to call the hospital. And find a baby nurse, the hell with the money.

"In the dark I woke up. There was a cry echoing in my head. A series of frightened cries. Frightened myself, I got up in a daze, head pounding. Harry, by some miracle, was content; he made slurpy sounds sucking his knuckles. I ran down stairs as fast as I could.

"But nothing had changed. Noel lay in the same position, the desk lamp turned away from his face. His expression so peaceful. Even giving little snores, like his own baby's sleep-noise. I went back upstairs and soon dozed off. When I again heard someone crying—more a moaning—I didn't jump up but opened my eyes and listened and heard nothing more. Another nightmare, I decided. The way worries worm in between sleep and waking.

"The next thing I knew, Harry was grizzling in his bassinet, and daylight shone through the curtains. I felt such a rush of relief! As if making it through that night was a victory and everything would be better and clearer from then on. Noel would get well."

Claudia hugged her ankles and propped her chin on her knees. It was a pose I remembered. I laid my arm over her shoulders.

"You're shivering."

"I found Mandy. She was dead."

I didn't take the words in right away, because she spoke low and flat, toward the lake. When I asked her to repeat what she'd said, she flung my arm off and shouted, "Don't you understand? She was dying that night while I lay in bed listening to her! Mandy down below, calling for help. All night long."

"But she died *how*?"

"Necrosis, a word you'll know. But isn't that just another word for death? The coroner's verdict. Maybe some bacteria she'd carried from Africa, and the exhaustion following her delivery gave it an edge. Maybe. But sometimes I blame all those chemicals, her own corrosive emotions eating at her."

"Oh, Claudy." I pulled her closer, her head against my shoulder. Her fuzzy cap fell and her rich hair tumbled loose. It felt like charged silk in my hand. I saw gray in the parting and shut my eyes, only to picture Claudia discovering her daughter-in-law's stiffening body—in what state, with what expression? I saw her phoning, finally, for a doctor, then tending to the infant. Concealing the truth from Noel as long as possible? Answering the questions of the recording physician, then of the police. Of her son.

She was sobbing against me. Grief refreshed by telling.

I asked about Noel, where he was now.

"He's all right." She was sniffling, composing herself with the help of my handkerchief. "He's at Mt. Sinai. They have a new protocol."

"Good. That's a top-notch hospital."

"Mandy was calling for me. A glass lay on the floor. I think she desperately wanted water. Olen, say it. You are horrified. Disgusted. Do you despise me?"

"Knock that off. You tell me now. What can I do to help? I don't have much clout in New York hospitals."

"It's not about Noel's illness. It's . . . a kind of favor. A major favor."

"What? Say it!"

"A birth certificate. Write me out a birth certificate. Please. For Harry. To prove he was born here. Here in Torwald."

"But citizenship should be no problem. The mother was American, and—"

"Noel too. That's not the problem. No, Olen, it's because of them. Her people. They don't know Harry even exists! Because she hadn't been in touch with them since the elopement. I wrote them about her death and sent the body to Connecticut at my expense. Noel and I, we held our own small memorial service in London. But Olen, it's dangerous. If they come to London and snoop around . . ."

"Snoop? Are you suggesting the mother's family shouldn't know they have a grandchild?"

"They must not! Because they're like her—self-righteous and possessive. They'll find a way to take him! *Money,* Olen. Top lawyers can win any custody case. Harry won't be safe, safe and free, unless he can have a new identity. Born right here, in this perfect small town. Why not? As my own child."

"Your child?" My gaze on the gray in her hair.

"It's not impossible!"

"And it's not true!" My mind was churning. "What does Noel say?"

"When he's done with treatment we'll find a place together. The three of us."

"And for now? Claudia, where is the baby?" But suddenly I already knew.

"Harry's here. Back at the Piney Point. The desk clerk is babysitting. Olen, I want you to see him. Will you help us?"

"Give me some time to think. This isn't as simple as you apparently imagine."

"I need to get back. But call soon? It *is* simple, Olen. It's only a piece of paper."

A quarter past three. The shadows stretched long. "Would you believe," Claudia whispered just as we parted, "that when Harry cried from hunger, I felt my breasts tingle, like milk letting down?"

I CALLED THE office with a glib lie and drove home, thankful that it was Deanne's library afternoon. Exhausted, I lay down on the floor of our bedroom, not wanting to muss the quilt.

After all these years, I knew where Claudia was. I could go to the Piney Point any hour I wanted. "Call day or night," she'd said. She would stay there as long as I needed, waiting with baby Harry for my answer.

On the screen of my closed eyelids a catamount prowled the path circling the lake. Oiled shoulder blades. A gaunt she-lion near the end of winter.

I had to think. The room was darkening. Someone unafraid to fight a wild cat. What else did she have the nerve for? To ignore laws.

"We won't presume, won't bother you," she'd said. She didn't know what she was asking. Or perhaps she thought, compared to her, I had little to lose. Was I afraid? Not as much as I should be. What would it mean, with time? What would I become a part of, and responsible for?

Do you despise me? For what, Claudy? For being exhausted, convinced the cries were tricks of your overtired mind?

Childbed fever. A catch-all diagnosis from a nineteenth-century textbook. This mother who had waved her baby away. Had she called out in terror, sensing death in the room? Or were those only pleas for water, in her peevish whine—

A sound jerked me into the present. My face was covered in sweat. I felt the carpet scrape across my cheek as I turned. Those familiar steps outside the room. The door opened, fanning light.

"Ols? Hey there. Hey, sweetheart . . ." Deanne was kneeling beside me before I could struggle to my feet. Her hand pressed my forehead. "What's going on? Are you sick? What the heck are you doing on the floor?"

Noel's sweat-drenched forehead under Claudia's cooling hand.

"Goodness, Ols, will you say something? Here, okay, heave ho, let's stand up."

"Watch out! No heavy lifting."

That got a laugh. We both stood, swaying a little together. On the bedside table the phone rang.

"Oh, for God's sake! Just leave it! Can't these people ever give you some peace?" Deanne tried to catch my arm, and failed. Her tone darkened. "Who is it, do you think?"

"Nobody. Nobody we know." I held the phone to my chest. I could see her, my nobody. Hunched on the edge of a motel mattress, cradling the infant. Alone yet not lonely, anxious yet certain, pressing the phone's racing heartbeat to her ear.

Mrs. Trefoil's Parlor

HALF-DAZED BY A cyclone of red maple leaves outside her kitchen window, Amber heard a sound like a baby's high-pitched gurgle or the dream-yelp of a dog. Then silence took over the house again, the night aide having left already, the day nurse not yet arrived. The sound came from the hospital bed in the front room—the house being so old and narrow that they couldn't drag the rented bed further. It was her mother calling, but not wanting *her*. Mom hadn't summoned Amber in weeks, no longer showed a twitch of recognition. Amber guessed her mother was calling her own Mamosh, that high-living heartbreaker whom Mom had reviled in healthier days. Or maybe calling God? Recently, while her mother's voice still held some power, Amber had been shaken by cries for both: "God! Oh Lord God above, help me! Mamosh, where are you?"

The spell of the leaves was broken. After setting the kettle on its wreath of blue gas—hot water for her own Nescafé, sterile water to thin her mother's Isolac for the feeding tube—Amber walked down the hall, counting gouges in her bare pine floor left by the steel bed. She and her ex, Ramon, had spent a long night sanding these boards on their hands and knees, only to rush and botch the final job of sealing. Later they blamed each other for the damage, but now she saw that no amount of sealant would have mattered.

The front room was the bright one, sun-drenched by windows along opposite walls. Amber missed having its use. The sofa set she and Ramon had chosen for sleek sophistication now appeared predestined: clinical white. In a corner, flanked by the tube stand, dangling pouches and a metal table crammed with drugs, stood the bed, foot aimed at the door, head hydraulically raised. In May, during the settling-in stage, Amber's mother had referred archly to the high railed bed as her throne. Her kind of joke.

"Mom?" No response. "Something you want? Are you comfortable? Are you awake?" These days she spoke to her mother mainly to clear the cobwebs from her own voice. She didn't expect any answer, answers already belonged to the past. She was sure her mother did hear, when not freshly sedated, and that her stubborn muteness stemmed from anger over dying, an anger that had hit Amber full force, splattering her with its venom, just before communication ended. Or had her mother given up speaking only because her throat was raw from the trachеotomy and she had no will left to fight the pain?

How to help someone who won't or can't speak. All Amber could do was check her mother's position, make sure she hadn't thrashed her bones—all she was now, bones—into a disjointed huddle. Amber wondered if she straightened the hips and limbs mainly so the day nurse wouldn't think her callous or neglectful. According to her few relatives, she already did far more than was owed to a mother who, when a young and vigorous alcoholic, had thrown the daughter into the night over and over, until the message got through. So why Amber's dread of disapproval? Alone in the house, she conjured up some sympathetic listener she could confess to: about how even straightening her mother's legs (which looked thin as pipe cleaners but were surprisingly heavy) she felt guilty. That furious burbling of the tracheotomy pipe—groans? How to be sure the pretzeled position wasn't the one her mother wanted, the only one that gave some relief?

Amber stood in the doorway. The faint ridge of her mother's body lay perfectly centered in the bed.

"I'll fix your pillows, okay? Find the cool side?" As she crossed the sun-warmed floor, her mother's small head, stretched upward in profile, changed from an ashy smudge to the particular: the streaked auburn hair turned white in two months of summer. Mottled skin spanning knobby cheeks, beaked nose. A stunningly swift aging toward a stranger who with each day of her transformation became easier to pity, to forgive.

At first she didn't notice that the trach tube no longer bubbled. Her mother's lips were what stopped her: colorless, drawn back above tobacco-stained teeth in a fierce grin Amber hadn't seen in years.

Her best feature, her mother used to insist, was her eyes. In her off-key falsetto she used to warble "Beautiful Brown Eyes" and later, "Don't It Make My Brown Eyes Blue." Now Amber pressed the lids down over her mother's protuberant eyes with a gesture learned from movies. Amazingly, it worked.

"Goodbye," she said. And after a while, "Bye, Mom. And . . . bon voyage." Time passed, or not. Smells of sweet infection and sour excrement still rose from her mother's bed. For once, no chores were pressing. The day nurse was late, but that woman's irresponsibility would never drive Amber up the wall again. From the corner of her eye, she saw vermilion leaves streaking across the window. She had no tears, was dry as a ditch, but ached to hear something else said, to continue their new habit of one-sided conversation.

The face cradled by the pillow seemed to alter and reform itself, sinking into the hollows of extreme age, then relaxing as if lifted by a memory. Next week would have been her mother's fiftieth birthday. Even though no one else knew her exact age—twenty years single, no close friends anymore—in September she'd wept big fat tears at the prospect of turning fifty. "Honestly, Hon, do I look *that* over the hill?" "Christ," Amber had said, "*you're* the one holding the mirror. Anyhow, I'm your kid. How do *I* know what you look like?"

Years back, while still childishly convinced of her own powers (if she could only, only, find the magic words) Amber had prodded her mother to grow up, get off the street, find a steady-paycheck job, an apartment. Start taking some kind of care of herself.

"Mom?" she said now. "Hey? You look so young. You still are young! You didn't—you didn't get a lot of time."

She sent the day nurse away at the front door. "We're all set here. Tell the agency we're cancelling. Thanks, sorry, okay?"

BEFORE AMBER'S MOTHER went into her silence, she had often demanded a pencil and pad to make a show of writing "my last will and testament." The scraggly letters grew loopier and less legible with each draft. The pages were handed to health aides who squirreled them away in the bed-table's cabinet, along with the patient's handbag and Medicare papers and mystery paperbacks. Given the inheritance at stake, Amber didn't bother snooping. But now she wheeled the table out with cautious jerks—still in the habit of not disturbing. She found the bankbook first and checked the total: $610. Welfare savings. It had been only to placate Ramon, the champion of Family Values, that Amber had offered to *maybe* take her mother in at home. At which the hospital social worker had exclaimed, "What a world it would be if every adult child was like you!" And then set to finagling a financial horn of plenty. That the government would pay for Mom's support flabbergasted Amber. She wished she had caught on sooner. After Ramon walked out, the US Treasury checks covered her mortgage. After a lifetime of Mom's self-absorption, she deserved this shot in the arm.

End of shots, now.

In the black plastic handbag, a pack of cigarettes so dry they might self-ignite. Lipstick. Matted hairbrush. A snapshot of herself at nine or ten—pole-thin in overalls, raccoon circles under her eyes. She pictured her mother displaying the photo to fellow street people. The purse held three subway tokens. Mom had never learned to drive. Small mercies.

On the top sheet of the yellow pad Amber found a shopping list: Maalox, Kleenex, TV Guide, Sunday Globe. The next page was filled with the meandering script of what Amber realized was an attempted diary. She pushed it away like something diseased.

A pile of recipes torn from the newspaper. And here: an address book. The entries were smeary, mostly in pencil, hard to decipher. Doctors. Amber's own changing numbers. A few unknowns. Friends? Who, then?

Under the paperback novels, she finally found a folded yellow-lined paper. The edges were taped together and on the outside some nurse had printed: Confidential for My Daughter, Amber. To Be Opened Only After I Am No More.

Amber sliced the tape with her fingernail.

The handwriting inside was her mother's, from past the point where she could form letters. It swayed around the lines like a preschooler's effort. Amber stared at this maze. No clue, no bag lady's hidden treasure. No last word. She felt let down but resigned. Just what had she expected?

At the bottom of the page in the firm nurse-letters was printed: Trefoil & Sons—Fun. Parlor—Dorchester. Her Personal Wish. Very Important The Patient Says.

Amber's knees ached from the hard floor. "Why didn't you tell *me* that?"

In the kitchen, blue smoke stung her eyes. The kettle had boiled dry; its bottom glowed fiery orange. She leapt to shut off the gas and when she threw a pan of water over the kettle, more smoke and steam billowed, and black chips of smoldering metal dropped to the floor. It was funny to think that on her mother's death-day she might have also burned the house down. The irony brought her to the edge of tears.

She dialed a number from the dog-eared address book. Her uncle in Seattle, whom she hadn't seen since the days of the photo he'd taken of Amber that her mother had kept. She heard a distant clatter, throat-clearing. "Yeah?"

"Uncle Lou?" She fixed her eyes on a spinning tornado of falling leaves.

On hearing the news, her uncle became energized. "So, Sis went faster than you had us thinking," he yelled. "You know I was meaning to come out to see her. Next month, in fact. Say, Amber, you holding up okay?"

"Yes. I'm not sure what to do next."

"Do 'bout what?"

"Well, her—"

"Oh, all that stuff," he said. "That's what undertakers are paid for, right? The service we'll want out here, of course. Seattle's where her roots are. Listen, I'll deal with the burial arrangements on this end. The least I can— Hello?"

Amber stealthily hung up. Dizzy, she drank a glass of water and opened windows, thinking the kettle smoke had poisoned her a little. She pulled out the yellow pages and dialed again.

A warm voice answered. "Trefoil and Sons. Thirty years of service to the bereaved." The woman's voice was multi-chorded, like a jazz singer's. "Good morning! How can we be of assistance?"

"I, um—my mother died."

"I am sorry to hear of your loss. May she rest in peace. Now when was that, dear?"

"An hour ago? Or two. Not by accident. I mean, she was ill. But nothing contagious. Throat cancer. Somebody recommended you so I—"

The woman interrupted, gentle and firm. Did Amber have a death certificate? Amber was grateful for this practical reminder. She felt more anchored, speaking to this woman for whom one death was like any other. She gave her name and address, and driving directions out Route 2 from Boston for picking up the body. On hearing her mother's name, the woman's voiced soared.

"You're the daughter. Well, you poor dear child! I knew your mother. Last time she called me up was only—now, when was it? July?"

"She told me," Amber lied.

"You did right to call us. My boys will be out no time at all to look after every single detail. You only need that certificate and— Let's see. Today's Friday. When do you want to come to my store?"

"Your store?"

"Why, to select her casket, dear."

THE DOCTOR ASSURED her that the death had been an easy one. Amber asked, "How the hell would you know?" He palmed her a sample pack of Librium along with the signed certificate.

She raked leaves while waiting for the undertakers. The garden shouted out her neglect. Ramon had been the one who had weeded, limed, macheted back each summer's growth. Raking, she thought about how it wasn't her mother, or the stress of advancing illness, that had driven him off. After all, he had pushed for Amber to take her mother in. Let bygones be, he'd preached. Who else has she got? And if you don't, could you ever forgive yourself?

Maybe her seesawing feelings about the breakup were inevitable: as long as you're alive, separations are never finished.

The leaves leapt at her, grabbed her clothes, swirled overhead. *I'm such a jerk,* she thought. *Can't even rake.* She glared at the glossy windows of the neighboring houses, each surrounded by a crew-cut, leaf-blower tidy lawn.

Neither she nor Ramon had been prepared for the disruption home nursing brought. The bedpans, Alps of laundry, emergencies, medical procedures to be learned, the parade of aides. The lack of sleep. Recriminations exploded at dawn, at midnight, hissed between clenched teeth. Those tensions, they both eventually realized, had other, deeper sources. "You were just the catalyst," Amber said aloud, embracing a cloud of leaves, stuffing what she could into a dirt-streaked plastic barrel.

In one sense, bringing her mother home had turned out to be a smart move: Ramon had signed her his share of the house. He was not the kind of man, he told the mediator, to take the roof from a dying woman. But now taxes were coming due, and the roof had two leaks.

Amber looked up at the silvery shingles, still sheltering her mother's remains in the noon silence. Would she have to sell? All summer, her days had melted together, sealing out the abstract *afterward*: the question of how to manage alone, on what. In a small town, with limited work experience and no college degree. Crying "Shit, shit *shit,*" she pulled leaves from her hair, angry at the ending of summer.

LIKE A BLACK pirate ship the hearse crested the hill road and sailed down toward Amber's house into the empty driveway. Its gleaming bulk surprised her—not to mention the gaiety of tasseled purple curtains, a pastel dashboard Virgin, sconced yellow flowers. Two tall, slim men in close-cut black suits swung out from each side. They wore tiny fedora hats and black string ties. For a second, she saw them snapping their fingers, breaking into a joint-popping dance.

There was no dancing. Stepping forward, the men took off their hats. One reached out his hand. All the corpses these manicured, slender-boned fingers had touched. She shook his hand firmly, apologizing for the dirt on hers.

"You just stay on out here," the driver said. "Let us manage." He wore gold-rimmed glasses; he wasn't young; his skin, set off by white shirt cuffs and collar, was black with shimmers of blue. The man behind him—twin? younger brother?—nodded. "The deceased have oxygen equipment? Rental, no doubt. Number will be taped on. We can call the company, remove all that too. Save you the hassle. Time we're done, you'll find everything back to normal, Miss."

"Are you sure I can't—"

"You leave everything to us. You've had a grief, understand? Go back to your garden work, if that's what's needed. You done your part." He touched her arm. His brother squeezed both eyes together, as if in sympathy.

They filed up her front walk, entered her house. An occasional click from the hearse's cooling engine sounded. She rested a hand on the warm waxed hood. A luxurious machine. She looked around at her neighbors' windows, at first shyly, knowing these inner-city undertakers were bound to be gossiped over, and then defiantly.

The man was right: she did not want to see her mother's body being carried out. She wandered to the back of the house.

An orchard of gnarled apple trees abutted her lot. No one owned the trees: when the last farmer died, his land had passed to the town. The air was pungent with cidery fumes from the fallen fruit. In the spring, gazing out at the ground-skimming clouds of apple blossoms, her mother had said, "Make you a deal, sweetie pie. Come October, I'll teach you applesauce from scratch."

And Amber had said, "Sure you will," marveling at how illness can alter both memory and personality, because in all the years, her mother had never prepared anything homemade.

She toed wormy Macouns rolling through the grass but found none worth keeping.

Suddenly sure the undertakers must be finished and were probably waiting outside where they were exposed to suburban stares, she headed back, mentally going over phrasing the delicate question of their bill.

The driveway was empty. Inside, in the front room, tubes had been looped up, the bed stripped, all ready for removal. The men, her mother—everyone was gone.

On a chilly Monday Amber drove into the Dorchester section of Boston, early for her appointment in case she got lost. No highway led toward the neighborhood she wanted—*ghetto* used to be the word. Arson-gutted buildings and weedy stretches of rubble. As she drove down Blue Hill Avenue, trolley wires sizzled overhead, trash tumbled, the few people walked with backs humped against the wind.

Following Mrs. Trefoil's directions, she now recalled having been on this street once before. At least five years ago, just after she and Ramon moved in together. She'd taken the trolley from downtown for a reluctant reunion in a thronged self-serve cafeteria, a pretend-casual lunch in her mother's chosen hood.

How her mother's skinny frame had stood out among the sturdy black men and women whose turf this was. Everyone lined up for collard greens and wings with red gravy. "Home cooking, baby!" Mom had urged. Her lumpy plastic shopping bags were propped under their table. People carrying trays veered around them. *Bag lady!* The words hit Amber in that moment as a revelation, and from then on, they stung her through stand-up comedians' raw jokes, sob stories, and random flippant remarks.

Amber pressed the written directions against the steering wheel. She peered for street signs but many were missing, the poles bent right to the ground.

Ramon had never seen this neighborhood where her mother had lived. Amber had made sure of that. In their own circle he'd referred to her mother as eccentric, which to him sounded aristocratic. Amber soon realized that Ramon considered himself an aristocrat. His parents had emigrated from Cuba "with gold coins sewn in their shoes." His pocked complexion was "Spanish, back to a Moroccan prince." For her part, Mom—invited to the engagement party at Ramon's insistence and chugging champagne like it was Poland Springs—announced how tickled she was to see Amber flout prejudice with a brother. Thanks to mutual mis-recognition, and sparse contact, a bond flourished between Ramon and Amber's mother. Amber was left out.

Prospect Terrace. The sign was intact, not even a bullet hole. Amber turned her rusty Fiat up a steep side street. While the engine bucked and struggled, the neighborhood brightened, as if she'd crossed a border. Bow-fronted homes gleamed in the sun, trim fences enclosed chrysanthemums, a splash of tricycles were dropped in mid-play. Amber rolled down her window. The Trefoil & Sons sign stood before a white mansion at the top of the hill.

She parked in back, behind the hearse. An Office sign with an arrow was tacked over wooden stairs. Before Amber could knock, she heard a rattling of bolts. The door swung open.

"Well, well! Better we meet late than never! Amber—such a lovely name, I always did tell her. No trouble finding us, I hope?"

Amber stepped into darkness. Sweet smell of chemicals in the air. "Mrs. Trefoil?"

"My Lord. If you aren't her spitting image. Don't be timid, child—step on in."

A dim, unbounded space. The only strong light glowed from an enormous aquarium tank. Schools of tetras and angelfish hovered in swaying pink reeds over gaping treasure chests. As Amber's eyes adjusted, Mrs. Trefoil settled into a high-backed wooden chair. Threads of daylight straggled through a gauzy curtain behind her. She wore gold-rimmed glasses like her son's, whose face Amber recalled as lively and dimpled, not an undertaker's mask at all. Broad-shouldered and large-bosomed in a navy skirt and jacket, she tapped the top of desk between them. "Sit down, dear Amber. Relax, now. I made us this pot of tea."

AMBER, NIBBLING PECAN wafers and having trouble tearing her gaze from the tank of brilliant fish, responded to Mrs. Trefoil's onrushing conversation as best she could.

"Originally your mother and I met when she cold-called for that insurance man down the Avenue," Mrs. Trefoil said. "The business side naturally brought us together. Oh, she had some juicy bits to tell on her boss. No wonder that gig didn't last. Oh my, your mother could imitate folks, right? Make you laugh till you cried. I miss her. Not like you do, Amber—but she knew how to chase away my blues. We had ourselves some crazy times, right here in my parlor."

In the beginning, Amber's mother had wheedled for extravagant gifts, as if dying should be a kind of super-birthday. Once Amber and Ramon had gone out to price aquarium kits. Amber estimated Mrs. Trefoil's ichthyoid investment at a few thousand dollars, minimum. A successful business person then, a worldly woman. The opposite of Mom. The stream of bubbles, whoosh and burble of the filter really was relaxing. Client therapy?

"I recall your dear mother did mention family in Seattle."

"Yes, but we moved east when I was little." Collecting herself, she turned to confront Mrs. Trefoil. "To be honest, my main problem is, I want to get her—her body—to Seattle. For burial. If I can."

"Air freight," Mrs. Trefoil said.

"Isn't that . . . kind of complicated? Expensive."

"We do what must be done," Mrs. Trefoil said. "Now you follow me."

THIS—THE CHOOSING OF the casket—was what Amber had been dreading. Mrs. Trefoil led her down a long hallway, past what looked like a miniature chapel where artificial candles glowed, to a second large windowless room. Mrs. Trefoil snapped a switch. Caskets, stacked one over the other against the walls like rowboats, jumped out in the glare.

"Here we have your Royal Windsor," said Mrs. Trefoil. Her hand fluttered along puffy primrose satin lining. Amber was reminded of the boxes fancy dolls used to come packed in. She had never had a doll. "An exquisite model. Guaranteed to preserve for the maximum time possible. We'll come back to that aspect."

Aha. Here's how they do it, thought Amber. The guilt trip. How they shame you into splurging on a splashy ten-ton crate that's only going to rot a little slower.

Amber would not be shamed.

Mrs. Trefoil guided her on through the display, pointing out satin versus silk, brass fittings versus stainless, lecturing on the insect- and moisture-repellent virtues of rosewood, cedar, oak. Amber halted her, bent down to examine a simple lozenge-shaped box with a smooth white lining. "What's this wood? Pine?"

"I'm afraid so. Southern Yellow." Mrs. Trefoil sniffed.

"It's pretty," Amber said truthfully.

"This version's really only for . . . a special category. Charity cases and whatnot. Victims. Not for your mother, Amber!"

"So." Amber straightened; her knees made a loud click. "Is this one the best value?"

"All depends on your notion of value." Mrs. Trefoil folded her arms. "She did have taste, your mother." The room was in fact very cold.

"I don't have a lot to spend. She didn't leave much money."

As if Amber hadn't spoken, Mrs. Trefoil flicked at the white lining. "This," she said. "Feel here. Rayon." Her voice dripped disdain.

"Still. It's what I want for her."

Mrs. Trefoil inhaled deeply, as if gathering strength for an argument, but then let the breath out slowly, through puffed-out lips. She led Amber back through the house to the parlor, for a last sip of cold tea, discussion of details, and the filling out of papers in triplicate. She would need time, she said, to estimate all the expenses, especially considering Seattle, but was certain Amber would find her terms very reasonable. Seeing Amber frown, she pointed out the waived deposit and mentioned an extended payment option. Amber gave in. They signed.

Mrs. Trefoil's natural friendliness returned. "Blue was always far and away her best color. But you know that." Would Amber look through her mother's wardrobe for something in good condition with a high neckline in blue? Amber nodded, her eyes drawn to the neon pastel streaking of fish, while mentally marking for sacrifice a dress of her own. She intended never to touch the bags and sagging cardboard boxes stowed in her basement. Just imagining the musty junk inside made her queasy.

Amber stood, folding the contract copy into her purse. "Are we—is that all I have to do?" she asked.

Mrs. Trefoil dimpled. "Far as I'm concerned. Unless you come to change your mind on the Windsor?" She rounded the desk and opened her arms. For a moment Amber floated in the warmth of a stranger's hug.

Ushered out the front door onto the broad porch, Amber turned back to Mrs. Trefoil. The rush of wind and sunlight awakened her. Questions swam in her head: is it true you and she were friends? You *liked* her? Or did you make that up because . . . or at least exaggerate for the sake of—

"This certainly is her kind of weather!" Beside her, Mrs. Trefoil breathed deeply, nostrils flared. "I'm gratified she got one more taste of fall. Her favorite. She told me about all the nature out your way. Apple trees. That old house you worked so hard to fix up for her—"

Amber flinched inside. Mrs. Trefoil knew things. Including fibs, Amber would bet. Skewed, self-aggrandizing stories her mother had told. But why care what Mrs. Trefoil believed she knew?

"She was a true nature lover," Mrs. Trefoil said. "Nature—and children, too. She was one of the young at heart."

In silence, Amber exploded. *She didn't even ever want to visit me until she got sick.* "You've got your scene, baby, I've got mine." She changed her tune in the hospital. She hated the doctors calling her by her first name. She ninja-tossed an ashtray at one guy's head. She thought they were all out to get her, and by then they were. I took her home, no choice.

"All those leaves." Mrs. Trefoil gestured with her chin. The yard was stenciled by the shadow of a massive spreading oak. Under the oak lay drifts of brown curls. "Last Thanksgiving your mother raked those leaves. She and my grandson Amarr, together. Amarr's four now. Quite a handful! He's blind. Your mother had a special gift with that child—I still hear them giggling, rolling in all those leaves!"

"I'm sorry," Amber said.

Mrs. Trefoil stared. "About? The blindness, you mean? Amarr? Oh, yes, well. A handicap's not so terrible. You quickly get accustomed."

Time to leave. Amber's mind ran away, out of the city, back to her own yard and house.

"Another memory I have of that day is your mother making her famous applesauce. Spicy! 'Finally something good enough to cover up that embalming smell,' my son said, although I seldom notice the chemicals, myself."

The wind whistled in Amber's ears. She heard shrieks rising from a stick-thin white woman sitting half-buried in brown leaves, her legs outstretched like a doll's, her arms reaching to a curly-haired boy whose white sightless eyes matched his milk teeth. From inside the house came a strong whiff of cloves and cinnamon. There were people moving in the parlor, people in the kitchen. She glimpsed the curved back of a thin woman who was poking a wooden spoon into a kettle. For the last few nights she'd been wakened hourly by dreams in which her mother appeared. Now she took a panicked step back, into empty space.

"Amber, *child*!" Mrs. Trefoil grabbed her arm. The hold was as firm as a man's. Amber pivoted, the ground below dipped and blurred. She was swung upward until solid wood slid back beneath her feet. Mrs. Trefoil leaned her up against a post, before letting go.

Inside, a phone rang.

"Never mind that call. Whoever it is can wait." Mrs. Trefoil frowned. "You'd best come back in my parlor, now. You need to sit down a while."

"No, I—"

"Now listen here. You're in no state, child. You can sit quietly by yourself. I have plenty of business to attend to."

"I'm *fine.* Clumsy is how I always am!" Amber's fingers clasped her stinging arm. "It gets dark so early. I really do have to get back."

"All right, then. Looks like you are old enough to know your own mind. Though I'm not convinced."

Stiffly, holding the rail, Amber descended the steps. Her purse had landed on a heap of leaves. Nothing was lost. The funeral home director, her skirt snapping in the wind, stood on the porch above her. "Mrs. Trefoil?" Amber called. "I just wondered—around here, in this neighborhood? Were you the only . . . Or did my mother have any other friends?"

Mrs. Trefoil's face creased like a Greek comedy mask. "Amber, darling. Your irresistible, charming mother? What do you think? What on earth kind of question is that?"

On the plane back to Boston from Seattle Amber rubbed her cheeks to ease the paralysis of two days of phony, mournful smiles. She understood, with a new intimacy, why her mother had left that city. Already the funeral service, the numbing hypocrisy of aunts and second cousins, the chill of incessant rain, were fading into a deserved haze. What she did remember vividly was the sound of her own startled cry in the vaulted church, when as first mourner, approaching the casket with her armload of lilies, she recognized the Royal Windsor.

A massive carved mahogany tomb. A funeral barge already loaded with wreaths, mostly from anonymous donors, taper-lit and out-glorying the altar above. The image of the Royal Windsor, a vanity fit for a gangster or a billionaire, haunted her on this night ride back. Only when a series of thunderstorms set the plane rocking violently did Amber fall asleep.

Once home, she scrabbled anxiously through her mail. Was she liable for that extravagant, unauthorized expense? Maybe. No one ever said laws were fair!

But for weeks the mailbox offered only holiday catalogs, Cancer Foundation requests—and then a black-bordered condolence letter from Ramon, which she tore in pieces. Had she missed Mrs. Trefoil's bill?

She landed a job in the town insurance agency, with health benefits.

In November, in the confessional cubicle of the local bank manager, she laid out her financial situation. She did not mention the pending, unspecified debt to Trefoil & Sons. She couldn't stop staring at the red-faced manager's gold tie clip. He told her that her situation looked brighter than she supposed, that his bank was about people serving people, and Amber profiled as a good risk, someone able to keep her equity and her head above water.

That afternoon he called to invite her to dinner, to a restaurant two towns away, where she guessed he hoped not to be recognized. She suffered through the farce and the groping for two more dates until the loan was approved, then ever after said she was busy.

In the breathing space that followed, she thought about calling Mrs. Trefoil. Maybe she could offer a compromise payment. But part of her simply wanted to hear Mrs. Trefoil's voice again—and yes, even to go back to the funeral home, to the draped parlor lit by the fish tank. She saw herself sitting with knees pressed together like a schoolgirl, nibbling cookies, listening to the undertaker's stories. Mrs. Trefoil might even sing to her—yes! Songs about crossing the river Jordan. About death being life's reward.

But February turned to March, and more than the hovering, unknown debt, the possibility that Mrs. Trefoil might simply have forgotten her made Amber hesitate. Soon, she told herself, someone will review the accounts. Any day they'd send an overdue notice. She'd call Mrs. Trefoil and say she'd forgotten, too. A rough winter. Mrs. Trefoil would understand.

One Saturday, sitting on her white sofa in the sun-drenched front room, Amber considered driving out to the mall. But there was nothing she wanted to buy. Now and then her mind's eye dove down into her basement, to a stack of taped boxes forwarded from a YWCA rooming house. Her mother's name scrawled above her own address.

The March wind rose, and there came to her the creak of old wood scraping on stone foundation. She heard her unstoppable heart. She pressed her fists to her eyes.

When the phone rang, she froze, then lurched up, slipping on the polished floor in her rush to reach the kitchen.

"Hello? Yes, hello?" A hope, then certainty, flared in her. "*Hello?* Don't hang up! Please, if this is Mrs.—?"

A dry click in her ear. Wrong number? Or a prank call? Happened to women known to be living alone. Amber wasn't afraid of harassers. But she heard an odd sound, her own hiccup or sob, as she set the phone back down.

The caller could not have been Mrs. Trefoil. From the beginning, the undertaker had never wanted any payment. And the contract? For form's sake, to spare Amber the pain of feeling beholden, on top of grief. All Mrs. Trefoil had tried to win from Amber that day was one extravagant expressed desire: the Royal Windsor, price be damned.

There would be no further communication between them. No tea, no flashing fish, no dimpled smile. Mrs. Trefoil had long since balanced her accounts.

Far Bangalore

"ALL OUR REPRESENTATIVES are busy helping other—Good evening! Thankyouforwaiting."

"Three fucking hours, robo-voice!"

"Sir, all calls are recorded for training purposes."

"'Sir?' Are you a real person?"

"Monica speaking. And can you kindly confirm that you are Mr. . . . Ellie Wandel?"

"Eli, okay? Hey. Sorry. After moldering on hold for—"

"Three hours, Mr. Eli?"

"It's kind of a miracle to hear a—you are a human?"

Silence.

"Wow. A fellow sentient being. Look, I guess you can see my file already, but—"

"Mr. Eli, sir?"

"Just Eli."

"Might we start with a few security questions?"

"Oh. Homeland Police. Haha. Fire away."

"Excellent. What was the name of your first pet?"

Eli has always hated pop quizzes. He squints at the swirling screen saver on his useless laptop. *Come on, man. Picture the dog. Shaggy brown mop. You pulled its ears. It bit you on the—* "Trifid!"

"Exactly! And your favorite movie?"

Why do they demand such a personal factoid, moreover one he can't recall? People change. Tastes morph.

"Eli? Are you still with me?"

"Oh yes."

"The movie?"

"Wild guess. *Blazing Saddles*?"

Silence.

"Uh, *Avatar*?"

"Brilliant! My sister loved it. And lastly, your zip code."

"One three eight two seven."

"Match again! So that's done." That silliness, her voice implies. "Now, Eli, describe your problem to me."

Overwhelmed by this invitation, Eli puts his feet up on the dining room table and closes his eyes. His problem. His so-called life. One year out of college he camps solo in the house he was born in, which now has a for sale sign stabbed in the crabgrass, in a formerly one-company middle class town, now a no-company town, where even the Dollar General is about to fold. This deep-porched house won't sell until hell freezes over, and hell, thanks to Big Oil, just keeps getting hotter.

"You are unable to connect to the Internet. Correct?"

"Right! For two days. Your techie came and stomped around outside but after he hightailed it, still nothing. Power, but no signal."

"Hightailed it?"

"Left very fast."

"Unprofessional. He should have tested the line."

"Right? Did he even splice the wire? We're dealing with nineteenth century technology here. I live in a—"

"Rural zone."

"Kind of. I'm on DSL. There isn't even an icon anymore on your website for DSL. We're like extinct up here. Not that I can open the website—"

"Clearly not!"

"You get that, Ms.—? I forgot."

"Monica."

"Monica! But the robo-voice kept telling me to go online for faster service. Anyway, the point is, me getting back online is a matter of life and death."

"Mr. Eli! You are not injured? Not ill?"

"Sorry. Hyperbole. Like in, exaggeration?" Although Monica sounds well educated, highly educated even, with her bubbly post-colonial British-Indian accent, she and he can't possibly totally share a vocabulary. Although it is amazing how many cool Hindi words have found a home in English. Pajamas. Bangle. Juggernaut. Avatar!

"Hyperbole, yes. I'm an offender myself." A smile illuminates her voice. "However, were there some medical issue, Eli, I could triage you into a higher—"

"Honestly, no. I just really need to be online. It's critical. To my job."

"Of course. As it is to mine. More and more to all of us."

"It's the only way to prove I've showed up for work."

"I see! Your work is remote?"

Dear God let her not ask what kind of work.

"Hm. Your cell phone functions. You might engage your phone as a hot spot, to connect with your employer?"

"Have you ever tried to download forty filled-out questionnaires over a phone?"

"No—"

"Plus, here in rural American I'm lucky to have two bars. Plus, my data plan? The last time I used this phone as a hot spot I got hit with an obscene bill from the wireless carrier, which has the same name as the Internet provider you work for. It's like robbing Peter to rob Paul!"

"This sounds quite unfair. Eli, I will do all I can to expedite your file."

"Will you, Monica? You're being amazingly—"

Sharp pings announce a new call coming in. He unglues the phone from his tingling ear to read the screen. Janis. Tap green dot to accept and put Monica on hold, or red to decline. He has never, ever, declined Janis before. Red.

"Eli, you are with me?"

"Absolutely."

"I need to conduct tests of your landline for the DSL. Is your phone plugged into the wall jack?"

"No. Because I don't own a land thingie. Who does, these days?"

"I see. No problem. Will you please stay with me while I set up the test?"

"Sure! It's not like I'm expected somewhere." With that, he remembers talk with Janis about eating out at RedRibs Roadside tonight. But Janis, for whom movie streaming is like an IV feed, will understand. "I'm all yours, Monica. Test away!" Semi-flirting with a call center rep definitely beats yelling at a robo-voice, which has to be the definition of impotence. A subject on which Eli is becoming an expert.

But why has Monica gone silent? Has he tumbled into some cultural no-go zone? "Um, do you see anything bad?"

"The test takes time."

"No worries!"

"You know, Eli, it's so true what you said about automated menus. How my customers curse when they think only a machine is on the line. I expect some day to hear someone in the throes of a heart attack, and then the company will—" She stops. Uh-oh. This call is being recorded. Her amiable impersonal voice returns. "Well, Eli! I see from your zip code that you live in New York State. How is your weather today?"

"Hot. Humid. Even for July."

Ping ping ping. Janis. Who else ever calls? Except once a week, his mother. Janis can text if it's so urgent. Eli's thumb squashes the red dot.

"And thunderstorms. Climate change, you think? Which might be why my Internet—" *Zip it, Eli. There's probably an Act of God clause in the contract, ready to stick you with the repair bill.*

"So, where are you, Monica? Let me guess. India?"

"Where many people also don't have landlines." Again, that bright smile in her voice.

"I know, right? Next guess. You're in Bangalore."

"You are familiar with India! Tell me, Eli, did you enjoy visiting my country?"

"Um . . . so much. I'd go again in a heartbeat."

"It does my heart good to hear this."

Eli blushes. "I mean, India was always top of my wish list." That much is true. Ever since Mom read him *The Jungle Book*.

"Bangalore is hardly a tourist destination."

"Bangalore is real! The center of technology, the hub of modern India—"

"You get it!"

"Bangalore's so . . ."

"Say it?"

"Electric. I had some life-altering experiences there."

"Tell me one!"

"If only we had time. But what it comes down to, Monica, is, there are two kinds of people."

"Right? Those who hate India, and those who love India." As if she can see him nodding, she adds, "Wow. We think alike." The blush in her voice sails across the Pacific.

So easy to forget Big Brother. In her business voice Monica says, "Your test is nearly complete. We appreciate your patience." On reality TV shows, people get so used to 24/7 cameras that they screw on screen. *Stop, Eli. Do not think about sex. Especially not the mechanics of it.* It's all been ruined by his job. He ruined it for himself by taking the job. As money-hungry as the TV stooges, but he's only paid a fraction of what they got. *Smaaart.*

"Monica?"

"Mr. Eli, I regret that this is taking unusually long."

"No, please! I'm happy to wait. Only, I have a question. Do you want the Wi-Fi search thingie on or off?"

"It doesn't matter. I'm simply testing the signal."

"Got it."

For a split second his free-floating screen frames a bowed head, fluorescently haloed in her cubicle. "Hey. It must be around 4 a.m. in Bangalore, right?"

"Five minutes past, to be exact."

Graveyard shift. But his call center representative's work hours are none of his business. Inappropriate questions will be recorded.

Does she drive or walk to work? Alone? Each way in the dark? Recently the news has carried stories that don't fit his ideal India at all. Women gang-raped in buses. Young girls raped and murdered in country fields and city elevators. Children. How can humans do these things? He tries to avoid news that makes him feel powerless against cruelty, depravity. Normally he speed-censors CNN online, but since his computer died, he buys the *Times* at Onundayga Variety, which survives by selling scratchies, chaw tobacco, and one paper a day to Eli who, walking home, absorbs the horrors before he can stop himself.

"So, Monica, how is your weather? Must be forty Celsius in Bangalore."

"Hardly!" She laughs. "We're in monsoon season, Eli. It rains buckets. Quite chilly, too."

"I forgot. Monsoon season." Thinking of the droughts plaguing India he almost blurts, I guess you guys are happy to have water. Then his swirling multicolored screen saver conjures up a recent AP photo of flooding in Karnataka. Bangalore's state. He sees roiling green water that soaks like ink into thatched roofs. Kids cling to trees above frantically swimming dogs and snakes.

Thanks to global warming, weather is no longer a safe conversational gambit. Monica must now suspect him of having lied. Anyone who'd been to Bangalore would know when the monsoons come, for crap's sake!

"I saw some serious flooding when I was there. I hope you're not in any—"

"No danger at all, Eli. But you are kind to ask." On his screen for a nanosecond: a coppery glowing face, shiny black hair, slightly snaggled, alabaster teeth. "Bangalore is a well-managed municipality. Comparatively."

"So well run." Is she telling him the truth? Company employees don't reveal to customers that people outside the call center are drowning.

"Excuse me, Eli. For the next phase I must put you on hold."

Meaning silence? He takes a deep breath. "No problem."

"You must be weary from holding the phone. Don't hesitate to put me on speaker."

A happiness Eli didn't know he had is suddenly seeping away.

She's right. Stand up. Stretch. Water Mom's gardenia. Like a houseplant, a lie wants care and feeding. His fib about having traveled to India—was it to spare Monica embarrassment over her leaping to a wrong conclusion? But she seems too confident to embarrass easily. Anyway, so what—he knows more about India than ninety percent of Americans. Was it to fake a connection? Everyone's trying to fake-bond, in the Internet age. He pictures online connecting as an infinite helix of names/handles/avatars kissing up and kicking down. Everyone knows how but Eli. Is that why he lives in the boonies in a house no one will buy? His mother doesn't care; she's moved to the city with a boyfriend so gaga over her he has put his NoHo condo in her name. The power of womanhood is awesome. She was nineteen when she had Eli. They grew up watching late movies side by side, sharing popcorn and giggle fits, sampling weed.

"It's great that your Mom's found a guy," says Janis. "She won't be your responsibility anymore." But she never was.

For college, Eli commuted to nearby Binghamton State. He has never traveled farther than New York City, except for a recent free weekend to South Beach where Eli and Janis oscillated between obligatory time-share pitches and the pool ringed by helium inflated breasts. Was that even a place?

"Hello? Monica?"

His mother's gardenia looks doomed. Pale, stillborn buds dot the soil. Too much water?

He needs the Internet! For so many reasons.

"Monica? Hello hello hello?"

The corporate hold music is some ancient TV earworm. When he was a kid, his mother took all the overtime she could get. In the too-silent house he'd turn on the box and do his homework with laugh tracks and gunshots for company.

Janis pings. Red red red!

What's the command to block unwanted callers? Not that Janis is unwanted. But tonight, everything depends on Eli's line to Bangalore. If that gets cut off—

Where has Monica gone? To aid another caller? To the bathroom? For some water? A sweater. "Chilly," she said. What are her surroundings like?

Janis works in a fulfillment center. That euphemism for mail order warehouse cracks him up, which annoys Janis. Her job is to match terminally unfulfilling stuff with orders, pull said junk from shelves, Bubble Wrap it, and expedite. They both work shitty jobs for unpredictable hours to save up for the down payment on an RV, which they will drive west then south to the end of the continent, to far Patagonia. At least—the thought stings Eli like an inadvertently roused wasp—they tell themselves this is why they live and work this way.

Eli pictures a corporate call center as something like a vast airplane hangar, with workers in semi-cubicles wearing headsets and chirping like starlings. But maybe not. Maybe entrepreneurial Bangalore has small mom-and-pop call centers that sub out to corporations. *You wish, Eli. You just don't want her going home alone in the dark.* So obviously an independent career woman. In any country, plenty of men hate that.

"Monica? Hello hello hello hello!"

Why doesn't she respond? *Because, smartass, Monica is not her real name! Only an imposed Western alias.*

What is this earworm tune, anyway? Bum-bum-bum-bum BUM . . . *Law and Order!* Suspense is the last thing he needs.

He takes what yoga-student Janis calls a deep, cleansing breath. He needs to get online soon. Because an all-too-familiar dreaded Thing, the No-Thing to be precise, is preparing its approach, expanding, ready to engulf the hours to come. Featureless and shapeless, it stalks Eli as daylight fades, when inky dusk spills from under the Norway spruce. The silver bullet that can halt the No-Thing, disperse its suffocating miasma into harmless particles, is a fucking live Internet connection. The whole outside LED-lit world trickling in through his ISP at a snail-pace twenty megabytes per second. Which is still way faster than the phone.

Doesn't this communications monopoly realize there's an election coming, a planet burning up, racist bozos toting AK-47s? Not to mention the growing pile of scuzz work waiting for Eli to log on. At five bucks per questionnaire, he can make around $250 a day. He writes the whole house off as his office, at an above-market rent, market being zero. The IRS doesn't scare him. There are .0006 IRS workers per US taxpayer, a ratio Eli himself worked out via Google.

Another reason he needs the net is to shop. Not that he buys, but he scopes Indiegogo for cool off-grid gear. He and Janis scroll, Coors in hand, seeing themselves in far Patagonia on horseback with this water-filtration bottle or that insect-repelling poncho. Eli's also not above checking the zero-nutrient sites: Facebook, Instagram. He's not on TikTok. That's like urging a heroin user to try meth. Which in Onundayga happens daily.

And movies! Eli was deep into *Taxi Driver*, just after Travis shoots the stickup guy who the shopkeeper is bashing to a pulp with a steel pipe, when his signal died. He has DVDs but this new MacBook, bought for the new job, has no built-in drive. That's the scam: entice you into upgrading and drop the drive. Your old laptop ran great and tossing it only added more toxins to the choked earth.

What's wrong with this picture, Eli? Why do you need the Internet against the No-Thing if your goal is to unplug completely?

The hardest part of being on hold is controlling your own thoughts.

Eli justifies his choices as the means to the radical end of unplugging from the soul-sucking grid. But suppose Eli is not the prisoner of Big Tech overlords? Suppose he is the grid, an integral element, a flashing, popping node that, except for time spent sleeping or using the can, is incessantly sending and receiving bytes?

Except for these past three days.

He's been on hold for an eternity.

Text buzz. Janis.

Hey puppy u ok? y u dont answer?

Sorry. Nets still out. Talking tech serv. On hold. U ok?

U cd toggle.

What?

Toggle call btwn me & tech u dummy. Ok?

The phone shakes in his hand like a rattlesnake. Call from Janis.

It's too risky. If something slips, he could lose Monica. Forever. Tap red.

Cunt toke baby sorry.

His face burns. Where is spell-check when you need it? Janis won't care. She's a good sport.

Who r u with Eli?

What?

U cunt talk damn it. So who r u with? Her name?

U r so wrong bereave me.

"Hello, Eli? Are you there?" Monica's irresistible accent, blurred on speaker. He tones it down fast, as if anyone else could hear.

"Definitely! Any luck with my line?"

"The good news is I have managed to place your file on a fast-track basis."

"Fantastic. And the bad news? Please don't tell me you can't fix it."

Silence.

"Population one point three billion and no one in India can figure out what's wrong here? I don't want to be, like, Why Me, but every other subscriber in Onundayga—"

"Excuse me?"

"Onundayga. Where I live. My little town. There's a song about a dying burg like mine.

"Simon and Garfunkel. Garfunkel's *Breakaway* album. You don't like your town?"

"Do you like living in Bangalore, Monica? The monsoons? The floods? The beggars and lepers, the pollution. The crime rate?" *Are you nuts, Eli?*

If u dont call me rite now

Wriggling dots. Janis is typing again.

Monica laughs, eyes crinkled, he can tell. "You do know my city!" The shadow on his screen tosses gleaming locks. "I like Bangalore well enough. I ought! Unemployment is high. It's hard to find a position, even with a university degree. Especially with a degree!"

"So, you studied—?"

I want the truck, eli. No truck truth! im coming oven.

"Physics. My father calls me a romantic. Not as a compliment."

No. U r crazy. Eli texts in one world while talking in another.

"But they supported me. Now I owe them, after they helped me achieve—"

"Do you live with your parents?"

"Yes, do you?"

"Hunh. In a way."

"In America? You must be a dutiful son, Eli!"

U r a dick

Wriggling dots . . .

PIMP DICK. NOT PIMP LIMP DICK! IM COMING NOW!

Since shortly after he took his job, Eli has been unable to have sex. For six months she's commiserated with his problem. They try; he fails; he masturbates her; she comes, cramped and sobbing; he feels like a bastard for having caused such sadness; she promises they'll get the magic back, be even better together than before as soon as he quits his pervy job and they hit the open road.

Only now, because for once he can't take her call, she's convinced he's found someone able to perform sexual voodoo on a guy whose job is to pass or fail detailed questionnaires filled out by guys wanting to order erectile dysfunction meds online. His required reject quota of thirty percent, to make the FDA happy, is not hard to satisfy. He can't stop these wordplays, they pop up like . . . *stop!*

Many fields are left blank. Understandably, given the questions. Other guys exceed their word counts with tales of hydraulic malfunctions that wipe out marriages, affairs, egos, careers, plus the lengths. *Ugh.* The applicant has gone to in his quest for a stiffie. TMI.

The company website claims that his validated questionnaires are sent on to real MDs who issue the scripts and—bingo. But is there anyone backing Eli up, or is Eli himself the only "doctor" in this grossly profitable venture? Grossly, because a mis-cc'd internal email mentioned that the meds are sourced for pennies on the dollar from . . . oh, India.

He deserves a raise.

"What, Monica? I missed what you said."

"Nothing of importance. Your phone connection is failing now too?"

"No, no. You sound fine and clear!"

Ask about the flooding. And who walks her home.

"Excellent!"

"I've been wondering—"

"Eli, I need to discuss your results with an IT specialist who has not yet arrived. May I call you back later on this line? My shift runs until seven. Are you reachable until then?"

"No! Wait! Don't hang up. I'm fine with staying on hold. I'm not that busy."

"But I have to free up this line."

"Monica, I don't want to lose you! You understand my case, you are an exceptionally intelligent— I can't start all over again with someone else!"

"Eli. I will call you back before 9.30 p.m. ET. Trust me."

"Give me a number. Or a code, some way to reach you in case we're separated. Please. Please."

"I'm afraid the system doesn't permit that, Eli."

He knew that already.

"Trust me."

NOW IT'S IN the room with him. The No-Thing. Shoving up close like an obese commuter, squeezing his breath, his brain. While on the phone he never turned on a light. Now he navigates by glints and window-glow around the shadowy dining room and kitchen, the only rooms he uses, except to sleep. Other doors stay shut.

Relax, man. He sits down, plugs the phone into the laptop to juice it. A new earworm, some folkie classic, painfully distorted.

It's 18.25. Could be three hours until she calls. *Get up, get a beer. Smoke a joint. Something to stop this laugh coming up.* It's not really funny, turning impotent because his job is selling erectile dysfunction meds, is it? *Sure, it is!*

Eli's head goes down on the table he Crayola-ed on as a toddler. He is gasping, and how long he gasps doesn't matter, because Monica in Bangalore won't call back. He is alone like before, like never before, tangled up in the fucking system. Either all his own fucking fault or a trap he never had a chance to escape from, no more than Monica is free to give him her number.

Patagonia. Take a mortgaged RV, and stuff, and Onundayga Janis—aka, haul your whole past to the final stop? *Are you serious? That's all you got, Eli?*

The Coors goes down quick. Then its littermate, freed from its plastic collar.

You're okay. Chilling, waiting for a call from an ISP trouble-shooter. Basta.

How many minutes? Twelve. *It's only time, man. Ignore it.* But the No-Thing oozes into every second, making each one an immense balloon of emptiness. His stomach sits in his throat. He can feel his heart there, too. Bopping like a maniac.

It's getting crowded up in Eli's throat. Another beer. What if he throws up again? Like last night, swimming in sweat. Was he ever glad to see daylight. Damn, the bedroom must stink. *So, sleep on the porch. On the roof. Dive off the roof, soar into the giant arms of the spruce. Imagine goodness, Eli!* But his face is twitching. *Got to get this shit together—*

"Eli! Hey! Are you trying to fool me into thinking you've gone out? Your car's here, stupid! I know you two are in there. Open the fucking door!"

Bang! Unlocked, the door swings open. He hears Janis half-fall into the kitchen. "Ow! Shit, Eli. What the hell are you doing, sitting here in the dark?"

He shakes his head.

"Where is she?" Janis strides into the dining room. The No-Thing retreats to a corner. For now. Janis heads upstairs, slamming into rooms that have been shut since his mother left. Comes clattering back down. "Your bed looks like a cyclone hit it."

"Like usual."

"Really? Would I know how your bed looks?"

"Come on, Janis, can you please just. Want a beer?"

"You've been drinking your own Kool-Aid, am I right? Taking those meds?"

"My God, Janis." They've had that painful argument. There's no way he'd ever take that crap. He knows too much about it.

"You can't talk to old Janis, huh? Something's going on! Damn it, where is that bitch hiding?"

This is how defendants in show trials must feel. Hard to prove a thing didn't happen. If Monica calls back now, will that be proof? Or fake news?

"I was on the phone, is all. Trying to get the fucking Internet working so I can access my fucking backlog so I can—" Have Janis standing here, listening to him and Monica talk? Never.

"You're not even glad to see me." Her sad voice. In the dark, she's hardly visible. She sits down opposite him, pushing the No-Thing aside.

"So I can make some money so we can get out of here like you want!"

"Like I want? You know something? I'm actually grateful to that slut. Tonight's given me a chance to do some seriously overdue thinking about what Janis wants. Damn it, Eli, will you quit checking your phone! Show me that fucking thing. Now."

"No."

"Give here, you little shit. I have a right to see who's texting you!" Janis lunges at him across the table. She lands on her chest halfway, fingers stretched toward the phone.

Eli jumps back, toppling his chair.

"Come on, Eli! What's her name?"

He once read that revealing names matters deeply even to modern humankind. A holdover from the primitive belief that finding out a person's true name confers shamanist power over them. He grips the phone tightly behind his back, closes his eyes, and sends three syllables into the silence. "Mo ni ca."

TEN DAYS AFTER Janis smashed the chair on his head, causing lacerations and a fleeting concussion, the seldom-used front doorbell coughs like a chain-smoker. Eli sprints. Out in the driveway a giant in black leather straddles a motorcycle fat with saddlebags. "Eli Wandel?"

"That's me. You are—?"

"Bob. From Sherpa to the Rescue Inc. Express dispatch service. Here: your passport back from the Indian Embassy. The visa's inside. Look kosher? Sign here—use your finger."

Eli's crammed backpack stands upright in the hallway. Both the fridge and his bank account are scoured clean. The visa fee and the airfare left nearly a thou in cash from his Patagonia savings. All changed to Lakh now, stashed in a blade-proof body purse, the last thing he will ever buy off the Internet.

FROM KENNEDY AIRPORT he tries to call his mother twice but gets her machine, so he voicemails tons of love and goodbye.

The plane is full and celebratory. Indian was always his favorite take-out. Bye-bye, Big Macs. After three beers, he dozes in and out for nine hours. He has slept like a Onundayga black bear ever since the No-Thing cleared out, which was ever since Monica called back to say his system was up again and would he please go through these precise steps with her to reinitialize and he did, juggling, sponging blood off his forehead. He kept her on the line, laughing at his jokes, as long as he could. From then on, the Internet did work perfectly, not that he used it for vetting questionnaires or watching movies. The house he grew up in is full of books. He pulled out Tagore and Gandhi. While waiting for his visa to come through, he noted: "Live as if you were to die tomorrow. Learn as if you would live forever."

He orders Indian breakfast. Lassi and flatbread and honey and spiced sweet chai.

A chorus of oohs rises as plates slide in response to the plane's sudden thirty-degree tilt. Eli laughs, tummy-tickled. The 787, righted, soars over sparkling blue seas, then into a blindfold of cloud. A ragged gap reveals far below the gray disc of a city without limits, etched with roads and tin roofs, veiled in rain and saffron smog. Bangalore. Population eight point four million but that's a rough estimate; half the people down there living, loving, fighting, and dying are uncounted. Outside the grid. The India that sells call centers to the West is still nowhere near being inside the system. Any system.

The plane drops by giant steps. Rain lashes the windows. The buffeting wind and corkscrew dips elicit whoops of fear and excitement. Seatbelt lights flash and latches click obediently. Indians, he has noticed, are normally not fans of seatbelt use.

Another jaw-breaking jolt. High-pitched screams as overhead bins explode, cascading bags and coats, bottles of duty-free booze.

Eli is glad he doesn't have to fly this thing.

When the cabin goes completely dark, the megacity below leaps to life. Sheets of rain magnify necklaces of diamond headlamps and ruby shanty fires, all hurtling upward toward the plane at intoxicating speed. Somewhere in all that pulsing humanity is a woman named Monica.

Or not. Because *Monica* is merely a company alias. Her true, birth name is a sound he has yet to hear—a tangle of syllables, liquid and long.

In the dark, some passengers are sobbing, some retch, others chant. Hindu prayers, presumably. Eli feels no urge to pray. The plane rocks rhythmically, as if cradled in the hand of a playful deity. Finally, Eli has begun to make the right choices. The plane is descending faster and faster. Sooner or later, somewhere below in glowing Bangalore, he will find her. And she will teach him her name.

Ursa Major

We live in the long hills. Miles of rock spines running north to south. Climb one high peak if you have the head for that, and you will see the others lapped like scales out to the milky-white horizon. It's only tourists—we do still get a few in the warm months—who say *Long Hills* in a capital-letters voice. As if everything wants a label, like soup cans in stores. Back when there were stores.

My kids still use their label-names at school, but at home "Girl," "Little G," and "Boy" work fine.

Our home is a split-log, brown locust wood. Everything in the long hills is brown. The leaf litter underfoot, the streams eeling through that spongy mattress, the ponds down low where slopes come together to make a funnel, and an upwelling pool round as an unblinking chestnut eye gazing skyward. Normally we don't go down to that water. Too far. Too steep. Too dark.

The tree trunks are slabs of gray-brown, red-brown. The needle sprays on the borer-infested pines are greenish-brown, whereas the oak and poplar leaves, shredded to lace by larvae, are brownish-green. Everything here fights to survive.

My skin is the brown of tea left to steep too long. When I was young, I was lighter, like Girl, whose shoulders shimmer nougat. Our neighbors—the closest lives a mile north along the ridge—are either weather-cured or born brown. They wear oiled leather, they carry oak-handled hunting rifles.

Brown is the final color. Mix together enough colors, you will end up with brown. Try it!

Our cabin sits on a log foundation to keep out the creepy-crawlies, for all the good that does. No cellar, so bone-freezing cold in winter. Three rooms, all length, and go find the width. As if whoever built it used trains for a model. Or these long hills.

Our neighbors hunt deer, possums, and ground birds for food and crows for sport. But not bears. Like us, bears come in a rainbow of shades of brown. Silky and sinewy, they roam the sides of the long hills. A small adult female weighs three hundred pounds. They drink from the deep pools. We recognize and avoid their pathways—the scavenged berry bushes, the scoured trunks of trees. As they avoid our signs and smells. Bears are scarcely ever seen. It's said they only come out boldly in one season: fall. Or spring. Or midwinter. Each year, someone swears to a different season.

THREE DAYS AGO, while out digging for the last of our winter vegetables, I heard rifle shots. Crack-crack . . . Craack! Downslope and dangerously close. No one with an ounce of brains hunts near the few homesteads still occupied in the long hills.

I ran around front. At first, I saw nothing unusual. Then I looked up across to the next ridge. Five, then six, rolling tear-shapes, beige and amber and molasses—the bodies of bears in motion. I was too awestruck to move a muscle.

Just below where I stood, a breeze parted the mountain laurel branches. In the second before they furled shut again, I saw a person flat on the ground. A second later I was airborne, hurtling downward through the trees before landing—almost falling on top of him. Of both of them, I should say. The stranger lay face upward, arched over a big spanking-new, orange backpack. Both ears torn off. Drained white face pockmarked as if by boils. Or nails. By nails, then. Claws. I looked away from the bulging eyes and the open black mouth of the mauled man to the hunter who must have fired the shots, who squatted beside the stranger, hot rifle across his knees.

Opposite us, splashes of blood on leaf-litter led into the forest. Scarlet patches on brown, bright as flags. "Bear," said the hunter. "A young sow I'd say." His boot tapped a silver box near the stranger's hand. "Making a video movie, he was. Sending it out."

"Why? Damn fool reporter, maybe?" The stranger's moaning was making me dizzy-sick, and where was this wounded she-bear?

"Or worse." The hunter squinted up at the early April sky, where a flying black bug was growing bigger. We felt the gut-stirring vibrations of the MediVac.

Back at the house, I told the kids, "Everyone stays indoors. Don't you stick even a fingernail outside."

"But why, Ma?"

To scare them serious, I told the truth as far as I knew. "Bears are about. They're moving." Then, for comfort, I built up the fire so sparks shot through the chimney like it was the Fourth of July. Boy, who I'm starting to think is simple-minded as a saint, clapped his hands at each burst.

That night I couldn't sleep for being haunted by the man without ears, his pasty city face punched full of holes.

Girl couldn't sleep either. "I can't catch my breath," she panted. I shushed her and gave in; we went out just far enough to sit on the entry step. I leaned against the door with her on my lap like a big straight-legged doll. A clear cold night, a gazillion stars stacked up behind each other like Heaven could hardly hold them all. And if you looked hard enough, winking and blinking like they had something urgent to say. Though maybe not to us, who knows? "Look," I said. "There's the Big Dipper."

"That's baby talk," said Girl. "It's Ursa Major."

I laughed at Miss Know-it-all, and she laughed too to keep me company. You've got to love school.

TWO DAYS LATER a visitor dressed in a badly-fitting suit jacket knocked at our door. A lawyer? We hadn't had a social worker bother us in years. A politician? A preacher? I prayed neither.

I stepped back to let him in.

He leaned on our table, all business. "You'll want to fill out this paper, Ma'am. It's to claim your rights." He showed me where to put Xs. "To document how terrorized you are. By those bears. Dangerous predators. Breeding out of control. Since the attack, you have to pay for a taxicab just to go buy your groceries, isn't that so?" I pictured a flatland taxi mired in these steep rutted roads, beeping out SOS. And grocery store? Here we barter, homespun and meat and preserves for stuff like sugar and penicillin and knives, "liberated" from stores far away in the flatlands. I laughed to show that I appreciated his clumsy attempt at humor.

When I saw he wasn't joking, I reached for the paper. To show him I could read.

Was I afraid of the bears? I listened in on my fear center the way you'd take a pulse. No more than normal, I concluded, pushing the paper back. He said I'd be shooting myself in the foot if I refused to apply for my share of the Border Zone Defense Fund. "Every other household here in the Long Hills is signing on!"

One by one I checked the boxes. Watched him multiply each box by a factor and divide by the total number. He said my indemnity would amount to $905.59. "As close as I can push it to an even one-K, Mrs . . ."

I shook my head hard. That crazy kind of money? Was he some kind of maniac? How to get rid of him quick, before the kids came home?

He added, "Per month, you understand."

My heart rocked between my ribs.

"Call me Gideon," he said.

MR. GIDEON DROVE us to the Public Affairs Station, three hills away. It's an outpost of the County Ag Extension. Green cement blocks, and inside, the eye-stinging reek of toilet disinfectant. A place where pot-bellied ex-cops eternally infatuated with guns and uniforms can play at being rangers while still pulling their pensions. I was surprised the Extension was open. Generally, they lock up tight in the cold months when local people might actually need some help.

The officer in charge had a stack of more papers waiting. "Sign here, Mom."

Mom? I shot him a look. Mr. Gideon was off near a window, trying to get reception on his phone. You try not to laugh at them—laughing at strangers is rude—but I could've advised him to give up. Anyone there could've told him.

"And here too. One more weensy little Jane Hancock." My scratched signature looked totally different each time. "You're stressed, you're in a panic—right, Mom? How you people can complain the government has forgotten you out here, when we're risking our own—"

"No one asked for you. We don't give a flying f—"

"Well, here's proof the government cares about your situation. Sign here, where it says you don't dare let your kids take the school bus. Right? Because of the homophageous bears. Even the kids need taxis! You folks need assistance!"

This time I didn't know whether to laugh or run. Or tell the truth: I love putting my kids on that yellow school bus. Same one I grew up riding. Dented steel sides painted the color of kindergarten happiness, the bus even longer and skinnier than our house, belching black farts, revving off into the future just before sunrise. With me, the phys ed coach, sometimes jumping on behind them. And what was this leg-pulling about taxis? Maybe German Panzer tanks could handle these mud-rutted roads but not city taxis.

I wanted to ask about the pasty-faced man. Had he made it, was he alive? If so, where? Who was he, and what had brought him out of season to the long hills? Had he frightened the she-bear, crept up on her too close? Or done something worse? I wanted to know his name. "Say, that fellow who got his face mauled—"

"He's all taken care of," said Mr. Gideon, joining us. The officer gave one of those significant choking coughs.

"What was it brought him here this time of year?"

My officer leafed through the papers. "Surveying. That's what he . . . does. He surveys."

Survey. Surveillance. Spying, then. On whom and why? But I cared more about the she-bear. Was she alive still? Hurt bad, or not? Was she pregnant, or did she already have little ones who'd been watching, hidden in the bushes? Bears tend to birth twins or triplets.

I wondered: Do bears seek revenge? Did they band together, like vigilantes? Probably not. They're loners and vulnerable because of that, like us. I probed my fears again, the dark corners of my imagination. I was wary of the bears as always, but no more now than before.

"Last page," said Mr. Gideon. I had him pegged for a lawyer by now. Or a government agent. Or both.

On the last page I signed that I had testified freely without coercion. Nine hundred and change, per month, does that count as coercion? More money than I could dream of how to spend. Although, once you start making a list . . .

WHEN ALL MY papers were signed and stacked in a trunk with the others—were there that many people still living in the long hills?—and the trunk stashed in back of his top-down Jeep, Mr. Gideon drove me back home.

At first, I was enjoying the ride, whooping with the bumps and slams and high on the idea of having all that money. But the closer we got to home, the lower I felt. Was my sworn statement true? Near enough? Is there a compromise called "near enough?" How many pages had I initialed without reading? What did I swear to? And why was my signature on anything worth a single penny to anyone at all?

But what did it matter?

A person can lie when lying's justified—like, say, figuring what to tell her kids, in case they notice telltale signs of fresh money around the home.

Mr. Gideon pulled up in front of the cabin. He cupped his pillowy hand around the back of my skull. "You did a fine job in there, Mom. You won't be sorry." He poked his bristly nose in my ear. "Welcome to the party. Now, you going to invite me in again?"

"Get your dirty mitts off, mister. There's no party. My kids are inside." Immediately I wished I hadn't told him that. I pictured my three babies peering at us from behind the flimsy protection of a winter-dirty window.

I braced both hands and vaulted out of the Jeep.

He wiped frantically at my spit on his cheek. "You filthy, illiterate, no-name, fucking outlander!"

"You fucking ignorant pussy-livered flatlander!"

He opened his door. Walked toward me in his thin, mud-caked loafers with a wired-on smile. Jabbing his finger at me. "Your first check should get here in a week. You owe me, mamacita. Bigly."

She came roaring out of nowhere. Barreling between us. Her shaggy dreads streaming. Brown bears can clock thirty miles per hour. A rank hurricane of greasy hair, mud, sour milk, and caked blood. I stumbled backward, fighting to stay on my feet. Mr. Gideon's scream came high and undulating, like a red-tail keening on the wing.

I wiped my eyes. She had vanished. Mr. Gideon was moaning like his video-packing predecessor. Careful not to look too closely at him, I reached into the Jeep for his cellphone, which was not much different from the old kind I remembered. I punched in 911. Here, high on the ridge, turns out, there's pretty good reception.

I dragged the trunk of papers inside. Locked the doors and windows. My kids were pawing at me to pick them up. I hugged and rubbed and soothed them so we could listen for the ba-dum ba-dum pulsing engines of the MediVac.

It landed right out front, shaking our walls. Somebody banged on the door. We stayed crouched under the windowsill. Somebody cursed a stream and went away. Finally, the copter lifted off. The Jeep started up and rattled downhill. After an hour, I lit the fire. The kids took turns feeding it all that fancy paper, dancing and laughing.

IT'S THREE WEEKS since I found the surveyor mauled. My nails have grown too hard to cut. In our tarnished mirror all I can make out of me is shadowy features, bright eyes, and hair that's grown out, thick cocoa-colored locks that warm my neck and shoulders.

Girl is right: indoors it's become harder to breathe. I'm not nervous about going into the woods alone for a short while, though I don't stray too far from the cabin. I walk with long strides, pushing away notions of what a person could do, might have done with that kind of money. Even leave the long hills. It was some kind of scam anyhow, a bait-and-switch, and soon enough I'll learn the real reason for the surveyor's solo hike and Mr. Gideon's visit. We all will learn.

My eyes throb from scanning the trees for a glimpse of her golden coat. I sniff the air for her complicated, comforting smell. Thirsty, I pull off my boots and set them on a stone and splay my bare feet in the cool leaf-litter before starting down the ever-steepening bank to drink from a round, dark pool.

Evangeline, Or Theories of Childhood Development

EVANGELINE

Bellied down on the bottom bunk, with the door barely ajar, the children are invisible to the three grown-ups in the big room outside. Evangeline is boss of the iPad. Seven years old, she is mostly in charge of *whatever*. But sometimes she lets Winnie who is four, or Oliver who is three, pretend to be the boss. Because it makes them happy. And stops them from screaming so loud that she can't hear what the guys in the iPad are saying.

Saying, and singing. Together, Moana and Evangeline now sing the "How Far I'll Go" song, which is about sailing past the reefs that surround Moana's dying island. Evangeline knows all the words. Winnie, face screwed into a hate-curse, headbutts her. Oliver slurps loudly at his juice bottle, showing off. He is only supposed to have one bottle and not until bedtime, but when he whined Mommy said, "Just this once." Which she says, like, ten times a day.

From the big room Momalee's voice, sharp and unfamiliar, pierces the Evangeline-and-Moana world.

"Isn't it time to call the kids to the table?"

"They're happy. Leave them," answers Mommy. Evangeline nods fierce agreement.

Momalee, whose real name is Lee, who wants to be called Momalee instead of Grandma like everyone else's grandmother, hardly ever visits them at home. But she has joined in on their vacation in this house Daddy rented in Puerto Rico. Puerto Rico has beaches and palm trees and wild chickens, so it is actually like Moana's Polynesian island, as Daddy promised, except for being garbage-y in places. And up to now, not magic.

Momalee says, "I probably shouldn't ask, but did you consider making this a screen-free trip?"

"Sure. For about five seconds." Mommy's voice.

Evangeline's insides scrunch together. She clutches the case of the iPad and cocks her ear to the next room.

"Honestly, Lee, do you think we three would be enjoying this peaceful adult moment together if we didn't let them watch? If *that's* the vacation you wanted—" Mommy makes an impatient whooshing sound.

Momalee says, "I'm not criticizing your parenting, Annie! But can you dismiss the science? The negative correlation between the amount of time young children spend interacting with screens and their social and intellectual develop—"

There's the dragon hiss of Daddy opening a beer. "Puleese, Mama! No lectures, okay? Not here. This is vacation."

"Oliver has trouble making eye contact!"

"Maybe with you, Mama."

"You always say such sweet things."

"I was kidding! Hey. I'm sorry. Smile?"

Momalee is silent. Evangeline closes the iPad.

Daddy says, "So, did I turn out such a basket case? You used to let me and the bros watch TV every single night."

"For one hour, Hugh. Monitored. After homework and chores."

Evangeline has no clue what "chores" is.

"Oh, Lee," sighs Mommy. "These kids—our kids?— watch way less than your seven hours a week! No screens allowed on school nights. Strict rule."

Evangeline rolls her eyes and slaps her hand over her mouth. "Mommy lied," she whispers. Winnie copies the eye roll perfectly.

"You *gu-uys*," Momalee calls in a chirpy voice. "Want to show me your movie?"

Slow-motion, like a prisoner obeying orders, Evangeline rolls off the bed, balancing the iPad in two hands. Sand from her swimsuit drizzles on the sheets. Oliver howls and throws his bottle full force, hitting Winnie who howls louder and more fearsomely. Evangeline is proud of how fearsome Winnie can be.

This is a real-life test. Momalee has powers. She has already rocked the normal ways of their family: what they can eat and when. Whose lap who gets to sit on in the rented Jeep.

Evangeline has to prove the iPad is a good thing. She sets it on the dining table where everyone can watch. Moana and her pig set sail against all the rules to cross the barrier reef. The waves are, like, black and miles high. Smiling, Evangeline sways back and forth like a sea-fan.

"This one could be a dancer," says Momalee. "So tall and graceful." Evangeline stops moving. *It's true I look like Moana*, she thinks. *Except that my skin stays white from too much sunscreen.*

"Watch!" Evangeline knows what is about to happen, but still she jumps when Moana and the pig are pushed off the catamaran by the whacking boom. The catamaran breaks to pieces. Moana is trapped miles underwater with her foot stuck in coral.

"This is terrifying," shouts Momalee over the cries of Oliver and Winnie. "Typical Disney crap! Do you have awful nightmares, Evvie?"

Evangeline shakes her head. "Wait for the next part, guys. Will everyone be quiet, please?" Her sister and brother pipe down.

Moana smashes the coral with a rock. The waves gather, they love her, they lift her and save her.

"Annie, how often have they watched this movie?"

"Tonight is only the second time," says Mommy.

Winnie throws up, just a gob, from excitement. Daddy swipes her chin with a kitchen towel.

"*Four* times." Evangeline holds up her fingers proudly, knowing it's dangerous. But four is the truth.

Momalee sighs. "Let's close the machine now, sweeties, okay? I'll read you a story instead, a brand new one—" She reaches a shaky hand toward the iPad. To shut it.

But Evangeline is quicker, darting between the grown-up bodies to snatch up the iPad and protect it behind crossed arms. She walks backward firmly on her heels toward the bunkroom. Inside the iPad, Moana is waiting. Evangeline's other sister. No—Evangeline *is* Moana. If they decide to take away Moana, Evangeline will die. Already she can hardly suck in a breath. Oliver and Winnie walk backward on each side of her, like guards.

They are all in the bunkroom. Outside the windows the sky is black, not pinky-gray like at home. She mouths to Winnie: *Shut the door.*

Through the closed door she can still hear their voices. "You let her behave like that? You let them get away with— Never mind. Sorry. You're the parents. I'll stop. Not another word out of me. Ever."

"Jeez, Mama! We all love you! Don't pull that martyr thing."

Evangeline slowly lifts the iPad's cover, like Aladdin opening the treasure chest. The screen blooms blue and orange. She flops on the bed with Winnie and Oliver. They watch, breathing hard, head to head.

HUGH

THE TRIP WAS Hugh's brainstorm. Two working parents, three winter-stressed kids, all in need of air and sun and a break from DC's postelection mourning. He booked the cottage for five days, saving the final night for an ecolodge in the National Rainforest. What could go wrong? He would happily drive his kids up a hundred switchbacks to the top of El Yunque for them to experience the riches of this stupendous sanctuary.

Doubt kicks in at 6 a.m., as they bag up wet swimsuits while the kids murmur wistfully, philosophically, about *how sad* to leave the cottage, the iguana at the bottom of the garden, the tame thrush in the lime tree, the sea turtles and jacks and parrotfish—in five days, Evangeline has become an intrepid snorkeler—Rocco's Tacoria, and can they at least keep the hermit crabs?

Oliver squats in a corner, scratching a bloody bug bite. When his grandmother approaches with Benadryl he shrieks in terror. They spray the kids 24/7, but arthropods find chinks. The word *Zika* is taboo. How bad are the mosquitoes in the rainforest?

One selfish Daddy. Obsessed with wanting to show them the pulsing, steaming world of El Yunque that he discovered at age seven, on an impromptu escape with Lee. Small boy, single mother, both awestruck at seeing plants known only as tame window decorations in the States—ferns, poinsettias, orchids—exploding up to the clouds like Jack's beanstalk. Citric green, red, yellow, oozing purple.

This won't be the first time he has pushed the envelope to turn a vision into reality. *But hey, Jerkface, there're times you nailed it,* he reminds himself, heaving pink plastic suitcases into the back of the Jeep.

Casa Galena, nestled into the verdant flank of El Yunque, could be the set for *A Hundred Years of Solitude*. A ramshackle warren of outdoor corridors and low-railed terraces that a boisterous child could easily tumble over. Treetops two hundred feet below. Somewhere close by, a cataract roars nonstop, only its high-spiraling spume visible.

Are they the only guests? The grim proprietress, aged somewhere between eighty and infinity, shakes like a spider thread in a breeze. Her hefty son, on his knees, fiddles with a balky modem. "No internet, so no phone. Sorry, folks."

"Oh, no problem!" Hugh assures, looking around. *But no restaurant here?*

Winnie whispers, "Daddy, I'm starving."

Hugh lifts her up, a slimy bundle of car-sweat. Jealous Oliver tackles his leg. "Easy, soldier, I've told you, don't pull Daddy's shorts down." Annie haggles with their hosts for food.

Evangeline moans, eyes rolled up white, clutching her little stomach. She is ninety-fifth percentile in height, and perilously beautiful. A Botticelli maiden, one friend said. Hugh suffers nightmare flash-forwards of his daughter at fifteen being abducted by aliens to a Vogue photo shoot on Mars.

His mother, her expression unusually content and concentrated, is spooning the last cup of yogurt into three kids' eager bird beaks. *Now* they will let her come near them!

Something velvety caresses his leg. Startled, he looks down at shimmering copper feathers. Puerto Rico must have more chickens than humans! They are everywhere, pecking, flying, perched in trees to scold the mangy cats below.

An hour later, the proprietress's homemade chicken sandwiches taste delicious.

EVANGELINE LEADS THE way down toward the first rock pool, her sequined sneakers sparkling on the sun-dappled path. Winnie at her heels. Next, go Lee and Annie with backpacks. Hugh covers the rear, wearing a massive pack stenciled Sea Raiders from his service days. Oliver straddles his shoulders.

"An easy hike to the first rock pool," the proprietor assured them. But under the tree canopy the path quickly narrows, steepens. Patches of wet leaves big as pie plates alternate with pea-shot pebbles. The children are laughing, slipping, accelerating. Lee says, "Watch your feets, you guys! Don't go head over teacup out here. We don't want any sprained ankles."

"Listen to Momalee. She's giving you some good advice." Hugh smiles at his mother's back. She is a trooper, patting the rock face for handholds, bracing herself for a leap from root to root. She's as thin as Evangeline. But not as strong. Maybe it's his mother he should be worried about out here on the climb, not the kids. He tends to forget her age—

Well, just as she does.

Suddenly the waterfall surrounds them. Above, ahead, and rushing down-mountain to the far sea. A perpendicular whitewater torrent, sluicing over boulders big as elephant rumps. Hugh, peering up-mountain into the sun's glare for the indiscernible origin, is unbalanced by the clamor, the brightness, the height. The relentless power of the churning water. He crouches, to set his son down on solid ground.

Although the rock pool here looks calm and inviting, it unnerves Hugh. On the north edge a wide lip pours like a tipped cauldron over boulders and razor-edge crags down to where the next pool waits, invisible, maybe a quarter mile below. He and Annie wade in, struggling and slipping, to cordon off the lip. Teamwork. The kids have put each other's water wings on and are already splashing into the shallow side. Their grandmother, testing her footing and the current, and preoccupied, as often, with her own situation, pays them no mind. She even throws Hugh a look he reads as scoffing, as in, *aren't you two being a bit overprotective*? She's thrown that look before.

Evangeline dog-paddles upstream against the current to his outstretched hands, piping with pride like the lime tree thrush. Winnie's silhouette darts above him along a boulder, like a goat scrambling over the rocks, herded by her biped mother. Momalee holds naked Oliver up to examine a purple orchid that hangs from a crevice like a fancy hat.

This is the other Hugh, the one constantly tracking and checking those he's responsible for, those he loves, vigilantly swiveling 360. The Hugh who trained as a Marine Sea Raider and served in a jungle that was Hell's answer to this rain garden's Eden, where no one knew or would ever admit US operatives were present. The Hugh who was lucky not to have come home with full-blown paranoia like too many of the guys.

With the Raider appeased, Hugh the Vision Maker returns. My God, look at these kids! They're in heaven. A day of shared discoveries and future memories. What makes a family.

He lifts Evangeline high out of the water and calls, "Hey, everybody! Who's feeling the burn? Who wants to push on to the next pool?"

To pick up the trail again they must still traverse two thirds of the waterfall, scaling slippery boulders. Hugh shoulders first his pack, towels dangling from its davits, then his son. The girls and Annie are nimble as geckos, but Lee, chary of heights, struggles and falls behind. Dropping to all fours she eventually progresses, spider-like. Hugh watches with pained tenderness. His mother won't give up her ratty bikini, while Annie, lovely and rounded after three pregnancies, wears a modest one-piece.

It's Annie who leads inland now, holding Winnie's hand. Here, lower in the canopy, only isolated rays of sun strike through the giant bamboo and ferns. Rope-thick lianas loop downward from roots anchored high overhead. The ground is puddle-pocked, littered with enormous palm fronds, five or six feet long, and clubbed at one end. Winnie and Evangeline try to lift one. Too heavy. A mudhole sucks off Evangeline's sneaker. Her complaints are ignored. "There's no turning back now, guys!" *Why not, Daddy?* he asks himself. Because . . . giving up is not part of the experience he planned for them.

"There! I see it! The next pool!" Evangeline arrows her arm down through the green toward a silvery glow.

"Good job," praises Annie. Winnie prances. But his mother stops short. She looks back at him. Is this too much—has her stamina suddenly run out? The narrow stretch of trail ahead is nearly thirty-five degrees steep, paved with rotting mango leaves.

Evangeline begins a controlled sideways slide down the chute.

"Do like me, guys. Momalee, don't be nervous."

Yes. They are beginning to include Momalee. Let her call herself any goofy name she wants. He sets Oliver down in order to reach for his iPhone. They'll want this picture.

"Lee, don't do that!" Annie's cry of warning. "Those vines won't hold your—"

Hugh glances up from his phone. His teetering mother has grabbed a handful of vines to steady herself, but the improvised rope shreds. She slides down the chute, grasping in panic for another vine. This one, for the moment, bears her weight. Lee swings back and forth on it like a bell clapper.

And then comes a clattering racket, like a downed helicopter crashing through trees. A projectile six feet long, clubbed at one end, fans his face, barely misses Oliver and his mother.

The scream comes from Evangeline.

She lies sprawled, head downhill in the mud, the palm frond across her back. She is howling, panicked high-pitched cries. His mind flashes on the caged macaws at Rocco's, the green and red screamers. His daughter in her red bathing suit under a green frond. In his mind he sees a jungle insurgent: green cammies, bright slashes of blood. Slight as a schoolboy. Hugh's textbook rifle shot.

The flashback comes and goes in fewer seconds than it takes to reach his daughter, yank away the dead weight of the palm frond. Later he will wonder at how the mind roams, infinitely quick in time and space.

"Daddy. Help me."

Evangeline stares straight ahead into the forest, wide-eyed. Seeing what, or whom? Blood trickling through her light brown hair. Red stripes down her cheek. The blue eyes spared, thank God. Shoulder, an open flap. Darker, venous blood welling on her thigh.

Annie kneels in the mud beside him. "Hugh, my God, her leg."

Evangeline whimpers. "I'm scared."

"Hush, baby, it's all right, you're going to be fine, you *are* fine. Mommy's right here, Daddy's here, we're all together—"

Try to gauge the extent of injury. To comfort his terrified firstborn, as he was able to do in her first hours as he discovered the healing power of his low, slow voice.

Deep gash. Scars. No future model, this one. *How the mind roams.*

"Evvie, hey, can you move your arms for me? Hey, that's excellent! And your legs, just a little? Fantastic." *Wrap the leg tight in a twisted towel. Pressure bandage. Safe to lift her in his arms. Careful with the bloodied leg.* Evangeline sobs into him, shaking.

He turns to his mother. She reads his livid face.

"It wasn't my fault, Hugh! I didn't make that branch or whatever it was, come down—I wasn't anywhere near her—" Defensive. Self-obsessed. Not a glance for the child. His mother doesn't give a shit about them. All that matters is her fucking self-image.

"You could have killed my daughter."

Annie's cool palm on his back. "Sweetie. Deep breath, okay? Let's just—not blame. It wasn't your mother's fault. I saw it happen. These palm leaves fall all the time. Lee, her pulling on the vines was, a coincidence."

Hugh looks around. The littler ones stare back, somber. He starts to climb the trail with Evangeline in his arms, her low keening in rhythm with his steps. His mind flashes on an illustration of Abraham and Isaac. At the first pool he will wash as much of the mud and debris from her wounds as possible. Christ knows what kind of bacteria breed in this mud. Or should he not touch the leg? *Decide, damn it!* The innkeeper boasted about the purity of the El Yunque Falls water. Drinkable, in fact. The peasants trek all the way up here with canisters, for this water. Believe her? *Decide.*

LEE

"You are shaking, Señora. Everything copacetic?" The driver has been watching Lee's attempts to regulate the air-conditioning vents.

"More or less, Maximo. Been a long day. You should know! I'm fine. No worries!" She folds her arms, resigned to the freezing AC blast. Embarrassed by the echo of her voice. When did it become so shrill? And why not tell him the reason? *I have the shakes. The neuro says there's no cure.*

The truth wants out. "It's age, that's all," she says. "I'm old."

Maximo, swooshing the van in and out of the left lane to pass a jerry-built truck full of mud-caked cows destined for the slaughterhouse, pays no mind. He is reassuringly burly, fifty-something with gelled hair, knobby features, a creased neck and, under his pale blue-striped polo shirt, a drum-taut beer belly. His cell phone rings for the umpteenth time. He answers in Spanish.

They've been together since seven in the morning. They've used up weather and food, and bonded surprisingly over politics—apparently Trump is manipulating the Puerto Ricans so they'll vote against statehood. Now the sun is setting over the vanishing point of the highway, throwing a burnt-orange wash over the strip malls, chicken joints, weed lots, frail houses, and occasional shiny beige windowless US megastores (CVS, T.J. Maxx) that line the approach to San Juan. Since they left Lee's family at the hospital, the van feels haunted in its hollowness.

The evening before, after the accident and their exhausting trek with everyone in shock back up-mountain to the inn, Hugh drove Evangeline in the Jeep to the nearest hospital, in Caguas. Annie and Lee stayed the night at Casa Galena with the small ones, battling squalls of mosquitoes and watching anything Winnie wished on the iPad. In the morning, Maximo's van, sent by Hugh, was waiting to fetch them.

On the drive down, Winnie and Oliver, each clenching a bottle by the nipple between their teeth, clung to their mother, crying off and on. Annie tried in vain to reach Hugh on her cell. Only Maximo addressed a word to Lee, the pariah. She tried to chat, her stomach awash with apprehension.

When they finally entered the hospital lobby, Lee saw only Evangeline. Wearing double johnnies, her thigh swathed in a plasticky bandage, the girl was practicing hopping on a single crutch. The leg wasn't broken! Lee's left hand started flapping more wildly than usual—emotion made the tremor worse. She swiped at treacherous tears. Evangeline's determined face, cleaned up, had scrapes around the forehead but no stitches. So, no scars. Or maybe a slight one, more like a beauty mark.

"Sweetie, come here, let Momalee see you!" Lee dropped into a catcher's crouch, arms spread wide.

Evangeline turned away. Annie and the children flew to Hugh. Hoisting up Oliver, he turned to Maximo. "Man, we've already missed our flight. But my mother's plane, back to Providence? Doesn't leave until seven tonight. How much more to drive her to the airport in San Juan?" His lowest, gravest voice.

Lee straightened, useless arms dangling. Hugh passed Maximo a folded hundred- dollar bill. Annie said, "Safe landings, Lee. Be sure to call." Hugh touched Lee's shoulder. She had no idea what he wanted to convey. Did *he* know? Evangeline hopped diligently back and forth, long hair swinging to hide her face. The people Lee loved most—the only ones still alive who she *can* love—shut her out.

"THAT WAS MY son calling." Maximo slides his cell back into its carholster. "I have two girls and a boy. Like you. But all three grown up now."

"Those aren't mine, you know that. I'm only the grandmother. Maximo, I apologize for all the crying and whining this morning. It's not the way *I* raised my children—"

"Oh, tell me about it! But you can't say zip, right? Just makes for bad feelings all around."

And so *they are off to the races*, as Lee's own mother would have said. Lee about the iPads and teeth-rotting bottles and lack of responsiveness, Maximo about talking back and shoplifting and dope and hanging with the wrong gang. "And now, will you believe it, here in PR they passed a law you can't physically discipline on your own child."

Lee says, "Well, I don't think spanking accomplishes much. My kids were sent to their rooms. Or—sometimes a look was enough." She is proud of that, still.

"When nothing else works? My boy I just talked to. Diego. Today he has a good job and a family but a couple years ago he was on the wrong track, smoking weed, cutting school. He said, 'You can't stop me!' My wife said, 'You going to let him do that, talk to you like that?' I waited. One day he came in stinking drunk. I hit him across the face. A few times. He said, 'You can't do that! I'll call the cops, they'll put you in jail!' I said, 'No problem, you go ahead and call them. While we are waiting for them, I'll give you a beating like you never had. *Then* they can put me in jail. And when I get out, I'll come beat you all over again and maybe worse for your disrespect!' And I laid into him at that point. I let him have everything I'd saved up. My hands hurt for a week after. He was hurt very bad, bleeding on the floor. '*Now* call the police!' I said. He just lay there crying. For days he didn't talk to me. He lost a couple teeth, couldn't hear too well for a while. And you know what?"

The last thing she wants is to know more.

"One day he comes to me and says, 'Dad, I am sorry. I was wrong. I want your pardon.' *He thanked me.* He saw he needed the discipline. After that, he never smoked or got into any kind of trouble. My boy Diego. See what I'm saying, about raising kids? Give up the authority, you have failed the job. You and me, Señora, *we* know."

Lee stares ahead at the red ball of sun suspended between the sturdy high-rises of San Juan. Seeing the man beside her in a cold, animal rage, smashing the face of his son who is down pleading on the floor. A shiver grips her from head to foot. Incomprehension. Revulsion. Let him think it's the blast of the van's AC.

She pictures her three rooms in Providence. The windowsill plants dried out in her absence, maybe past reviving. And then she realizes what the driver has just told her: in families, terrible, terrible things are forgiven every day.

What she did wasn't terrible! Stupid, maybe, and clumsy for sure, and thoughtless—if she *did* anything at all. What do you bet that when she walks into her apartment, the phone will be ringing like crazy? Her son Hugh calling, eager to hear that she's safe.

EVANGELINE

The iPad only has 16% left. That is life-threatening. *Life-threatening* is one of the powerful new words Evangeline has learned in the past week in Alexandria Hospital, which is a gazillion times bigger than the one in Puerto Rico. Also *IV drip* (the yellow tube taped into her arm) and *vancomycin* and *rehabilitation* and *staph infection* and *prosthesis*. Except she doesn't yet exactly know what *prosthesis* means. But she will figure it out. She always does. When they talk to each other, do they think that just because she's watching the Moana movie, she can't hear?

Before the accident she was such a baby, thinking they couldn't hear her and Moana singing together. She's wiser now, growing up fast like Moana does: first a baby saving baby turtles, then the Chief's daughter in the councils—Evangeline is *so* the Chief's daughter!—and soon the courageous one who against the Chief's rules will keep on trying to sail beyond the barrier reef until she makes it—

Evangeline slams her fist on the button next to her bed. Finally, a nurse comes. "What now, girl?" Evangeline holds up the iPad. The nurse shrugs and plugs it into the wall for her. Evangeline can command these nurses without words.

The grown-ups here don't like her. She won't let them! The nurses change all the time. The doctor calls her *we* and *us*. "We have to be brave," he says. He is a crazy dude. Here, they won't let her get down from this cage-bed, let alone practice going fast on crutches. She's not sick! Just that her hurt leg has a beat in it, like drums on Moana's island. Just that she is tired. Who wouldn't be? They make her stay in bed!

Evangeline misses Winnie and Oliver. A lot, actually. She cry-sings their names when she is alone. When they're allowed to visit, they reach hands up to hug her, but the IV and bandages are in the way. The three of them can't get back into the iPad's world together. But they huddle close, and they stroke it like a pet. The ceiling light is achingly bright and the grown-ups stare.

She begs Mommy and Daddy. Let's go back to Puerto Rico. I don't care if it's garbage-y. This room smells worse.

Daddy says, "Absolutely we'll go back. Hey, it's not like Puerto Rico is about to disappear!"

"Moana's island disappeared."

"That was only a *movie,* Evangeline. Hey, want to see our photos again?"

"Promise me, Daddy."

"We'll go back, soon as you . . . can get on a plane."

Evangeline hums "How far I'll go." One thing she learned from Moana is, if you want something bad enough, you can make it happen.

Prosthesis. That's the magic word. To open the swinging doors, to let her out of this bed, out of this hospital. Prosthesis.

Moana was trapped under water by the coral. She got out easy; she smashed it with a rock to make it let go of her foot. But what if the coral was stronger and the only way for Moana to escape drowning would have been to smash off her own leg?

The warm iPad humming against her cheek makes her teeth buzz and tickle. She laughs quietly. She's completely ready for the life-threatening adventure ahead. It's the one way out from here, the only way Evangeline and Moana can push past the reefs into freedom. Into the fierce and beautiful wide-open sea.

The Investigations

Late on a July evening the three main Harvard Station subway entrances buzz like wasp holes. Only a couple of blocks away is this narrow stairwell for townies, exit only.

Clio and I lean against a warm brick wall, eyeing the arrivals. Pink dusk pulses over the clock outside the Coop. Our sandals vibrate with the trains that discharge uphill waves of passengers.

They are tired but we are teenagers: inexhaustible. We'll know our subject when we see her. Or him. It's intuitive, an experiment. But it's not a lottery.

A man emerges from the exit. Bowed head, sloped shoulders. Alone.

With a shared glance Clio and I confirm that he's the one to follow.

The subject aims straight for a lamppost. I wince as he shies away at the last possible moment, and jot in my small notebook: 9.14 pm Tues Aug 1. white male dark jacket/jeans/loafers. 35-40? Jaywalks Mass Ave. What's on his mind?

Clio—Clothilde Albertine Devereux, who hates her name—lopes beside me. Her hand covers the notebook in her back pocket as if it might jangle.

When we met earlier that summer, I was almost fourteen and she fifteen. Not much difference, you'll say. But Clio, five foot eight, already had a ripe, languid air about her. And cello-shaped hips. Breasts that billowed her C cup bra. "Call me Clio. Same as the muse of history." I knew that, thanks.

What else? Banana-yellow, shoulder-length hair. Pimple-free complexion. Dark chocolate dots nestled in that creamy skin: a trio on her jaw and in other places I'd find. "Witch-marks," I'd say later. Long tangled lashes over violet eyes that seldom opened all the way.

And me, Kirsty? Dishwater hair, chopped bangs. Monthly breakouts. But construction workers had started to whistle. At fourteen who knows what she looks like? Mirrors only add confusion.

It was Spence, sprawled on a dolly under a red vintage TR7, who had introduced us. Hammer banging, free hand scrabbling amongst the tools laid out on the asphalt. The moment I walked into the leafy alley where Spencer Voss and his mom lived in their carriage house, I stiffened. Who was this interloper talking to my best friend's legs? Her silver sandals touching his boots.

Understand: there was nothing between Spence and me. Minor correction: four years later he would ask me to marry him. But not then. His being a senior did not impress me. But he had a way of being there for me when things went batshit. Which was why I'd come over on that June afternoon.

The intruder crossed her arms.

"Hey, Kirsten. Que pasa?" Spence had recognized my sneakers.

Silence. *Go figure, Elephant-brain.*

"Clio, my buddy Kirsten. Kirst, meet the new kid on the block."

"Hello." The stranger blinked at the sky.

"Clio just moved from Californ-i-ay. You two—agh!" He grunted; I heard metal being ripped loose. "You two have stuff in common. Clio's dad is a lit prof."

"Cool," I said, showing my good manners. "What kind?"

"Twentieth-century French." To the faded lilacs.

"Sartre? Camus? Beauvoir? Although *she*, actually—"

Now Clio saw me. "Camus is his field of expertise."

Spence snorted. "Kirsty reads ten books a week. *And* writes poems."

I wanted to grab the wrench and bust his knees. I would find a way to kill Spence later. "Gotta went," I said.

"Call me later. Promise." So, he had an inkling about why I'd come.

Clio said, "Kirsten? Will you visit *me* sometime?"

My eyes were still dimmed with rage.

"I don't know anyone. We're at 39 Hawthorne. Why are all the houses here so dark inside? And made from wood? Wood attracts mold. Don't break your neck on the porch. My sisters' toys are all over. The bell's out, so knock. We're only renting. Papa's on sabbatical." She sighed. "So he can work all the time."

It was the longest speech I would ever hear from her.

I walked home. Where else? Don't horses run back into a burning barn?

Home was the ground floor of a triple-decker in a no-man's land of weed lots and warehouses. Three rooms, a kitchen, and a bathroom with tiles missing like a panhandler's teeth. Once upon a time Spence and I had lived next door to each other in the alley, but while the Voss family fortunes held steady, my mother and I were slaloming down the economic hill.

I'd started calling her Jean. The purpose was distance, but she was thrilled. A teenage daughter is not a dating asset.

The kitchen screen door banged no matter how you eased it. Jean looked up, eyebrows arched. She was ensconced—one of her favorite words—at the kitchen table, gripping a bottle of Sam Adams like it might go poof. Wearing a sundress instead of her ratty teddy. Her pencil hovered over the *Globe* crossword.

"School out early, Bean?"

"It's Saturday. Also, summer. We got out for good last Monday."

"Sheesh, nobody tells me nuttin around here!" She squinted against the glare. Clumped mascara under aqua eye shadow. Pancake makeup over neon spider veins. "Ouch, baby! Tell tech to dim the houselights, will you?"

Fey. That was my mother in her upbeat moments.

I smiled. Tonight might be all right. I might actually get some sleep. "Did you eat that breakfast?"

"Every yummy bite, hon. You spoil me." With sudden certainty I pictured the eggs buried in the garbage, her revenge for my pouring her gin down the drain before putting the empties back behind her bedroom curtain. This is how we dealt with each other.

"How do you feel today, Jean?"

"Tippy-top. Should I not?"

Glad you feel so great, Jean. Do you remember attacking me with your razor last night?

Her forgetting was better for us both.

A plastic blue *Venus.* What freaked me was how filthy it was. Dried soap and black hairs. *You're going to cut me with that?* The blade only grazed my shoulder—thanks to patented three-way swivel action—before I got away. I locked myself in the bathroom and jammed one foot against the door while squeezing the scratches to make them bleed clean.

Jean had started blubbering. "Baby, let me in, Bean, I love you, I'm your mama!" Then came, "You lying bitch nymphomaniac" and hammering on the door.

A YELLOW PEDAL car. Pink Big Wheel with streamers. Barbies worse for the love. I was all about observation. The bell was jammed. Clio hadn't lied. I knocked, waited, turned to go.

The door with the brass knocker opened. "Hi. I saw you from upstairs."

Clio pulled me in. She piloted me down a hallway, past a study where a man with a badger-striped beard was reading under lamplight and past a dining room. She never loosened her grip.

In the kitchen sat a little girl crayoning with thick strokes. A toddler crawled around a woman with a faded blond braid who was ironing clothes tugged from a basket. I'd never seen a real live maid before.

"Maman! Dis bonjour a ma nouvelle amie."

The woman glanced at the clock. So that's where Clio got her smile from.

"These are my bratty sisters. My next-oldest is at solfege. Four girls and no sons. Pauvre Maman!"

So, Clio was the oldest. Fated to boss. I saw her managing them all, siblings and parents, in their bilingual ivory tower.

Upstairs in her room she wrapped the doorknob in a web of white string to stop anyone from turning it. We unbuttoned our shirts without a word. She sluffed off her bra. I didn't wear one.

Her underpants were tiny, silky, pink. She pulled them down with one finger and a right-left slash of her hips. "You."

I half turned my back, bending, pushing my whities to my ankles. Her room was papered in a hallucinatory maze of rosebuds.

"Lie down." Did she say it, or did I read her eyes?

OUR SUBJECT TAKES the Broadway bus. Near Columbia he slips out the front. Clio and I exit rear. From inside an iron-grilled variety store we watch him hurry down the street. We follow.

Why do people who live in basement apartments leave their curtains open? They only see passing legs, but hey, strangers see in.

A ceiling fixture blooms. Our subject drapes his jacket on an armless, plaid upholstered chair, opens the fridge, takes out a rectangular box and a milk carton. He calls toward the room on our left. Its window is blank to us. He shrugs. Gas flares under a kettle on the stove. He vanishes. We hear a toilet gargle. He's back, no hurry zipping up, showing a streak of brown penis.

He pours something into a bowl, adds milk, hen stops. Listening? Does he sense the watchers *ensconced* behind the boxwood hedge?

A woman stands behind him. Come from where? Her long black hair is tied at the nape. She wears a shawl despite the heat. His wife? Daughter? Jean was only seventeen when she had me. The woman squawks so loud we can hear her, though not the words she says. He shakes his head. She heads toward the room on the left.

He is our third subject. The previous two shook us, one diving into a car, the other into a security office building. We had waited hours before aborting the mission.

This time, we sense the real thing. We can stay here as long as it takes, because Jean's sense of time flatlined ages ago and Clio's parents swallow her lies like aperitifs.

In her room that first visit. "My turn." Did I say it, or not have to?

There was an insistent throbbing inside me, a pulse where I hadn't known one existed. I'd already done the things Clio wanted. She commanded by nudging my hand or a syllable uttered through half-parted lips. It began with me brushing my palms over her shoulders and arms, then over the breasts that stood up like sugar cones on the diorama of her body. Salmon-pink nipples.

I obeyed. Running my hands down her ribs, the incurve that widened to lushly rounded hips. My hands slid down her flat belly to folds looped like necklaces above her—I had no word for it. All the names repelled me. Especially *vagina*. Hers was guarded by large, full, resilient lobes under a shiny pelt. Breathing in a scent like flats at low tide, I grasped her hips and lifted. With a long sigh, eyes rolled back, Clio turned.

Her back was long and muscular. Circling the pearls of her spine with my fingers kept my nausea at bay. "Lower," she ordered. I sat on her canopy bed with one leg curled under me. She raised her ass upward. More pleading than commanding. I splayed my hands on the two globes. Too rich, this flesh. I slapped down hard with one hand. Five red prints glowed on her skin. Clio whimpered and bit her forearm. I pulled the globes apart. Slowly ran a finger down the pink-brown groove to the shining moisture below. The throbbing was killing my head. "Go on. Do it again. Again!"

I stopped. "No! I can't anymore."

Clio groaned. "More."

"It's my turn," I said. I'd earned it.

LIGHT FLICKERS ON in the basement room to the left. Bed, dresser, and the woman raising someone small off the floor. She plops this person into a chair. A wheelchair! My notebook files open but it's too dark to write. She buckles straps. Pushing the chair into the kitchen, she elbows off the light switch. Our light bill, Jean's and mine, is two months overdue and either I donate my babysitting stash or we'll be cut off next week.

As if she can sense my mind wandering, Clio pokes me.

The man hunkers down, holding the bowl under the chin of the person in the chair to spoon in the whitish contents. Eggs? Oatmeal? The small head whips No. Goo splatters the man's jeans. The woman takes over. The man bolts to the sink and starts sponging his pants.

I'm holding my breath. I've never felt more alive.

GROGGY CLIO PUSHED herself up off the bed. "Your turn." I lay in her warm outline left on the quilt. I wanted to roll on my stomach, to cover my eyes, hide my face. But Clio said, "On your back."

Only later I asked myself, *Has she done this before? Who else has lain on the yellow quilt?*

I stretched out, knees pressed together, eyes tight shut. Surrendering to her scrutiny. Anything to avoid seeing Clio looming over me: her webby lashes, pouting lips, the breasts with areola broad as dolls' plates.

She started by trapping my ankles and ran her hands up and down my legs with a rotating motion, an odd caress. But that summer no one thing seemed odder than another.

I was painfully naked. This was not the nakedness of showering in gym class, or inspecting my skinny body for changes in a full-length mirror.

Clio murmured, "Ma gazelle." I tossed my head, meaning: No talking! No voice! Don't remind me that it's you making me feel this way!

The pulse was behind my pubic bone. A hidden drum. I wondered if she could see its waves rippling low across my belly.

Her hands moved farther up my legs, thumbs digging into muscles. From the knees to almost all the way up. But not to where the drum was beating—instead, the touch stopped. I wanted to cry out. Her hands skipped on me like birds and landed on my breasts—almost flat with me on my back, but tender. The nipples, which she rocked back and forth, stiffened hard as pencil erasers. Suddenly her mouth folded down on mine, warm and liquid. Sucking. Nipping. I was outraged and nearly comatose with pleasure. How can a person freeze and burn at the same time?

"Tell the truth," she said. "You never help yourself feel good? Just a little, like this? How I'm doing now?"

Her fingers threaded through my pubic hair, which was skimpy and straight as cornsilk. Among other embarrassing things about my body was that the slit beneath my pubic hair was so visible. Other girls' slits, as glimpsed in the gym locker room, were set low, hidden modestly between their legs. Mine was cut high.

"Not once in your life? Are you maybe repressing?"

Repressing. That was an insult, in our Freud-worshipping town of intellectuals.

What's more, I'd answered that question for nosy Clio already. And she had laughed, which riled me, because I knew all about masturbation. In theory. And found it kind of pathetic and also more for boys, with all that equipment at hand, so to speak. Did Clio think I wasn't normal? Let her.

"Relax," she said. "Now, move your legs apart. Are you afraid, Kirsten?"

No. Only my legs were paralyzed.

"Don't be nervous. Don't do. Anything. I won't, you know, make you finish. Unless you beg me."

Through all the deafening blood rushing in my ears I could hardly hear her words, let alone make sense of them.

THE WOMAN JABS her spoon at the boy in the chair. His frizzy halo of hair had me uncertain, but now it's clear he's a boy—all hunched shoulders and jutting knees.

The man has stepped back to watch. The fridge wobbles as he takes out a beer. He levers the cap off against his loafer. Cool. Maybe he is not the drudge we took him for.

I bend double, nearly check to the ground, to see his face. Crow's feet. Pointy features, sandy Elvis sideburns.

The spoon flashes to the floor. She slaps the boy's cheek. The sound of the slap carries through the closed window.

The boy starts keening, flopping back and forth.

The man snatches the bowl from the woman. He scrapes the contents furiously into the sink. I picture my scrambled eggs in the garbage.

Clio's cool, soft arm settles on my shoulder. I shrug her off, thinking, *Don't touch me outside! You make me sick.*

The night turns fiery blue. As if we're inside swirling ice. Squad car lights rake the brick walls and fix on us, hunched in the bushes like robbers. We should have figured there'd be patrols—this neighborhood is even cruddier than mine. Tracking our subject, we'd passed an acre of grim brick projects.

In the basement apartment, he looks as panicked as I am. He grasps the wheelchair handles and aims for the bedroom, which is also lit up blue. Down go the venetian blinds.

In the main room the woman hurtles toward us, shielding her eyes from the hurtful light, to yank the flowered curtains shut.

"THE BOTH OF you. Get in back. Watch your noggins!"

A huge hand cups my head firmly, forcing me into the car.

"Seatbelts? Click 'em! Everyone settled?"

We nod. The cop riding shotgun turns around. "Say what?"

"Yes!"

"Yes, sir."

"Names! And talk loud. I'm hard of hearing." He says, "haad a heerin."

Clio says and spells her name.

"And you?"

"Kirsten."

"Kirsten *Devereux*. You two twins? Now, where's home, girls?"

Not: "What the hell were you up to, for Chrissake?" But: "Where do you live?"

No trip to the station? Straight home? Clio's parents will say I'm not their problem. And then? Wild horses won't drag my address out of me. Because if the cops drive me home and Jean is smashed as usual, I end up in protective custody. And after that? The first survival rule Jean had taught me was, be afraid of Family Services. Very afraid.

Clio recites an unfamiliar address in her languid voice. It takes me a second to realize that it's Spencer's. Spence is alone this week, while his mother visits family in Georgia.

Clio takes my hand in the dark. Our fingers intertwine.

"That's off a Hahthon, right? Nice neighborhood. Figahs. Got that, Jimmy?"

The driver nods.

"I am not even going to ask you girls what you were up to. Talk about opening a can of worms. Ask my own kids how I know. But you listen good—" He twisted around even further, his glasses misting over in the AC. "I catch you in District Four again and you will be two very sorry young ladies. We're giving you a one-time pass. Do I have to scare the bejasus out of you—we had a murder here last month. Black girl, fifteen, shot dead on her front porch. Appears like a gang mix-up. Now. You want to be someone's mix-up, hanging around here?" Pause. *"Do you?"*

"No."

"No, *sir*," Clio said.

I WANTED TO put a lock on Clio's bedroom door but she said that could give maman et papa the wrong idea. I won about the silence, though. There we used signs only.

Outside we didn't talk much either. TV, school, sports—as far as I could tell, Clio had no interests. None. Other than the investigations. And our two bodies.

What did she do when I wasn't there? I gave up trying to find out. And what we did in her room was never, ever acknowledged. Outside, it didn't exist.

But there, time stood still. According to the bedside clock we usually *played* (Clio in presence of her mother: "Kirst, let's go play upstairs") for about an hour. An hour dedicated to what had become a sort of ritual—you on your back, me face down, relax, don't clench, slower, my turn, your turn—with variations. Clio experimented with pinches, blood-beaded scratches. Squirmy tongue-kisses.

Once I was back out in the open, alone, I hated her. I walked away fast. The swelling in my belly ebbed. For days I stayed firm and sober. Until on another hazy afternoon I found myself turning onto Hawthorne Street.

Sometimes her mother would call upstairs to us, offering fresh lemonade. Parched and sweaty, we ran down to join Clio's sisters. Maman was a nurturer; I was beyond envy.

When the cops rang the bell at the Voss house, Spencer instantly sized up the situation. He played the exasperated big brother so well that I bit my cheek to keep from laughing.

Next day Clio and I stayed out on her porch, surrounded by beat-up plastic toys, our butts squashed into kiddie rockers.

Clio fished a Bic and a crumpled pack of Benson and Hedges from her shorts' pocket. I'd taught her to smoke. Since then, she bought B&H from the tobacconist in the Square. She sucked in nicotine, purse-lipped.

"We should have told the cops what we saw."

I reached for a drag.

"Are you kidding? That would've—" She frowned. "Spoiled the evidence. We can't turn over our first serious investigation for no reason. You don't want to strip away the hypocrisy anymore? Reveal people's hidden actions and drives. Their true motives? You'd rather ruin a case by calling in the cops."

I heard again the woman's slap on the boy's cheek, like a whipcrack. Jean might chase me around the room, but what kind of sicko hits a kid who's tied down?

"They're stressed."

"Come *on*."

"We don't know their secret yet! Their motives! For instance, what kind of problem—"

"They torture the boy! He was screaming!"

"He? That was a girl. What is her handicap, do you think? Cerebral palsy? Imagine, trying to raise a spastic kid. The mother probably has to work, too."

"Now, who's jumping to conclusions. Who says they're even parents? If he's their captive, a—" *Scapegoat*, I thought. Punished for the sins of others. "That makes us accomplices."

"Then do it—call the cops. My parents will be so furious. They'll lock me up."

I smoked, thinking, *Your strict parents let their daughter smoke?* Not to mention other things. Because I was sure Maman and Papa must have a clue about us. How could they ignore Clio's glow when we came downstairs, that mudflat odor?

Suddenly Clio's family seemed as opaque to me as her hooded, lavender gaze.

I said, "Maybe. But suppose we are witnesses to a crime?"

"You're right." She stubbed out the cig. "We have to go back. Tomorrow?"

We exchanged twitchy smiles. A current of connection. What was it we recognized in each other? This shared desire to tear away veils, dig below the visible world, break through the looking glass of the obvious.

WHEN I GOT home that night, no Jean. Which was a surprise, given her agoraphobia. I guessed she'd found a new boyfriend, one with wheels. I hoped she would stay over at his place. Forever.

I was deep in a dream about sailing on the Charles with Clio in a wheelchair when the screen door banged. My mother's trilled laughter mixed with a man's burred baritone. Tinkly iced-drink sounds from the kitchen. Then they barged into her room. Which is right next to mine, and the wall between thin as papyrus. They forced me to hear every sigh and groan as I lay rigid in the dark.

THE NEXT MORNING, I sat cross-legged on the asphalt next to Spence's scuffed boots with a book open on my lap.

"Today, Maman died," I translated aloud *The Stranger's* opening line. Spence would never hear another line written by me, that was for sure. But Camus was his kind of guy, I'd told him, "A master of understatement." Spence liked me trying to save him from being a total gearhead.

While I was still with Meursault in the Algerian bus, Spence scooted out into sunlight on his dolly. He sat up and fixed me with his starry blue eyes. "Listen," he said. "I like Clio. Don't get me wrong. But she's out of control and you're—" He laughed. "You're you. Kirsten. Don't let her rule. The last thing you need is cops."

I shrugged. *I'll hang out with whomever I want.*

"Okay. Got it. So, how're things otherwise? How's Jean doing?"

"She's in luuhve," I said. "He's moved in."

Spence's calloused, grease-slick hand on my arm nearly made me bawl.

THAT PLEIADES EDITION of *The Stranger* came from Professor Devereux's library. One afternoon I'd arrived at Hawthorne Street to no Clio. Maman said, "Wait in the study."

By the time Clio's father walked in, books lay scattered all over his leather-topped desk.

"Ah bon, ma petite? Tu sais lire français?"

"Read some, but not speak." I was not about to let him hear my accent, acquired from a Haitian tutor at the Y.

"Assez bien pour comprendre notre grand Albert Camus?"

"Some, yes." My mind raced for an exit. Huis clos. "Please don't tell Clio."

"Etonnante! Clothilde isn't aware that you read French? You girls are strange. Don't worry. I'm good at keeping secrets." He tapped my cheekbone. Then he scowled, pawing a hand down his beard.

"I have work. Go now." He glanced at the titles I'd taken out. "Quelle drole d'enfant. You may borrow three of these. Quickly, choose! And bring them back next week."

He picked up an ivory-handled desk knife and began slitting the pages of a fresh paperback, looking not at the book but at me.

THE YELLOW BRICK projects inside their high chain-link fence look like a state prison.

We're simply two girls out walking. Shades, sunhats, backpacks. Our cops won't be around. They're night duty.

Nearing the block of our subject, we slow down. My heart bangs. Clio licks her lips.

Our deal is this. We surveil the basement apartment at random hours until it gives up its secret. But if we see any violence, we phone 911. Anonymously.

I'm convinced bad things happen in the small bedroom. And the boy can't run, the way I can from Jean. But would he, if he could? Maybe he's brainwashed, terrified of the outside.

Part of me is wired, exuberant. I want to learn everything, see these people's lives exposed—emotions and motives open to our inspection. But I'm also feeling trapped. Because we can't turn back. It's like when you are responsible for someone not because you care, but because they have no one else.

We walk the length of the building. At the end of a cracked cement walk, a green glass awning shields the entrance. Iron bars protect the dirty basement windows.

Kitty-corner from this building is a small park. Dirt paths spider between clumps of crabgrass. A trash barrel brims with empty fifths. My feet hurt, Clio's starved, and the picnic table with missing slats is perfect. We perch in the thin shade of a weed tree, facing the building. The breeze licks away my sweat. From her backpack, Clio conjures sandwiches. Seven Up. I sink my fangs into homemade bread—and tears. Dijon tears for Maman, who believes we are hiking in the Blue Hills. I almost forget why we're here, picnicking in the park. Me and my summertime friend.

The ground shakes under the engine of a red and chrome Harley crawling up the street. Its two riders stop, leave the bike running, and stroll in our direction. One has a beard, the other's arms are stained with tattoos. Both wear red bandanas. Clio stands, shouldering her backpack.

Behind them there's a commotion at the entrance to the brick building. I recognize our subject because of the wheelchair he lugs down the steps and unfolds and tests by pushing on the back of it.

"Time we go, Kirst," says Clio.

Our subject vanishes inside the building.

The bearded biker smiles at the girls with pointy teeth.

I shrug. I'm on my feet too, but don't like to seem prejudiced.

"Stick around, girls. Plenty of room at the table."

"Buy you an ice cream, sweetheart. What's your flavor?"

"Nah. They going to treat *us*," the other biker said.

"Got that right!"

They slap five and pinwheel their hands.

In the distance behind them the man and the woman are lugging the wheelchair down the steps. Staggering. The woman's shawl slipping. The boy in the chair writhes and mewls.

The tattooed biker rubs a lock of Clio's hair between his two fingers.

The woman pushes the wheelchair to the curb. Our subject calls from behind her, "Please Anna, no! It's too soon!"

The bikers swivel to look.

A van pulls up. The driver opens its rear doors, and a hydraulic lift descends. Clio and I start running, heading for that van like kids in a race to reach the olly olly safety tree.

We reach the van, panting. No one takes notice.

Tears are trickling into our subject's sideburns. He kneels down awkwardly on the sidewalk. "Mamma," he says. "Forgive me."

The woman—for, it is a woman—in the wheelchair, whose knobby knees jut up and out, has stopped mewling. That gummy infantile O-shaped smile of old people. Her frizz is white at the roots. Currant eyes buried in wrinkles.

"Hello, you pretty angels. Such a fine day! Happy to be out in the sun?" We nod. "Come here to me, dears."

Clio steps forward.

A stringy arm shoots out and clamps Clio's wrist. Nails dig in. Clio half turns to me, her face contorted in pain and shock.

I react without a thought. I hear the slap—my hand registers the texture of the old woman's skin, her cheekbone's ridge.

Is there a limit to what a person can do, on impulse?

The man is on his feet, coming at us. "Why, you little bitch—"

The shawled woman cries, "Bobby! You want another frigging lawsuit? *Now* you see why we have to send her?"

Clio and I dodge his reach.

The old one in the chair chuckles and winks at me, meaning, We're in this together now.

The woman pivots the wheelchair toward the van doors. Our subject, his face shiny with tears, glares at me. Still, with the bikers watching us from the picnic table, he's the lesser of two threats. I beg mentally: *Please stay!* But he and the woman both squeeze in beside the driver, the doors slam, and the van pulls away.

The bikers stand on the table, facing us. The tattooed one holds up a tin can. It breaks in his grip like pistol shots, *crack-crack-crack*. They bounce down from the tabletop to lope in our direction.

But Clio and I see what they don't. A patrol car gliding from the vicinity of the projects, drawn by the sight of a riderless red motorcycle with its engine running.

Swift as snakes, Clio and I slip into the green shade of the apartment awning. We press together, watching the cops close in on the red bandannas. Clio's cool shoulder presses against mine. My hand burns from the slap. Our case is closed.

We didn't see each other for weeks.

I was house-bound. The same night I watched an old lady get shipped off to the final warehouse, Jean downed a fistful of Valium. I lunged to stop her. She fought back, pulling my earring half through the lobe. I froze a critical second at the blood ruining my shirt. Jean didn't weigh a hundred pounds but booze gave her the strength of a gorilla. She swallowed.

At Mt. Auburn, the ER staff pumped her stomach while I read *Health* in the lobby, holding gauze to my ear. Trying not to picture what Jean was going through.

Her own fault. After her first OD and pump-out she had sworn never to "pull that stunt" again. But physical pain is so easy to forget.

When we were back home, I changed her stained, yellowed sheets for clean ones. Jean curled up on her bed like a sow bug. I cancelled my babysitting gig. She sweated the fresh sheets sopping wet. The doctor had given her a shot that made her retch at the smell of booze. It soon wore off enough that she could sip some whiskey, to stop shaking.

I cooked Kraft Mac & Cheese. Side by side in her bed we watched old movies. Braiding my hair during *You'll Never Get Rich*, Jean deadpanned, "So how much is Rita in the hay worth?"

ONCE MY MOTHER was back to normal, I went to return the professor's books.

At the door Madame Devereux pressed a finger to her lips to show the baby was napping. A shiver gripped me. *I don't ever want to be like you—always worried about someone else!*

"Clio returns soon. Will you wait in the office, Kirsten? He is out, also."

"Sure," I said quietly, planning to put the books back and leave. I'd meet up with Clio later.

In the study there were three shelves of poetry. I beelined for Mallarmé.

How long had Devereux been standing behind me? I'd heard nothing. "L'apres-midi d'un faune" rose up out of my hands. He gave an amused cough.

"Le Faune: Ces nymphes, je les veux perpetuer. Si clair, Leur incarnat leger. You comprehend Mallarmé, Mademoiselle, do you?"

I shook my head, not turning.

"Charmante—a girl who won't lie. "*Aimai-je un reve*? Do I love a dream?"

I felt the prickle of whiskers, his lips on my neck. His belly against my spine. He wasn't tall, but solid. I grabbed a bookshelf for balance.

"These nymphs, I want to perpetuate them. So fair—" he stopped. His tongue flicked inside my ear. "Mmm. Salt."

I felt a kind of cool derision. Had I been anticipating this moment? Plotting it? Was Devereux my next subject? I swiveled to face him. He'd shut the door. Locked? I buried my head in his starched, striped shirt to hide my smile.

His hand pushed inside the waistband of my shorts, paused, then swiveled lower. He was as practiced as an angler casting in the dark. His warm fingers were thick, exploring.

"You should not be ashamed of positive sensations, Kirsten! Au contraire, one should take pride in one's capacity to experience pleasure."

I drew my head back. His eyes were hazel with radiating red threads. I whispered into his breath, "Do you do this only with—"

He shoved a thumb in my mouth before I finished, With Clio? Or your other daughters, the littler kids?

He needed both hands to work his belt buckle. I slid sideways.

"Stop," I said. "You must be crazy. I could make so. Much. Trouble."

"Really? Trouble for whom, dear Kirsten? But I know so much. About you. Your deplorable home life, your alcoholic parent—I'm merely tutoring my daughter's disadvantaged friend." His trousers were the old-fashioned pleated kind. Underneath he wore nothing.

"Caresse-moi, cherie! Ah oui, tu me fais du bien." His hand closed, forcing my hand to squeeze. "I ask only for what you have already given elsewhere. Regarde!"

I had never seen an adult penis up close before, let alone touched one. His seemed enormous, a rigid, grayish-pink, silky worm. Oozing liquid onto my wrist. With my free hand I reached behind me, feeling for his pretty paper knife on the desktop.

I took a strong grip and stabbed at the bared, puckered flesh of his lower belly with all my strength. To my amazement the blade sank deep. Devereux gasped. He fell backward into the bookshelf, clutching his wound. Hissing and moaning through clenched teeth. Blood trickled through his fingers.

For the second time that summer I felt a long, unfamiliar shiver of happiness. I dropped the knife and slipped out of his study, out of his house.

I SCRUBBED UP on the banks of the Charles before walking to Mt. Auburn cemetery with the idea of hiding out and sleeping there. But the gates were already locked, so I turned around, drawn to Hawthorne Street despite Spence-voice warnings in my head. *The last thing you need, Kirst, is cops for real!*

Yes, but guess what? Perpetrators can't resist revisiting the scene of the crime. I listened for the howl of an ambulance. Was Devereux alive?

But the house on Hawthorne was still, folded in on itself. A dim light shone only in Clio's room.

TWO DAYS LATER Spence found me asleep in his cellar. I couldn't tell him. It wasn't guilt—I simply couldn't find words for why I had let Devereux get that far. Was it what I'd wanted? Power? Or the opposite? Was I scared by his threat? I only told Spence that I needed a break from Jean and her raucous boyfriend. To lie to him hurt like hell. He led me upstairs and fed me Cheerios. While I was looking out toward Hawthorne, wondering if the police would come searching here where once they'd dropped me off, he chatted. I caught the word *professor*.

"What did you say?"

"Clio's dad. Someone broke into the house and tried to kill him. Stabbed him in the gut, in broad daylight."

I felt my mouth twitch. "They call the cops?"

"Well, *yes!* But there's not much to go on. No weapon found."

The twitching turned uncontrollable. I pictured Devereux cleaning and hiding the damned paper knife before he and his wife even called 911. "Thanks, Spence. I better go."

"Where—to Clio's?"

"No. Just home."

AT HOME I locked the bathroom door. The boyfriend had walked out on Jean, leaving her to lunge around like a wounded hyena. Now the bathroom door bulged under her fists. I was a slut, a vampire, a thieving nympho. I stole every man she loved.

I opened a window to the night breeze, scrubbed the slimy tub with Ajax, and turned on the water full blast. Clio. Had she tattled to her father about my fear of the System? Or had he eavesdropped, spied through a peephole? Didn't matter. Nothing mattered. I tapped along the top shelf of the medicine cabinet for a razor blade, pristine in its wrapper.

The first slice across the violet vein in my wrist was only a test, to gauge resistance. The second had to count: I might not have the courage for a third cut. I bore down hard. A red smile gaped up at me.

I could no longer hear Jean yelling. I felt uplifted, purified.

Poppy-red blood spilled down my arm, over my shirt and bare legs and feet. I took a step, slipped, skidded, and nearly did a split. How ridiculous! What a mess I was making, and who would clean this mess up, if not me? Was I pulling a drama stunt, like Jean? I started giggling. Then angry, I tugged the cord from her bathrobe hanging on the door and managed to loop it just above my elbow. Pulled the tourniquet tight while mopping the floor with a towel under my feet. Almost dancing.

I shouted Spence's number through the door.

As it turned out, not a completely stupid stunt. Not that I ever want to find that emptiness again. But after Spence disinfected my arm and taped butterflies over the two gashes—I liked that medical term, "butterflies"—and wrapped my wrist in gauze, two wonderful things happened.

First, Jean went on the wagon for three weeks. She fussed over me like I was a rescue puppy. Scared that I could leave her, one way or the other?

Second, when I went to Hawthorne Street sporting a bandage on my wrist, Clio came out with two books. "These are for you he says." *The Stranger.* And Mallarmé.

She and I smoked in silence. I couldn't ask and why would she tell me? During my R&R at home, I'd been torn between acknowledging Devereux as the perverted despot and seeing the family as inscrutable, exotic, uninhibited Europeans. It was like looking at an Escher print: the stairs kept switching direction.

The more you ask, the less you know. What about the three people in the basement? Was the old woman a victim of granny abuse or was she a manic bully? Were the other two caretakers or sadists? One thing was sure. There had been a slap. Instead of reporting it, I had repeated it.

Did I truly give a fig what happened to Jean? Did she in any real way love me? Or were we each simply terrified of facing the world alone?

In my head I questioned Clio. Was I the lucky one? Was my roachy apartment in no-man's land a gentler, safer place than 39 Hawthorne?

Three weeks later Spence waved me goodbye from his packed Triumph, heading to Worcester Tech. "Call for anything," he said. "Or for nothing! Especially nothing. Worcester's no distance."

But it was too far to walk.

A year later Mrs. Voss sold the house and moved to Atlanta.

Clio was admitted to a fancy girls-only boarding school in Connecticut. *That* felt like distance.

I started ninth grade at Cambridge Latin. Spent nights on the street, beneath bridges, in church basements. But I managed to stay under the System's radar and graduate.

I WAS PEDDLING comedy skit scripts and living on peanuts in New York when Spencer tracked me down online. The next week I took the Chinatown bus to Cambridge. First time back there since Jean died.

At the Central Square Starbucks, I asked for a small plain, which always drives the baristas nuts.

Spence: corrugated forehead and thinner hair and the same starry eyes. He pulled my hand close, stroked his thumb over the silvered scar. He nodded at his DIY doctoring.

"Kirst, you won't guess who I bumped into last week in LAX. I was on a consulting gig and—"

"Who?"

"Your old pal. Clio."

"Clio Devereux?" A somersault in my belly. "How's she doing." As in, *so what?*

"Still looks like a gas station pinup. She's a forensic attorney. Go figure."

I had to smile. "No kidding." Through the far end of a telescope, time x distance, I saw a high-heeled professional striding in a gray pencil skirt, blond hair swinging.

"Funny thing. I expected she'd be gassed about us getting together! But she hardly seemed to remember you. Weren't you guys like Siamese twins for a while?"

"Me and Clio? So wrong, Elephant-brain." I bent over my coffee, drowning in the warm backwash of one hazy summer. "We had nada in common. I barely remember her."

And that, it occurred to me a moment later, was the truth. Because how can you remember a person you never really knew?

But Clio, I remember the things we did.

Bwa Teneb

"The bishop's map," hissed Père Emory, wrenching the Land Cruiser's wheel to avoid a foraging goat, "is utter bullshit."

Scobie agreed. For four hours, she, the père, and Ti-Bo had been bumping and crawling through the salt-poisoned flatlands of southern Haiti, and now upward on a tortuous track through cactus-studded bush, with the blue smear of mountains never coming nearer.

She scanned a cluster of huts leaning off a steep slope. "Maybe someone up there can give us directions."

Ti-Bo leaned forward from the bench behind her. His breath scorched her damp neck. "If ghosts give directions."

She saw his point: despite the goat, this inland part of Haiti felt drained of life. The lone mango tree among the huts had dropped its leaves in the long drought.

Père Emory yanked up the brake. "You two go look. I'll stay with the crate." Crate, he called their boxy vehicle with a pair of seats up front and behind those, perpendicular, two long benches running almost to the rear doors. But to any bandits who might be roaming this back of beyond, their nearly new

Land Cruiser must look like a fatted calf on wheels, begging for slaughter. "Be quick." He kept the engine running.

THE FIRST HUT they peered into looked abandoned. Packed dirt floor under a stoved-in straw roof. But the next one, only twenty yards away, swarmed with life. A dog roped to a slender leafless tree snarled at Scobie's ankles. A black torpedo pig, tethered to the same tree, screeched like a toddler in a tantrum. The children emerging from the shadows to marvel at the blans were streaked with salt, desiccated like the cracked ground under their bare feet.

"Bon swa, ti-moun!" cried Ti-Bo. Good evening, small people.

The children chorused enthusiastic greetings. Four girls wore underpants only. Their bellies protruded like small brown melons. Three little boys wore no pants, only ragged shirts; the fourth and smallest boy was naked. A youth, fifteen or so, clothed top and bottom, was making faces and miming. A woman thin as a stick bug, wearing a long skirt, came out of the hut. She held one stiff arm and its clawed hand up sideways. She bowed to her arm and smiled as if pleased to have reason to smile. She ordered the family's chairs to be brought out. Two rickety chairs appeared. And two cups of water! Scobie winced inside. How to tactfully refuse to drink? They sat on the chairs. Ti-Bo unfolded the map. The woman stood over it for a long time.

Scobie traced their best guess of where they wanted to go. "Est-ce que nous sommes sur la route juste? Bwa Teneb—c'est par là?" Bwa Teneb: Dark Forest. Literally, *Forest of Shadows*. A name from the long-ago, when Haiti still had lush forest. Sometimes Scobie's cobbled-together French seemed to communicate, sometimes not. Since arriving three weeks ago she had soaked up some notion of Kreyol, but she could barely speak it.

Bwa Teneb. That's where the bishop had said they'd find almost twenty hectares of high fertile land belonging to the diocese that he would deed to Père Emory to transform into a farm, refuge, and workplace for the kids overflowing his orphanage in Verseau.

The woman sighed. "My husband was a charcoal burner. All the woods have been cut down. Sick, he is. He lies inside." She flapped her paralyzed arm. Scobie eyed the hut, hardly big enough for one bed. Where did these children sleep? A sudden flurry of Kreyol left Scobie mystified. She fished a fifty-gourde note from the pocket of her intentionally drab skirt. The mother folded it small. "I can't say about Bwa Teneb. I don't know the places beyond," she said. "I keep to my place. I will give you advice, mezami: return to Verseau. Don't be found on this road. Not after nightfall." She eyed the sky.

"Kwa non?" asked Ti-Bo. He had a rough and practical sense of the language.

"Solda mawon." She looked sideways again, addressing her curled arm. "They find you, they steal your bodies. They sell your souls."

Scobie got that. Ti-Bo had told her about the plague of wilding soldiers. In the beginning, les soldats anciens had been mostly troops from Baby Doc's Army, disbanded after the elections in '91 were won in a landslide by the charismatic priest of the poor, Aristide. The anciens reassembled in the wake of Cedras's bloody coup, but were again sent packing after the "friendly" invasion of the US Marines in 1994. "The anciens were like the *Forty Ronin*, if you ever saw that flick?" Unemployed samurai on the loose. Thousands of seasoned bullies, nursing a grudge. Loathed and feared bands of predators and professional kidnappers. Some took to the streets or the hills, the most successful emigrated to Miami, helped by US personnel loyal to old counterparts. Recently, so the rumors went, the anciens had been regrouping. Neo-Duvalieriste radio broadcasts bombarded Port-au-Prince, while emigré cells of "patriots" threw lavish fundraisers in Brooklyn and Queens and plotted their return to power, promising: Then we will have law and order again, so US-blocked aid, 500 million dollars, will flow into Haiti.

Ti-Bo shrugged. "It's never smart to be out at night. But we have a very safe car."

The mother's expression didn't alter. "If you go far enough up this road, you come to Switchblade Mountain. The curves are sharp, the gorges fall straight down. There are no more farms. Beyond, who knows?"

She pointed to the southwest, to the spine of peaks they had been steering toward. Scobie guessed the first hump was Switchblade, its gently rounded top at this moment bathed in a delicate, greenish light. Ragged black clouds and flashes of heat lightning obscured the more distant peaks.

A little girl with the sparse orange hair that announces kwashiorkor, advanced malnutrition, pressed the chipped cup half full of water against Scobie's waist. Reflexively she grasped it, both tempted and resigned. Ti-Bo grabbed the cup from her lips and gulped down the contents, as he'd done with his own. "Regrèt, madame. Li se dejà malad." Sorry, madame. She's sick already.

He stood, pressing down on stiffened knees. Scobie stood too, noticing again that she and Emory's childhood friend Ti-Bo, this coal-eyed enigma (con man? godsend?), were the same five feet seven. They were both muscular and square-shouldered. Technically they were mixed raced, although Scobie with her brassy corkscrew mass of hair could and did pass for a deeply tanned blan, while Ti-Bo's skin never took on any other hue but sallow. She guessed, too, that they were both in their late thirties, even if she looked (she hoped) younger. Separated at birth? Two months earlier he'd been a stranger in a Boston bar who'd piqued her latent curiosity about Haiti with the prospect of a feel-good story about an ex-Marine who rescued street kids in one of the poorest countries on earth, a story that might earn her a Pulitzer or even a date on Oprah. How had he divined Scobie's dream that The Feature, the one that would justify her past near-misses and wrong roads taken, was still out there, waiting for her to find and write? Their minds, too, seemed to work the same way, in a mix of hunches and bullshit-cutting and spur-of-the-moment strategies.

As they waved goodbye to the children and plucked off the sticky hands of the tongue-lolling teenager, Ti-Bo pulled four Culligan water sacks from his pack. "This is for all you guys. Share." He nodded at the shrieking pig. "And give that goddamn animal some water. Any kind of water!"

There was no need for translation.

She and Ti-Bo slid and stumbled downhill like Jack and Jill, under a flame and indigo sky, between jutting jute and cacti, toward the giant beige capsule of the waiting Land Cruiser.

"WHAT DID SHE say to you?" Scobie clicked her seatbelt in place. "That sa ou pa thing."

"Means, what you don't know is bigger than you."

"How can she live in one place all her life and not know what's a mile up the road?"

"She knows," said Ti-Bo. From his perch on the right rear bench, he leaned up close behind her. "She's just not telling *us*. Wanna bet her old man has put his cows out to graze on the bishop's land in Bwa Teneb?"

"What cows? Those kids have never even seen milk. Anyway, her husband was inside the house, sick, remember?"

"Wanna bet?" Ti-Bo laughed, as if at himself.

Père Emory slowed the crate to a crawl before nose-diving into a washout left over from the years when the rains came. His bare arms tensed as he drove, tendon and muscle contracting under fine-grained skin. As he shifted gears, the back of his wrist bumped her knee, releasing waves of involuntary anticipation. Like a teenager out driving with a boy going nowhere and for no particular purpose except to sit this close, hip to hip, both looking straight ahead through the bug-splotched windshield. The bottom of the washout brimmed with white-glowing rocks. Moonrocks. The air-conditioning burped and fizzed.

"That was big of Gene, letting us take his fancy vee-hicle," Ti-Bo remarked. Gene Smithers, whom they'd left nominally in charge of seventy orphans back in Verseau, was one of the père's major donors, a Southern Baptist tobacco exec with back-slapping manners and a sore conscience. He had driven up from Port-au-Prince with his wife and daughter in the new-smelling, rented Land Cruiser for a week's visit.

"Gene's a man of mighty faith." Père Emory, the former US Marine turned de facto priest by popular insistence in Verseau, gave the road a wry smile.

"These rocks are murder on tires." Ti-Bo continued in the same upbeat tone. They were being jostled together and apart by the humps and drops of the road.

"Don't talk to me about tires," Père Emory said. The truck back at Lakay chews through four sets a year. At four hundred fifty US dollars a pop."

"The orphanage burns two grand a year on *tires*?"

Emory nodded.

"Christ only knows how you keep the show running!" Ti-Bo slammed forward against Scobie's seat.

"He might not, but you do. The cash you fly in covers more than half our budget."

"So why start up this kids' farm on top of everything else? You sure that's smart? I mean, you're going to need tools, seeds . . . Jeez, I'd bring over more if I could scrape—"

"I know you would, Ti-Bo. Look, the kids have to get out of the city. They sell their bodies, they steal and get beat or locked up, they come back to me sicker than before."

"What we need is a secure cash flow. We need to diversify. Let's get Lakay Bondonn on the map, stateside. Use Scobie's photos, let her spin the story, she's a writer, that's what she's here for. The pictures will grab people. We'll get endorsements—Gene'll know how. Stuff to prove Lakay Bondonn isn't just another post-flood, post-earthquake, post-disaster-of-the-month scam."

Père Emory swung the wheel to the left, then right. Scobie made a mental note: *the focus of a sharpshooter.* He could discern obstacles in the gully road invisible to her.

She rested her eyes on the distant stepping stones of mountain peaks. Though their outline seemed no larger than an hour before, surely the peaks must be drawing near. Held snugly by her seatbelt in the roughly rocking cradle of the crate, she let her mind drift. Back to Lakay Bondonn. To the clinic where she spent hours rolling bandages, sorting meds into baggies, listening to horror stories about the city hospital, where there were real doctors but no meds, no paper, no coffins. To the boys, escaped restavek house-slaves, laughing together, scooping their millet porridge two-fingered before going back to work fixing the busted roof. To Cannelle, the one-year-old so delicately pretty as long as you looked only at the right side. The mother had brought Cannelle in wearing a frilly, beribboned sundress, in hope of giving her away to the American lady. Scobie, holding Cannelle on her lap, remembered the abortion she never, ever thought about. Her first. Nineteen, not a cent, no insurance. Her boyfriend knew a private doctor. The bucket on the floor under the stirrups. Towel jammed in her mouth. No painkiller. "It's a girl, you slut. You're all selfish sluts, making me do your dirty work." Afterward she bled for a week. In and out of consciousness on the boyfriend's couch. They told her she'd been sterilized. No risk of adding to the infinite number of unwanted children. But that was a lie.

So many children, unwanted in so many different ways. When Cannelle reached for one of the vitamin bonbons Scobie always kept handy, Scobie froze, taking in the tumor that engulfed the baby's left cheek and jaw.

But now she was like a child herself, dozing, listening to the grown-ups' inconsequential quarrel overhead.

"Emory, come on. Since when did you ever quit halfway?"

"I'm not quitting! I'm saying it's time we turned back."

Scobie rubbed her face, blinking. How long had she been asleep? The setting sun cast thick shadows. The silhouetted mountains were still distant. Lightning flashed around the peaks like flames around a smoldering heap of charcoal.

"We came all this friggin way!" Ti-Bo shouted past her ear. "We're not turning around now!"

"But we haven't come far. Look." Père Emory tapped the Land Cruiser's backlit dials. "Nineteen miles in over two hours. That's all."

"Plenty of gas in the tank."

"But we haven't seen any of the landmarks on the bishop's map. There's supposed to be a school, a stream, a roadside chapel—"

"We passed a blue peristyle, didn't we? I mean, His Eminence is not going to admit the chapel is a voudun chapel—"

"Ti-Bo. Look. It'll be dark soon." Père Emory switched on the headlights. In that very instant, night fell. All they could see was what the two cones of light captured. "Ti-Bo? Lord knows I want to find this farm! But let's not push our luck, right? It's only one day lost, one botched day. Mea culpa. We should have started at sunup."

Ti-Bo exhaled hard. "I want to check out this farm with my own eyes. Is it for real? Or am I supposed to sink money on faith in that slimebag of a bishop?"

"And *if* we find it, what will you see, in the night?"

"We got headlights. We got flashlights. We got a nearly full moon. I want to see the land! And I know Haitian time. Tomorrow we come back? Ends up being the day after. Or next week. But me and Scobie are on US time. Hey. I've got two use-'em-or-lose-'em tickets right here in my pack. P-a-P through Miami to Boston. I got business. Peeps waiting."

Emory's hand dropped from the gearshift to rest on Scobie's knee. She felt the warmth imprint through her wrinkled skirt. "What do you think, Scobie? Do we go back?"

"Makes sense." She wasn't a sixteen-year-old eager to drive into the danger zone with a strange boy. "You're right. Let's head home." When before in her whole life had she turned back?

Ti-Bo said, "Wusses, the both of you. We don't *deserve* that land."

WHEN SCOBIE WOKE again, the men had traded places. Beside her in the driver's seat, Ti-Bo gave off a pungent smell, like a pepper vine.

"Are we there yet?"

"Daddy, we there yet? Huh, huh?" He mimicked in a falsetto voice. Up-lit by the dashboard lights, his face was an ashen clown mask. The clock flashed 21:10. She ached from hips to shoulders. The Land Cruiser lumbered like the elephant it was—teetering on a big rock or outcropping, coming down with a crash of springs. Her neck bones popped.

Ti-Bo must be still seething inside over not pressing on to Bwa Teneb. Now that they were retracing their route, she could see that the road sloped downward toward the sea. It was a far-off black band under the star-smacked heaven.

"Is that Verseau, way down there?" Tiny reddish flickers, probably charcoal fires, looked like a field of mirrors aimed at Mars.

"If that's Verseau, power must be out again. Or it could be Côtes-de-Fer, next village up the coast. Which'd put us on the wrong goat path."

Père Emory was rustling around in the back. She heard a window slide open, then close again. A brief gust of outdoor air circulated, hot as in the Boston subway. She thought, *Huh. We're lost. It's that simple.* But it wasn't simple: the change from being sure of the road to sure of nothing felt like falling in the dark.

Emory mumbled something. Ti-Bo yelled, "You talking to us?" And then Emory was leaning up close behind her. His chapped lips grazed her cheek. "I smell smoke. Don't you?"

"Cook fires out there, monche."

"No, no. It's not charcoal. It's like . . ."

Scobie sniffed. All she caught was the ozone of the air conditioner.

"Pull over, Bo," said Père Emory. "We better have a look."

"What, pull over?"

"In case the motor's on fire."

Scobie welcomed the stop. Outside, the night warmth woke her from the hypnosis of artificially chilled and dried air. She shook out her brown skirt and bounced from leg to leg and, hands on hips, stretched her head as far back as possible, to let her hair fall behind her and to absorb the downpour of stars. In the southern sky, heat lightning popped and danced like a movie marquee on the fritz.

Once her vision adjusted to the night, she clambered up the embankment. For about thirty yards, she guessed. Ropes of exposed roots offered handholds. Behind the screen of a spiky jute, Scobie crouched down to urinate. She'd learned to store scraps of paper in her pockets, in case there were no leaves, even dry ones. The stream of her urine trickled downhill, silent, invisible, but giving off a bold scent like bread soaked in tea. It seemed copious enough: Père Emory had taught her to be on guard for signs of dehydration.

I'm proof that humans are natural predators, she thought. Prey animals would never pee so carelessly, wouldn't advertise in other critters' territory.

Almost directly below, a pair of flashlights bobbed like fireflies. The two men were checking over the Land Cruiser for trouble.

Out of sight high in the bush, Scobie had a lovely, unfamiliar sense of being protected.

"I knew it. The oil pan," said Père Emory, back-crawling out from under the Land Cruiser.

Scobie blinked against the swooping flashlights.

"There's supposed to be a skid-plate but it must have sheared off. One of those rocks we bottomed on, probably."

"Could've come off anywhere," said Ti-Bo. "How'd you guess the problem?"

"Leaked burning oil. Never mistake that stench."

"What now?" asked Scobie. She thought, *If you'd stayed driving, Père, instead of Ti-Bo the cowboy, this wouldn't have happened.*

"It's only a slow leak. Not much on the ground. We might make it back to Verseau on what's still in there."

"But," said Ti-Bo, "suppose we drive on and do run dry—the engine will seize. Then we are screwed. And Gene Smithers gets a car rental bill for forty grand."

"So what?" fretted Scobie. "We can't stay out here all night."

"Sure we can." The père spoke softly. "And come morning we'll be able to see just where we are. We can send for help, flag somebody down—"

"Hey, Mo, who the hell do you expect to come find us? Triple A? On the other hand, there's huts scattered all around this gully. Could be some farmer's got a dose of oil stashed away. Even lamp oil. Whatever! Tide us through to Verseau. We got plenty of gourdes—oh *shitshitshit*—!" Ti-Bo jigged, slapping his neck, arms, ankles.

Mosquitoes had found them.

Inside the switched-off, already tepid Land Cruiser, Ti-Bo flipped open the lid-cushions on the bench seats. He hauled out bug spray, sunscreen, a stack of straw hats, assorted drugstore remedies, C- and D-cell batteries. Then came melting bags of ice, tuna-pickle sandwiches, cardboard towers of Pringles, bottled One A Day vitamins, bags of local peanuts powdered with hot cayenne, plastic sacks of Culligan, cans of Diet Sprite and Dr. Pepper. Ti-Bo held up a quart of Barbancourt rum. "First things first," he said.

They settled cross-legged on the floor, side by side, using one bench as a table. Ti-Bo propped his flashlight on a pack of paper napkins. It threw tall shadows of the picnic against the interior walls. Père Emory lowered his forehead to his fingertips. "Praise the Lord, O my soul," he murmured. "And forget not the good He has done unto you." This was not his usual formula for grace. Scobie and Ti-Bo waited, but no more words followed. Père crossed himself. "Amen."

"Amen," echoed Scobie, a habit of courtesy. But her hand sketched a line from forehead to breastbone, left shoulder to right. To keep him company.

Had she ever before been this thirsty, this hungry? She poured water from the torn end of the plastic sack straight down her throat. It splashed over her neck and into her shirt as well. Her teeth sank through white bread foam into the tangy goo of gherkins and onion, tuna and mayo.

Ti-Bo flicked the radio dial. Nothing but static. "I forgot," he said. "This vee-hicle is totally equipped." He beamed the flashlight into an armrest compartment, found a CD, and shoved the disc into the slot. Mahalia Jackson sang *Pass the Drinking Gourd*. "Hey! Is that perfect?"

Scobie sputtered a laugh through the tuna. She'd missed the music that in the rest of the world ran free as water. Here in the back country, like water, it was scarce. In Verseau, they at least had Père Emory's guitar.

"I thought you hated gospel," said Emory.

Ti-Bo set down three paper cups and fizzed in the Sprite, followed by a solid splash of Barbancourt. "Most of it. But I love her voice."

The two men had a tendency to disregard her presence, to talk mainly over or around her to each other, as if picking up some long-running exchange. She wasn't sure why this didn't offend or even bother her. Maybe it was the trust implied by their letting her this far into their friendship. A three-way unspoken bond.

"Your idea is to camp here all night, Mo? It's not worth trying to see if somebody around here can help us get out? I mean, a lot of these peysan have amazing skills. They're carpenters, masons, welders—problem solvers, period. Sort of like your dad was. There might be a blacksmith. We could get a patch on the oil pan!"

"That's unlikely. Let's wait for daylight. Get some sleep."

"Hey! I don't have the time you do! Besides being sitting ducks here in a disabled Cruiser some people might take for a treasure-laden shipwreck, we left forty kids alone in Lakay! You're not worried about what they'll get up to?"

"Smithers is on deck."

Ti-Bo snorted. "He don't even pale Kreyol."

"We'll all do better staying together." Père Emory began folding the second half of his sandwich back into its wax paper. There was a sound deep in his chest like a train in a tunnel. They knew that sound. Ti-Bo plopped more Barbancourt into his cup, but Emory waved it off. Then, heaving with the effort of a suppressed cough, he drank it down.

The crate was turning into an airless oven. "If we could just open the windows," Scobie pleaded.

"Are you crazy? We'll be massacred by bugs," said Ti-Bo.

"We're damned either way." She stored the père's leftovers in the cooler and collected their used napkins and paper plates into an empty bag. Crumbs from the bench she scraped into her palm. Later someone would be sleeping on this plastic-covered bench. Two in back, one in front? How in God's name could anyone sleep in this heat?

"Don't see why we can't run the AC, off and on," offered Ti-Bo. "This thing's got a power train could launch an atomic missile. AC won't make a dent."

"Not worth the risk," said Emory, very low, so as not to rouse the cough. He lifted his head, alert. A flare of lightning silvered the trickles of sweat running from his close-shaven, grizzled hairline down his jaw. Mahalia sang, "The-ere is a balm in Gilead, to maaake the wouuunded who-ole . . ." Scobie wanted to wipe his sweat with her hand. And taste it.

He said to her, "Listen. Kill the music. What's that sound? Outside."

Ti-Bo cocked an ear. "Bugs," he said. "Bugs hitting the windows. We're the best plat de jour since Napoleon sent his juicy white boys up here into the hills."

Scobie knew that tale, too: How the European mercenaries, maddened by heat and hunger, had lost sense of their mission to punish Haiti's claim to independence, lost faith in their paymasters, and dissolved into the impenetrable hill country the same way Toussaint L'Ouverture and the renegade slaves had, in order to escape torture and death. With local girls, they produced offspring who would never learn their fathers' native tongue. All that happened not so long ago. There were many kids in Verseau with eyes green as her own and hair the color of wet sand.

Thunder gathered far away and hurtled toward them. The crate shook. "Not bugs." Emory said. "What we're hearing now is the blessed event this whole country's been praying for. *Rain.*"

THE RAIN HAMMERED on the Land Cruiser's steel roof. Furious whips lashed the windows. With Emory in the lead, they piled out the back doors, whooping, squirting each other with mosquito repellent as they jumped down.

In seconds Scobie was drenched. Draping rain all but blinded her. Only the two rear windows of the Cruiser glimmered, a disembodied gaze. Scobie and Ti-Bo and Père Emory turned their faces up to the stinging rain and stretched out their arms and rotated like joyful drunks, drunk on heavenly water, bumping into each other, giggling and grabbing for support.

"This monsoon is likely to wash all our roof work away at Lakay Bondonn!" Père Emory shouted. "I should be worried, but—" He slipped, nearly fell.

"Worry later!" shouted Ti-Bo. "Or maybe you won't have to? Maybe it's just advance billing. Maybe the real rain is still a week or three away—that happens!" He pulled off his sandals. Scobie and Ti-Bo followed his example. Cloud water, rushing downhill, bounced and flowed over and under their toes and arches and ankles. They slid and slipped, holding hands. Dancing in the rapidly deepening and softening mud. Thunder cracks gave the backbeat.

A flare of light far down the road stamped itself on her retina, throbbing like a hallucination. Lightning wouldn't flash so low to the ground. She squeezed both hands holding hers, tightly: *Stop*. Then pointed their arms downhill. The light flared again and vanished. No—there were two lights now. Or four.

"No shit," said Ti-Bo. "Headlights? What is this, rush hour?"

"You're right. They're not moving," said Père Emory in a slow, measuring voice. "Tap-taps? Or trucks maybe, stalled in the mud?"

"What I want to know," said Ti-Bo, "is did they see *us*. *Our* light."

"Think they might be stranded?" Scobie, dizzy, still felt as if the ground were swaying. "Like us? Shouldn't we go check?"

"Curiosity killed the stranger," said Ti-Bo.

"Of course we should," said Père Emory. "I'll go down."

"Alone? But you said we had to stay together—" Again her voice rose against her will, almost a whine.

"Mo's right. We'd be idiots to all leave the Cruiser now." But Ti-Bo sounded uneasy. Emory had the upper hand. He spoke the best Kreyol, he was black as a pure Guinean, he could approach a stranger, or strangers, neg to neg.

"Wait a sec!" Ti-Bo dropped their hands. He yanked open the rear doors to dig into his horn-o'-plenty of a backpack. "Eh, eh, where you hide, baby?" he said.

He came back shielding a drawstring leather bag and pulled it open to give a glimpse of a handgun, ugly as a toad. "Our ole friend from way back, Mo. The Ruger."

Père Emory waved the bag away, with the pinched look of a reformed drinker.

"Go on, take it! It's not loaded." Ti-Bo flipped some well-oiled parts back and forth. "I mind the rules. Keep cartridges separate."

"All right. You load it," the père said. Under the rain's percussion they had to nearly touch foreheads to hear each other. "And you hold onto it. Guard the property."

Scobie noticed he hadn't said the property *and her.*

She watched him leave and felt herself smile and shiver at the same time. Rain-chill? Hero worship? On his third long stride, the rain crashed down like a steel gate to hide him.

Ti-Bo and Scobie sat inside the Land Cruiser, cool and wet as salamanders, facing each other, stripped to their underwear. Every few minutes a flash of lightning blanched the walls. A few counts later thunder grabbed the crate in its jaws and shook it—lifted it, Scobie imagined—to let the gabbling streams of water run unchecked beneath them.

"He's asking for—" said Ti-Bo. Rain-clatter erased the rest.

"What did you say?"

"He shouldn't stay out there so long. He could catch cold. I mean, he has one already. He's not going to get rid of that cough running around in the rain."

Ti-Bo's fussy tone irked her. "This rain is warm enough to steam corn."

"I shouldn't have let him go down. I should have at least made him take my gun."

"You couldn't have. Not a prayer." Scobie thought: *I'll worry about the père, okay? If and when worry is needed.*

"Here's maybe the good news, Ti-Bo. I'm thinking we could be a lot nearer to home than we figured. I'm sure I saw the sea again—pretty close—just before the rain started. Didn't you? So those headlights could be from someone on the coast road? Where a stalled truck is more likely. Which would mean we are already near the turnoff."

But Ti-Bo wasn't listening. He had grabbed one of the flashlights to shine around the driver's space. He punched open the armrest compartment, dug under the CDs. Gave a grunt of discovery.

Thunder made the Land Cruiser shake tip to stern like a dog trying to dry itself. Ti-Bo had pulled a molded plastic case from the compartment. He flipped it open. "Damn. I knew I saw something else. That was a box of clips, hiding under the CDs. Look here: Brother Smithers packs a Glock!"

She knew this gun, the Glock, from her old freelance days of chasing trouble. The Big Mac of automatics. So popular that it was liberated wholesale from NATO and UN depots. No prize for accuracy, but a fast repeat, and simple enough for a child to shoot. "Maybe a handgun comes as part of the standard Port-au-Prince rental package."

"Haha. Hey, Scobie. You know how to load, how to shoot this baby?" He was releasing the action and checking the chamber, the same as he'd done with his own gun.

"Not really."

"What's that supposed to mean—not really?"

"Let's see . . . I've shot air guns at Oktoberfest? I even won a giant stuffed panda. By the time I got it home all the straw-dust innards had leaked out. I could've cried. I mean, I was drunk."

"Sounds like your panda took a few hits before you got him."

"Oh. Also, I wore a gun like that for a while."

"Get out." A surprised grin in his voice.

"Just for looks? Deterrence. I had a job as night watch-person. On this huge construction site. Honest to God, even empty, the gun spooked the bejaysus out of me." Bejaysus—a Ti-Bo word. Funny, she thought, while he toyed with the Glock and aligned its sights in the near-dark. Funny how she tended to mimic others' speech and body language. Not with any intent to ingratiate. More likely, imitation came from traveling solo and wanting to blend in with whoever was nearby. "What're you doing?"

He had jiggled a clip up into the handgrip and was tapping the clip sharply to drive it home. "Loading, like Mo said. Now both of these babes are good to go. What's this about you working as a guard? Guarding what?"

It had not been her job, exactly. (If she had a bumper sticker, it would read, *Life is a Gig.*) She'd been moonlighting for a guy whose ID code she punched each evening at the gate below. She and the guy had been together for three months, but he'd gone off to Spain, a non-refundable all-inclusive booked pre-Scobie vacation with his ex-girlfriend. Scobie had carried the gun (weighty for its small size) in a holster snapped to the belt of a way-too-big Securitas S.A. uniform, while patrolling the half-constructed, skeletal floors of a high-rise condo development in Paris. Thirteenth arondissement, a sketchy neighborhood.

Sometimes in the endless nights, sick of cold coffee and the echo of her footsteps, she stretched out on a bed in a finished demo-room on the twenty-ninth floor. Next door was a lavish demo-bathroom with theatrical lights framing the mirror. Her own face startled her.

The main door opposite the bathroom opened to a hallway dotted with naked light bulbs on strings. A third door flapped open to—nada. To wind and night sky. Rosy heaven if the night was overcast, black space between stars if it was clear. Dizzyingly far below, the city pulsed in intricate loops of red and white and yellow flares.

Ti-Bo, who had been snooping through the CDs, trapped her in the flashlight's beam. "Why the crabby look?"

"You might use up the batteries," she said. "And what if someone sees the light?"

"We got extras, remember? This light is mini. Nobody'll see it through the rain." Invisibly, Scobie shrugged. "Anything good in that pile?"

"Gene's got a thing for Madonna. Plus, about twenty empty PowerBar wrappers in the glove compartment. Maalox Extra—that figures. Little red book: *Is Jesus on Your Board of Directors*? Not to mention a stash of skins."

"What?"

"Condoms, prophylactics."

"In Smithers's car?"

"The man is human. This might explain what keeps him coming back to Haiti très cheri. Brother Smithers wouldn't be the only misery tourist with an itch to scratch on the side."

"Stop. Maybe he keeps them to hand out. Driving through Kafou, to the truckers. You know. Against SIDA. AIDS."

"You go on believing that, sweetheart." She'd always been squeamish about condoms. The night's limp fingers washed up on all the world's beaches. And so awkward to use: rolled on like a stocking, removed with a silly little pop. Condoms were for others. Teens, the diseased, the poor. Mandatory for HIV-positives.

How many men had told her they couldn't do it with condoms. And how often she'd gone along, because she wanted what they claimed to want: trust. Real closeness.

"Shh!" hissed Ti-Bo, although she'd said nothing.

He'd shut off the flashlight. A strobe of lightning showed him shoving Smithers's supplies back into storage. Scobie became aware of a pounding on the back doors heavier than the rain. A thin voice. She leaned down on the lock handle, and the doors parted. Like a wave breaching a levee, Père Emory swung his dripping self up and inside.

He told them there were not one but two trucks stalled or stopped down the road. If you could call this roaring gully still a road. But were they in trouble? It didn't seem so. He hadn't actually spoken to anyone—had stopped before getting that close. He'd taken care not to be seen. Because you can't know. Two heavy-duty trucks with extra wide beds. Six men on the ground who were busy with whatever they were doing. You don't notice a person when you're not expecting an interruption, especially not on a night like this, and not when the visitor approaches from the least likely, least guarded direction.

Ti-Bo aimed the beam of the flashlight at his friend. "Man, what's the matter with you? You're shaking. You getting malaria again?"

Père Emory didn't answer. Scobie saw contractions ripple out through his limbs from his ribcage. He clamped his hands in the vise of his knees. Ti-Bo wanted to know if he had been keeping up with his weekly doses of Azulen.

"I'm *freezing*," countered Père Emory. He spoke through clenched teeth. To keep from biting his tongue, Scobie guessed. Her turn now to rummage through the bench storage. Who would have foreseen a need for blankets in Haiti in late July? She found none.

Despite the darkness they had a sense of who was where. A glint here, a stir of air there. Ti-Bo pulled Emory's wet shirt off over his head. Then he eased off the Pere's shorts and underwear in one bundle. Emory shoved his splayed hands between his knees again and bent low. His cough sounded bottled up, not the usual escaped explosion.

"Sit up tall," said Scobie. "You'll breathe better." She sounded bossy. Why not, if that meant he'd listen. With a beach towel she rubbed his back and arms, thighs and calves. Ti-Bo poured rum, glub-glub, into paper cups. One for Emory, one for himself. Scobie waved away the offer.

Emory drank, paused, and passed her the cup. "Two trucks, Ti-Bo."

"So you said."

"Stopped at a crossroad. What does that put you in mind of?"

"Are we near the coast, do you think? The Route Nationale?" Scobie downed the remainder of Barbancourt 5 Star. She knelt on the floor, one elbow propped on the bench beside Emory.

"No idea. I couldn't see more than twenty feet. But I don't believe we've come back that far."

"Were the trucks broke down?" asked Ti-Bo.

"Didn't look that way. Five or six men. Not doing a job I like to see, Ti-Bo. Hauling tires out of the truck beds. Stacking them. What do you bet they brought kerosene?"

Ti-Bo whistled. "Who do you figure? Anciens? Building a roadblock?"

"It will be huge. They're pros. Be finished before first light."

"So we can't get down from here?" asked Scobie. "Until the police come?"

"What police, Scobie? *They* are the police."

Ti-Bo said, "Sweetheart, until they decide to move their drive-in ATM elsewhere, we're stuck in these hills. Or we pay up. And they'll take everything."

Later Scobie would ask Père Emory if it was her fault that Ti-Bo's nerves had started to fray. He went from arguing the need to push on to Bwa Teneb to wanting only to get the hell down off the mountain.

Something malicious had stirred in her as she poked idly at a palmful of cayenned peanuts and the Land Cruiser rocked in the endless pounding rain. "We're sitting ducks for a flash flood," she said.

Ti-Bo sucked in a breath.

"These are perfect conditions. After four years of drought? The ground's sealed like wax. Where's the water going to go? Down rivers and roads. Gravity! I mean, that's what made this gash we're sitting in. You know? And there's no forest left to soak up the runoff. That's why the sea all around here is dead, right, all the fish poisoned by the runoff."

Père Emory murmured, "Don't heed her, Bo. The chances of a flood are remote."

"You'd be surprised," Scobie went on. "I used to have this friend? A catastrophe expert. I am not kidding. It's a branch of math: the statistical probability of extreme events. He loved for me to bring him news items about, say, a 7.5 Richter earthquake. Or two planes colliding in midair. Data. One story was a flash flood in the Italian Alps. This big riverbed filled with holiday campers on Easter vacation. Spring storms started up in the mountains at night. Around dawn more than forty people were swept away. No time to wake up and understand what was happening, let alone head for higher ground. The wall of water bulldozing all those tents and trailers."

She spoke lightly. Easy to be flippant about the long-ago. But back then, when she read the clipping aloud, tears had blurred the newspaper photo of floating folding chairs and beach toys. Real terror needs contrast. Looking at the photo, she'd pictured morning sunshine, fresh spring leaves. Had birds been singing when the water surged in, or had the birds already flown?

Ti-Bo snapped, "A disaster sadist. Scobie, you have weird friends."

"He was a scientist, not a sadist."

"Same difference."

"The event was mathematically valuable. Mystery is only a lack of data, he always said."

Père Emory said, "I'd honestly like to hear how statistics can put an end to mystery. What's your friend working on now?"

"Not the foggiest." She felt an obscure shame. How to think of him? As the persuasive sponsor of her second abortion? She'd heard he had made early tenure, was pulling down six figures as a Pentagon consultant, had been elected to the National Academy of Arts and Sciences. Married, with twins. "We lost touch."

Ti-Bo blurted, "Mo? We have to get to high land, we have to get the hell out!"

"Put on the red slippers," Scobie said, "and click your heels three times."

"You two can stay or come with. I am out of here." Ti-Bo half-crouched in the crate. Scobie could almost hear his mind racing to find a way out of the rattrap gully. "I'm going up the bank. What's a little rain. No, wait. Better to cut a deal with the roadblock. That's it. They've got the wheels, I bet a wad of gourdes'll buy a ticket out of here—less risky than sitting in this ditch waiting for the tsunami. *Wall of water*?" He screamed Scobie's hack phrase. "I can't fucking swim!"

Père Emory rested a hand on his friend's shoulder.

Scobie said, "Hold on. Stop, Ti-Bo. It's not going to happen, it was only Barbancourt talk, okay? I'm out of practice these days, leading such a righteous life."

Ti-Bo hitched his backpack over one shoulder. Père Emory grabbed his free arm so hard and fast that the shorter man staggered against the bench. “Stay here. The worst thing you could do is go down there.”

“It’s not like I’m leaving you in the lurch. I take the Ruger, and you got Smithers’s Glock now. You remember how it works, Marine. They say shooting a gun’s like riding a bicycle.”

“Monche, if they don’t like the look of you—doesn’t matter if they’re ton-ton macoutes or FRAPH or chimeres or plain-vanilla gangsters—”

“Listen. I’ve handled these guys before. They play a short game. I know how their heads work. Here’s my thinking: for enough grese pat one of them wants to drive a truck back here, with me, to pick you both up and take us to the main road. Wouldn’t that be sweet?” He backed to the rear door, clutching his pack.

“Like a fairy tale. Ti-Bo, hold *on*!”

But Ti-Bo had shoved open the rear door. He jumped. They heard splashing sounds, then only the rain’s full racket, until Scobie pulled the latch tight again.

“He panicked, Scobie. Not your fault.” Père Emory drew her down to sit beside him on a bench.

“I was trying to spook him, like telling stories around a campfire.” *How selfish*, she thought.

“You didn’t know you had hold of his biggest fear.”

“I’m so damn sorry. What if he runs into real trouble? I want him back.”

Père Emory laughed. “Believe me, Ti-Bo always turns up again. Not always where you’d expect. If he’s not back tonight we may find him in Verseau tomorrow. He’s set on you and him flying out of here, remember? I think Ti-Bo has had Haiti up to here. It happens. Not least to Haitians.”

“Not me. I don’t want to leave. Not yet.”

"Then you're the one with a fever. Listen. Tomorrow morning—"

His lips brushed her ear. His voice fell to a whispered burr for emphasis.

"Tomorrow morning you won't recognize this spot on the planet. The sun will be cooking again. Water steaming off the houses and fields like white smoke. Children and goats will be jumping and roosters cock-a-doodle-doo-ing and you'll see green spreading over bare ground where there hasn't been green in years. The higher we go—"

"So we'll push on in the morning? Find your new farm?"

"I have a hunch it's just up on the left, past the third set of lights."

His shivering had abated. They lay down face to face, stretched full length in the nest Scobie had made with the cushions on the floor between the two benches. Barely space for two, under their scratchy covering of beach towels. The chill in his core took her body's heat, cooling her. A perfect exchange.

He laid his head back on his pillowing arm, as if to regard her up close. She could hear the stir of his breath. Yet what could he see? Scobie stared into complete darkness. They could only find each other with palms, with fingertips. She moved her open palm over his angled arm, his back, and close-shaven nape in slow circles, as he had let her do one evening in the infirmary. *Is this better?* she wanted to ask, but knew the answer and also that, along with her hand's touch, the silence did him good.

She could not have forced down her smile if she tried. It rose from a sense of liberation. Lying on the floor of this crate in a rain-choked gully, she could float up into midair at any moment.

He did see her. Inside her. She felt perfectly perceived in every detail. Taken in, accepted whole, once and for all.

She raised his hand from where it rested on her ribs. Lifted the unresisting hand to her face. His rough fingers traced her lips, nostrils, dimples. She tasted salt, felt the broken nails, pictured in a rush all the things and bodies these hands had touched through years in this country.

"I don't want—" Her throat tightened.

"Shh," he said. "I know."

"I don't want to leave, that's all. I want . . . I *admire* you. Can I say that?"

"Shh." His hand slid behind her head. His lips touched hers, softly at first, then crushing her smile. For a moment she was afraid. Was he? The taste of him, tongue, teeth, saliva. She'd been starved. Finally, the embrace of a being more substantial than your unsteady, always-changing self.

"Baby." He spoke into her, his breath entering her throat. "I need you, baby." His strong hand cupping her cheek, holding her jaw exactly as he wanted for the kiss. He lifted, arranged her body under him. A towel falling away showered her with dry sand left from a morning light-years past. His hand smoothed her bare waist, covered her right breast, pressed hard, pushing and pulling against the nipple. Scobie inhaled. He froze.

"Tell me if I hurt you. I never, never want to hurt you."

"Nothing you do with me could hurt, nothing." Every part of her was intent on surrender. On finding the way to surrender. The channel they lay in on the floor enclosed them deep and narrow as a coffin. She pulled him tight against her. Would take him into and through her if only she could. Her flesh found his muscles and bones to melt against. The dense weight of him kept her from floating away up into the storm above them. The storm's din blurred their voices and made their eager, awkward, determined movements almost soundless. The storm gave permission.

His hands framed her hips. Guiding her. She reached down to touch his sex, long and warm through the layer of rough towel. He lifted her hand and pinned it over her head, and pressed hard against her again, slipped lower, parting her thighs and pushing at the soft pulsing between her legs, the thin wet barrier of her pants. She wrestled against his pinning hand for the reassurance of his strength. She thrust her hips upward, trying to find the way closer to him. *Baby, that's right. I knew you would be—this had to be—oh yes. Baby, move, stay with me—*

"Stop," he said in a raw voice. "I can't. Be doing this. To you."

"Do what to me—why, what is wrong, why not?" She locked her hands around him, pleading hands. "Listen, I can't get pregnant, if that's it. Impossible."

"I can't do this!" He broke away. But there was no room, no way to avoid her body. He hauled himself up onto the bench like an exhausted swimmer and coughed for long minutes, a dry hacking muffled by his fist. Now he was twice hidden. Even lightning wouldn't show his expression.

And there was no lightning. Only the rain continued to pour down, with the noise of heavy curtains being endlessly dragged open and shut.

She felt groggy. Lust, like deep-stage sleep, disoriented her. Her womb and her heart still pounded in tandem, bewildered and expectant. The happiness, too, lingered past reason.

"Scobie." His voice drifted down, as if calling to the bottom of a deep well. (This well had been dry for decades; all the water was outside; he would send down whatever she needed in a basket on a rope.) "I'm sorry. Forgive me. It's my fault. I thought I could control myself. Us."

"Control freak," she said. "I like mayhem." She put lightness, a skip in her voice. Because he needed to draw into himself, needed time to reflect, time to respond. How long had it been since he touched anyone because of his own need? How long since he had made love? Was he taking their embrace—taking *her*—far too seriously?

How strange to recognize happiness in present time, in the full bloom of the moment instead of later, too late, in some blue, nostalgic afterward.

"Come up here, Scobie? Sit by me."

Scobie crawling up out of the well. Emory collecting the towels to tuck around them both. He settled her head in the hollow of his neck and stroked her hair, her pockmarked cheeks. They looked toward where the windows must be. They wondered what time it was but made no move to find out. The waves of wanting slackened and rose between them like any other fever. His arm a rescue-ring around her; she was in no risk of floating away. Her whole body felt tender and throbbed in places, and she supposed his did, too.

"Feel my heart," he said. Her hand found the bird beating quick and steady inside the bars of his ribs. She asked him to tell her his sweetest memory. Some clue to what had made him who was.

"Where to start? I was born lucky, Scobie. Blessed. Maybe you're right, that's what gives me whatever stamina I have for the kids here. Clarksville, Maine. The farm, Mom and Dad, my bro Elliot. Denys, my sister. Hardly a cloud on this boy's horizon."

His arm a rescue-ring around her; she was in no risk of floating away. Scobie said, "I had a pretty good childhood, too." She saw that for the first time. "Compared to a lot of kids."

"Describe."

"Details? I can't. Ask me something."

"Tell me something you never put in words before."

Scobie closed her eyes, searching past the shouting and beatings and times she'd run away. "My stepdad had a new car, a Lexus. Russ had a zillion cars because he was a mechanic. Cars were his pets. The Lexus smelled like mint candy. I'm lying curled up on the back seat. Russ drives one-handed with my mother Greta scooted up against him. We must be following the Housatonic River because cattails and feather grass are scratching at the car windows. The sky is deep blue. Greta reaches around Russ's shoulders and curls her fingers in his hair. He has Elvis Presley hair, thick and black."

"Mine wasn't always gray." Emory lifted her hand to rub it on his own head. "And then?"

"That's it. Russ, keeping his eye on the road, leaned sideways so his forehead touched hers. I felt invisible. But still I was there—guarding them. Wanting them to stay happy together forever."

"I can see you."

They repositioned the cushions on the bench tops. Emory stretched out prone. She knelt on the floor next to him, still shivering, but only intermittently. The towels she'd covered with kept slipping once she began to try to rub warmth into him. She heard the rain calming itself like a cried-out child, winding down into small gusty sobs. Light was returning. The mercury glow from the water-blurred window might be either star glow from a shredded sky or the first sign of dawn. Her hands slid up and down his silvered torso, palms numb from the friction. When she moved the towel down his hips, he said nothing. When her hands suggested he turn over, he did so with a small groan. His erection was slightly curved. She bowed closer, but the moment her lips grazed the smooth tip, his hands gripped her shoulders and pushed her away.

She licked the salty-sweet liquid on her lips. Then, resting her cheek on his outflung arm, she stroked his ribs with her spread fingers. She felt heat flowing from him, steadily and generously, from some deep source. She brushed her flat palm across his nipples. Hard pebbles imbedded in soft skin. Her fingers traced the indent of navel and the shallow groove between muscle and hipbone, and encircled his rigid sex. She saw the pearly arc of semen pulse and vanish.

"*Baby*—" he rasped, and arched back his head and made a sound like a man tangled in a dream he can't wake from. He twisted his face away, cried out, reaching for her.

Scobie lay with her head on his chest. They were both still, listening to the thrumming of his heart.

A minute or an hour later he swung himself upright and locked his arms around her chest to haul her up onto the bench. She laughed—they both laughed at his sudden energy.

"Is there someone waiting for you to get back?" he asked. "In the States?"

"No." She didn't have to lie.

"I don't want anyone else to have this," he said. "From now on." His hand slid over her belly, then cupped the flesh between her relaxed, wet thighs. The fingers she had kissed pressed into her. Stroking her. She shuddered. As the sweet gathering explosion spiraled, she heard a rising wail, her own voice keening like a lost jungle bird. She fell forward, hiding her face against his shoulder. He rocked her in his arms, rocking them both.

"Baby? You're not sorry? Not sad?"

"Sad?" Bewildered. In the now-definite glimmer of dawn, couldn't he see the smile on her face? *Take this happiness, drink it, girl, rub it into your skin! They were only beginning.*

"You know what it's about. SIDA. I haven't been for the test in eight months."

"You're not much of a candidate for AIDS, Père Emory. Priest manqué."

He was silent. A sudden thought made her laugh again.

"What's funny?"

"How could I have been so dumb? We had Gene Smithers's condoms here," she explained, with a wave at the storage box. "Only an arm's reach away."

OUTSIDE, THE DAWN world steamed as Emory had predicted. The gully banks were smooth red chocolate, too slick to climb. They relieved themselves behind a pile of rocks, one standing guard for the other, though who on earth would be likely to pass by? They stood naked by the rear of the Cruiser, feet sunk deep in the sucking mud, washing off with drizzles of Culligan water and drying with the beach towels.

Back inside the Land Cruiser they lay down on the jumble of the blue plastic cushions, arms and legs entwined.

"I'm punch-drunk. I don't want to sleep," she said. "Emory?"

He was drawing a figure eight on her shoulder. "Mm."

"Seriously: Why are priests supposed to be celibate? Because they're so above passion? Or because loving a human takes something away from God?"

"I don't know. For me, loving a human is all that can prepare us for God. It's as much love as we can stand, for now."

"Did you ever fall in love?"

"Next question."

"How have you kept your faith, here in Haiti?"

"I don't know if I could have kept it anywhere else."

"What is faith?"

"Like the judge said about pornography. I know it when I feel it." She heard the smile in his voice. "I'll tell you a story that helps me get a sense of it."

Scobie nudged his arm with her tousled head.

"There was a family. Man, wife, their baby. They set out to drive through the desert from one city in Morocco to another. Forget just where. They're French, hip, well-off, and confident. They've got a desert-special Jeep. He has a Super 8 camera and she writes in her journal with a Mont Blanc pen. They have good new maps, but on the road they lose the way. The road is blown invisible by a sandstorm. The gas runs out and after some days the food is gone too. Finally, the water. The woman's breast milk dries up. She still keeps writing in her journal, day after day. At night the three crawl away from the Jeep to lie out on the cooling sand. She writes about the stars, the peacefulness of lying there looking into the heavens, the ecstasy, how the silent constellations swinging over the desert take the family outside of time, into the safety of eternity. At some point in their ordeal, fear simply disappears. They accept. The wife never felt such release, so sure of the rightness of things. Meanwhile, she cuts herself. Each day, small cuts in her arm, so her daughter can go on living. The baby learns to drink her mother's blood."

"And then?"

"She stopped writing. Weeks later, some Bedouins found the Jeep. No bodies, no bones. But in the sand, the journal."

Questions tumbled in Scobie's head. *What does that sad, terrible story have to do with faith? Was it really a true story, or a kind of parable?* The obvious parallels to their present fix made her uneasy. Was that the point? As Emory's breathing gradually slowed, she followed him into a sleep as deep as forever-after.

SHE WOKE UP alert, in what seemed like a parenthesis between dreams. Judging by the soft scudding light, not much more than an hour could have passed. Emory's silky skin slipped along hers as she rose on one elbow.

Had the woman in the desert bled herself only for the sake of keeping her baby going for a few more days or hours? Was that insanity or courage?

Scobie had bled. The painful scraping away of a possible life.

"Emory, do me a favor?" she whispered.

He stretched and turned, surprisingly awake. "Like, get us the hell out of here?"

"I want you to baptize me." She held her breath, stunned by her own words.

Emory laughed. "If you think for a minute that would make a difference in how I feel, you sure don't know me."

"No, I mean it. Please. You're allowed to, right? I saw you baptize a baby for a woman who came to Lakay."

"I may be a seminary washout, but I did make deacon. So yes, according to canonical law I can baptize."

"Then why not me?"

"Those children brought to our gate—they're dying. In an emergency, any person can administer the sacrament. But you? Oh, baby. Are you just saying what you think I want to hear?" He turned aside, dealt with a cough.

"Gene Smithers," she said when he'd finished. "He got it in his head I need salvation." She expected a snort from Emory. None came. "Smithers is so sure . . ." She hesitated, but then drove herself forward. "He says that baptism—by baptism, God—" *How can three letters be so hard to pronounce*? "Can forgive. No matter how unforgivable something is. You said that too. About starting as a new person."

"It's not like a study hall pass. Scobie, do you know what you'd be getting into, with God? Out of the frying pan, into the fire."

"Yes. No. But do it for me. Please."

"You heathens, Scobie, are supposed to take instruction first." He yawned and apologized and guided her head into the hollow of his shoulder. "There's a lot to sort out. Even instruction can only scratch the surface. Normally, an adult wanting a life in Christ begins the journey as a catechumen. Same as in Paul's day. Nowadays that means a year, maybe two."

"I don't have time! Being here in Haiti, living with folks who call themselves fortunate if they eat one full meal a day—isn't that instruction enough?"

His arms crossed over her back and tightened. "Miss Impatience! There's no emergency. We'll talk more. I promise. Now try to sleep a little."

She couldn't. She listened as his inhalations lengthened, trying to match hers to the rhythm. The sense of witnessing her own happiness persisted, as if she were looking back on this moment from some far future time.

Sometimes walking in Boston's winter, she ran across crows, those lone, angular birds that seldom flew away. For some reason crows reminded her of *them*. Even though she didn't have names for them, sometimes she called to them. The crows hopped and flapped oily black wings. Was there a fairy tale, where unwanted children turned into birds?

She could not tell Emory. Him, least of all. God might forgive her, but Emory was only human.

THERE WAS A frenzied hammering, fists battering steel. Scobie opened her eyes to stabbing morning sun. Raising her head, she saw Emory reach for the Glock nestled in the armrest. He said, "Shh. Stay down. S'probably just Ti-Bo."

Now his training showed. With the gun pointed downward at forty-five degrees he scanned the windows, put his ear to the rear door, then yanked up the latch bolt.

Ti-Bo jumped in like a giant locust, featureless against the flooding light, and remained crouched. "You guys okay? Nobody bothered you last night?"

Scobie sat up, snatching a towel to her chest. "Good to see you. Sure, we're fine. Never been better." She felt her blush spread.

But Ti-Bo had been better, she realized in the next moment. He held a red paisley bandana pressed against the side of his neck. When he pulled the cloth away, a crimson stream pulsed out, splattering one of the turquoise seat cushions. The bottom of his ear looked ripped, like a seam come undone.

"What the hell," said Père Emory.

"Don't give me that look, Mo. No big deal, just messy. The bullet zinged me in the dark. We were good, once I got close enough to talk to them." He pushed the bandana back against his neck, squeezing his eyes shut. "What did I promise? Huh? Ti-Bo delivers. There is a guy driving up here to fetch you. Us, I mean. Won't be long. Soon as they can spare a truck." He sank down on the bench.

Scobie had a bag of water ripped open, to wash the ear. But Emory stopped her from touching the bandana. "It's an artery. He's doing the right thing, keeping the pressure on." With his free hand Ti-Bo grabbed the water bag and sucked in its contents.

They sat facing each other. Emory said, "So it *is* a roadblock? And after someone shot at you, you crazy dude went on in, talked with them?" He gave a bark that sounded of incredulity and admiration. "What're you, some kind of Rambo?"

Ti-Bo nodded, wincing.

Waiting for an overdue friend is hard. A long wait for someone you only fervently hope will turn out to be a friend, is worse.

Stifling heat in the Land Cruiser drove them outside. Barefoot in the adhesive red mud that quelled up over their ankles, they leaned against the shady side of the crate. Ti-Bo and Emory each kept a secured handgun in their pockets that they fingered now and then. But the only visitors were goats and children. With pale ginger-ale eyes the goats sized up the three etranje; the human kids chanted, "M'bwan sank dollar! M'bwan sank dollar!"

Scobie handed out chips and vitamin bonbons. She was weary. Only Emory found the energy to joke with the children. They brushed shyly at Scobie's hands, while avoiding Ti-Bo. They hooted at their own daring and sprinted off, chasing spooked goats up the gully.

The rising sun shrank the shade patch, inch by inch.

Scobie tried to imagine where they would all be in an hour. In one day. She said to Emory, "Please. It's quiet now. No one's coming. Do it now?"

Ti-Bo's black eyes flicked a question that Emory caught before glancing down to brush dried mud from his legs. "Scobie wants me to baptize her."

Ti-Bo squinted down the silent gully.

Not even a drift of dust. *If he makes fun of me*, Scobie thought, *I'll make him sorry*. She would tell Père Emory everything about where Ti-Bo got the money he donated to Lakay.

Ti-Bo spun out into the sunlight, prancing from one leg to another, slapping his knees with his free hand.

"Stop jumping around with that wound!" Emory shouted. "You could do yourself real damage—are you absolutely crazy?"

Ti-Bo returned, to push his face up inches from Scobie's. Her nostrils flared; she could smell the brassy blood on him. "What's the deal here? You don't have enough problems, you need Catholic guilt? Sweetheart, you don't have enough sin in you to toast a slice of Wonder Bread."

Emory took Scobie's hand and studied it like a fortune teller. "Give yourself more time. I don't understand your hurry. I should, but I don't."

Scobie closed her fingers around his. A silent plea. Why wouldn't he give her what she needed?

Ti-Bo exhaled wearily. "Although I never did get baptizing babies. Original sin? Our species learns its nastiness growing up."

She remembered the proud, faded bumper sticker on the catastrophe expert's VW. Freewheeling: I Don't Know and Neither Do You.

"Emory? I've been thinking about your story. The French family in the Jeep. The mother got her sense of acceptance from the stars and at the same time she still hoped, hoped by a thin, incredibly strong thread that at least her child would be found. Because everything is possible, she had learned by then. She hadn't set out on their vacation thinking that two weeks later she would die in the desert. You said you could only do it in an emergency. Well, look at Ti-Bo. Another half inch and—see what I mean?"

That was all of it. Nothing more she could add. She felt woozy from the heat. None of them had eaten anything since the night before.

"There's still some chow left," she said. "How about Tang and potato chips?"

"Whenever someone is going to give—or receive—a sacrament, it's recommended to fast before," Emory said.

Pulse racing, gripping a canister of Pringles, Scobie stared at him. Finally Emory said, "I've only done this on rare occasions. Never without a missal in hand. But I figure the Holy Spirit will help me out. Wouldn't be the first time." Scobie felt a strange stirring where her ribs met. The start of faith? Plain old hunger?

She handed the chips to Ti-Bo. "I think I do get it. Original sin."

Ti-Bo gave her a look. "Well good for you." He carefully removed the bandana and studied the dark, stiff patch of his blood. "How's my neck doing?"

Emory scowled at the wound through his glasses. "Not so bad. You've got great coagulation."

Ti-Bo refolded and re-applied the bandana. "I heal up fast. Go on, sweetheart. Ti-Bo is listening."

She took him at his word. "The sin we are born with is wanting to be—believing you are—the center. Grand Central Me Station. Sucking in attention like a black hole. It starts out as survival, but it stays on justifying every kind of selfishness. A whole universe of only ones. That's hell."

She looked for Emory. His twitch of the lips, almost a smile. "I doubt the bishop would approve of what we're about to do here," he said.

"Screw the bishop. It's his lousy map that got us here."

Ti-Bo offered to take the role of sponsor, although he was not exactly a member of the club in good standing, he pointed out. But wasn't it right that he should serve as Scobie's godfather, considering he was the one who had talked her into coming to this island? In a way, he was already responsible for her.

He vanished into the Land Cruiser and returned holding a Tupperware bowl full of Culligan. "Besides, Mo. You maneuvered me into going to a few Masses. I guess some of the holy water could've splashed on me."

Emory said, "It's a fair bet." He dipped his index finger into the bowl, breaking the water's surface tension.

In a low, conversational tone he asked the Father, along with the Son, to bless this water. As if talking to someone who had just joined them.

Do you wish to be baptized in the name of Jesus Christ, our Lord?" he asked Scobie.

The alien words startled her. She wanted to break and run. "Yes. I do."

"Then let us give thanks to God."

"Amen," interjected Ti-Bo, loud as a small congregation.

Scobie's ragged voice chimed in. Unrecognizable. "Amen."

Père Emory gazed up at the fast-boiling clouds tangled in the distant mountains. Then, in the crazy music of morning insects, he grasped Scobie by the shoulders, pivoting her to gaze westward. It was an almost angry grip. "Do you renounce Satan, his evil ways, and all his sinful temptations?"

Scobie said, "Yes. I do."

He pivoted her again. Now she stared past his shoulder at the green glowing outline of the hills. "Do you believe in Jesus Christ, Our Lord?"

"Yes," to the cloud-rimmed hills. Was she telling the truth? Or was she only seduced by hope? Or benumbed on center stage, unable to say no?

"Do you, Scobie, believe in the forgiveness of sins?"

Against her closed eyes a vision flared. Fire. Mother-of-pearl. Fast-moving. She wanted to hold it steady, go into it, see clearly. "Yes," she whispered. "I do."

Her legs were already unsteady, and the pressure of Père Emory's hands was enough to force her to kneel on the ground. She hitched her skirt behind her as she dropped. The warm mud engulfing her legs was cool below the surface.

Père Emory's hand splayed over the top of her head, forcing her to bow lower.

"I baptize you in the name of—"

She hardly heard the word *Father*, as the shock of water hit her crown. She gasped. The water flooded her snarled hair, flowed fresh and cool down her forehead, cheeks, nose, and into her throat. She couldn't breathe.

Now the bowl was upturned over her. Water flowed everywhere. Suffocating. She knelt face to the mud, her mind emptied, dark and blank as the sky at Haitian cockcrow.

She opened her eyes but recognized nothing. A figure crouched beside her and cupped her chin firmly.

Père Emory whispered, "Scobie? Child? Are you all right?"

NOON. STILL NO rescue truck. The only shade was inside the back of the Land Cruiser. Scobie's mind was bright, flat and bare as a stretch of sand at low tide. Earlier, while she was laying out what food was left—a thermos of Tang, soggy Pringles, a bag of peanuts—"all the major food groups," said Ti-Bo—she'd felt like someone recovering from an accident, as if she was learning to move again, delighted by the freedom of her body. But now all three friends lay sprawled on the blue benches with doors and windows open, as prostrate as any of Hispaniola creatures.

Père Emory was proposing plan B, namely to climb up to a hut and negotiate the price of a few donkeys, when they heard the low grinding gears of an engine reverberating, lumbering up the gully.

"What'd I tell you?" said Ti-Bo. He high-fived them with both hands. He'd allowed Emory to rig a bandage for his neck wound out of rags, twigs, gauze, and Neosporin from the first aid box. "Two centimeters off the carotid artery," Emory judged. Ti-Bo said that with this bandage he could pass for a dog-collar padre, himself. But as he craned for a glimpse of the approaching promised truck, Scobie saw him as a box tortoise: round bullet-head poking out from its thick folded sheath.

The truck was all charred rust, beyond age. But it was equipped in front with the halogen lights that had cut so sharply through the rain, and fitted in back with a handmade, wood-railed bed. It roared up the gully, spitting streams of mud and rock, banging like a steel band. About thirty yards away, the brakes heaved an operatic sigh.

The driver swung down.

Père Emory watched straight-backed and emotionless through his metal-rimmed glasses. But like Ti-Bo, Scobie was already beaming, couldn't keep relief from turning into broad welcome. Their rescuer was a tall, tobacco-leaf-colored man in his thirties—large shades made it hard to guess—dressed in tan fatigues. No insignia. A red bandana much like Ti-Bo's circled his head, and a peysan's machete hung low against his hip.

"Bingo. That's my *man*." Ti-Bo edged past her. As he dropped out from the Land Cruiser into the sunlight, he tapped the Glock cradled deep in his pocket.

"Emory?" Sun-dazzled, she reached blindly. His hand caught and enfolded hers. The first touch between them since her baptism. "Are we good to leave? Is there anything we should take with?" She looked down at his hand, the place where two veins converged and crossed just below his knuckles, and all of the night before came crashing back over her in a single wave.

The rust-bucket rescue truck revved to show its impatience. Père Emory sank onto a bench.

"I'm not going back just yet," he said.

"What do you mean? They're waiting for us!"

"Someone has to stay. It won't be Ti-Bo: That wound needs attention. Chances are it's infected already." He didn't drop her hand but didn't seem much aware of her either. He watched Ti-Bo and the driver talking. "Don't you see? Otherwise, Gene's crate will be stripped and gutted within hours. We'd be lucky to find a puddle of oil here when we returned."

Where was her joy of only a moment ago? Her faith? Surely, she'd known all along this was coming, one way or the other—the separation. Even if only for some hours. Or days. Or forever.

"Why don't you ride back with them and let me—" She stopped. He would never agree to her being the only one to stay. She didn't want to see annoyance tighten his face.

She knelt on the floor between the benches. The mud crusted on her skirt was two-toned, half-dry. She reached her arms up around his waist as far as she could and rested her cheek on his thigh. The embrace was not so awkward. She waited, hoping, then shivered at the touch of his hands, first light on her hair, then diving through the mass of tangles to cup her head. Gently, like a sculptor taking an impression. She closed her eyes.

"Scobie. Listen. You'll be flying back to the States tomorrow."

"No! It's too late for that, we'll never make the flight."

"Don't underestimate Ti-Bo. You two could still catch the late plane out. Try! You can help us more from there than here."

"I can help you here. You need a female with the girls. You said." She rubbed her cheek fiercely against his leg.

"There is still the sacrament of confirmation to be received. Only a priest can give you that. Find an honest priest, baby. If you're not sure, call Father Ron Wylde. Our Lady's, in Clarksville."

"And then I come back here."

His hands tightened on her skull for an instant, and then were gone. What was his expression, above her? "The moment you two get to Verseau," he said, "send someone up to fix this beast. With tools."

"Right. Sure."

"Now hustle. They won't wait long."

She stumbled to her feet, tripping on her skirt, then moved to the back of the Land Cruiser, without turning around. She pushed the doors wide. She had no choice but to leave him.

"Orevwa," he said.

"Orevwa." She jumped into the bleached sunlight.

"Baby?" he called.

She whirled.

"You almost forgot something."

He leaned down, dangling three bags of Culligan by their corners. "Catch! Never forget the water."

From inside the truck cab, she recognized nothing. Clearly, they had lost their way the day before—somehow, they had become monstrously, inexplicably disoriented. Leaning forward on the shotgun side to peer through the dirt-fogged windshield, she concentrated on identifying new landmarks—whether to guide her own return or to describe the route to someone else. She was sure that Ti-Bo, outside in the truck bed, was doing the same.

The driver spoke some American. But he was busy steering, and she turned her face toward the open side window. Unusually for a Haitian, he smelled bad. Not merely of sweat. Maybe an infection. Or a fungus. Some minor disease.

Waved on by a jubilant machete-bearer who evidently recognized the truck, they zigzagged through the roadblock like a carload of sightseers touring the set of a violent action movie. A less fortunate tap-tap bus, forced to an emergency stop, balanced on three tires over the road lip. The letters of Christ Notre Seigneur were painted in Crayola colors front and sides, where in some duller land the end station would be indicated. All its passengers—the adults clutching bundles, with faces distorted by fear, the children round-eyed with surprise—were being herded into the scrub by a pair of rifle-prodding men in tan cammies like her driver's. The armed men saluted him as the truck jolted past.

The truck bounced around a last corner of the gully, landing on a remnant of pavement. "Bravo!" she said. "We made it!" The highway, at last. On her right, opened the brilliant, wave-winking, cool and vast sea. How could anyone's favorite color not be blue? Even the driver pushed up his shades, to let his eyes absorb the sea.

"That's Verseau, yes?" She pointed. "Is it far?" The driver shook his head. She strained to see into the far distance, to the pale, smoke-palled city.

She searched for familiar landmarks while eyeing both the clock and speedometer. Ten minutes passed. Fifteen. A fisherman holding a spear stood tall in a rocking blue boat, perfectly balanced, like a figure on a Greek vase. A thought snapped into her mind: *The sea is on my right. As it had been on their trip out, the day before.* Verseau could not lie ahead. It had to be behind them. Probably far behind, because they must be much farther south by now, down the coast road. The next large town—the last town on Hispaniola's southernmost tip—that would be Les Cayes. Or else—where in hell were they headed? Whatever this driver's destination, it wasn't Verseau. Her grubby torn nails pressed into the palms of her hands.

Dirty hands, but white enough to justify the expectation of a fat ransom.

Did Ti-Bo realize where they were, what was going on? She twisted to the rear window, to find his face up close to hers, goggling surprise on the other side of the mud-streaked glass. Then he whipped away.

"Whatcha looking for?" asked the driver.

"Excuse me." She forced a shaky smile. "Could we pull over for just a minute? I need to—to go—it won't take long, you know." She made the universal gesture of abashed embarrassment, with uplifted palms.

Her system was dry to the bone; she could not have pissed two drops if her life depended on it. But she had to stop the truck, get out, put distance between herself and the driver—exchange some word with Ti-Bo. Stand with Ti-Bo.

THE SLOWING-DOWN MUST have been sign enough for Ti-Bo. Behind her the rear window shattered with a sharp crack, sending a shower of glass slivers slicing at the nape of her neck. Ti-Bo's ropey arm, led by his small dark Glock, arrowed past her shoulder. She bent double to let the silvery blood-tinged shards slide off her skin. The shock wave surging through her had as much to do with vengeful, righteous anger as fear.

"Rete! Rete! Stop! Pull over right now, man!"

But the driver was already doing the Glock's bidding, steering the truck off onto a bulge over the sparkling coastline. Having begun the turnoff, he had to complete it. When he yanked up the brake his hand continued upward to slide inside his open shirt. *How slowly everyone moves,* she had time to think. Time wrapped around them like the cool, swaying sea. With what seemed the same deliberate measure she threw all her weight and strength and rage against the driver's arm.

Ti-Bo's Glock fired and kicked. Again and again. The explosions deafened Scobie. Glowing hot letters peppered her skin. Her head rocked and roared; her head was an iron bell no outside sound could penetrate. She watched the shattering driver's side window spew more glass.

He fell on his side across her lap, jerking and shuddering. She felt the complicated shape of his gun, still in its shoulder holster. His pinned arm began to relax against her chest. His unfurling hand stroked slowly down her right breast, dragging against her nipple. She tried to push away. Impossible. His head lay heavy on her thigh. His eyes fixed on hers while he licked and moved his lips. His eyes were a warm color, a light reddish-brown, the pupils tiny black wells. His rank odor mingled with a new smell, sickeningly rich. He was speaking rapidly, as if unaware of the dark blood blooming across his chest and welling from his cheek.

Bending closer, she was unable to make out a word. But within the alcove of her sheltering body, his heart beat. A steady *I'm here I'm here I'm here*, innocent and miraculous as the throbbing heart of a translucent newborn.

Until it stopped.

Notes

"The Age of Migration." A reference is made to the song "Smile" and its composer Charlie Chaplin, and slightly paraphrases a phrase in it.

"Far Bangalore." "Live as if you were to die tomorrow" is commonly attributed to Mahatma Gandhi, though sometimes debated.

"Bwa Teneb." A brief quotation from the African-American spiritual "Balm in Gilead" is included. The text and tune are in the Public Domain.

"Bwa Teneb." Phrases referencing baptism were loosely inspired by the language found in *The Book of Common Prayer* (1893 edition).

Acknowledgments

IN A COLLECTION spanning multiple countries, cultures, and years, each story has its own circle of supporters. Here are just some of the individuals and organizations who helped shape *The Age of Migration*.

This book is the first recipient of the annual Kevin McIlvoy Book Prize, which is sponsored by WTAW Press, and was judged by the luminous literary triumvirate of Nina Swamidoss McConigley, Joan Silber, and Peter Turchi. An honor underscored by McIlvoy's influence beyond his premature passing on the art and craft of fiction, as a writer and beloved instructor. My warm thanks go to WTAW Press publisher and editor Peg Alford Pursell for her meticulous and professional attention to every aspect of bringing this book to light.

The pioneering visual artist Vicky Colombet, collected in major museums, gave us permission to reproduce her original painting as cover art. An abstract expression of the flux and flow inside.

The months I spent in a rural Haitian hospital, during three years as a volunteer at Centre de Santé Fond des Blancs, taught me more than I can express—except through storytelling—about courage, kindness, and resilience, not to mention how to palé Kreyol. My deep gratitude to the nurses, doctors, and patients who showed me the way. Later, my work as head of the anti-poverty nonprofit Technology Exchange Lab took me to other places off the tourist maps, but on the migration trails. Stories everywhere.

Although I've taught in MFA programs, I don't hold an MFA, or a degree in English. After living abroad since my teens, I found in the US a mentor in the brilliant André Dubus II. André opened my eyes and ears to the searing potential of the short story. For two and a half years I was part of a group of acolytes meeting at his home. Salut to Jessica Treadway, Debra Spark, Jim Thomson, André III, Chris, Jack, and all the Thursday Nighters.

Without the individuals who have encouraged and published my short-form writing, this book wouldn't exist. The following stories were first published in different form in the cited journals: "The Age of Migration" (*Ploughshares*), "Mrs. Trefoil's Parlor" (*The New England Review*), "The Toubaab" (*Consequence*), "Evangeline, or Theories of Childhood Development" (*The Iowa Review*), and "Ursa Major" (*Prime Number Magazine*). My abiding thanks to the respective editors—Ladette Randolph, Heather McHugh, Cat Parnell, Harry Stecopoulos, and Joseph Mills.

Editors Sven Birkerts, Bill Pierce, Megan Sexton, and Askold Melnychuk have given other pieces, not included in this volume, an equally warm welcome.

Recently it dawned on me that through the magic of the writing life, one gathers amazing writer-friends. For their critiques, wit, and courage in these difficult times, high-fives to Margot Livesey, Pam Painter, Elizabeth Searle, Karen Chalfen, Missy Allen, Martin Edmunds, Nick Delbanco, Nick Owchar, Mike Mee, DeWitt Henry, Askold Melnyczuk, and Wilton Barnhardt, to name only a few. And *salut!* to fellow members of The Paris Writers Group: fearless leader Mary Duncan, Tim Smith, Keith Crawford, Laurel Zuckerman, Silver Wainhouse, and all the merry gang on the Left Bank.

Finally, thanks to my family. My parents, who sent me and my brother to sea at an early age in an ocean of books, and my own grown children, who continue the tradition with their kids. We are all travelers.

photo credit: Tom Dodge

About the Author

KAI MARISTED's books include *Out After Dark, Broken Ground,* and *Belong to Me.* Her work appears in *AGNI, Ploughshares, The Iowa Review,* and other journals. A translator and playwright, she has taught at Emerson College and the Warren Wilson MFA Program for Writers. She lives in Massachusetts and Paris.

About WTAW Press

WTAW Press is an independent, not-for-profit publisher devoted to discovering and publishing exceptional literary works of prose. WTAW publishes a carefully curated list of titles across a range of genres (literary fiction, creative non-fiction, and prose that falls somewhere in between), subject matter, and perspectives.

WTAW's publishing ventures include the annual Kevin McIlvoy Book Prize, the Alcove Chapbook Series, and the imprint Betty.

As an independent nonprofit literary press, WTAW depends on the support of donors. We are grateful for the assistance we receive from organizations, foundations, and individuals. WTAW Press especially wishes to thank the following individuals for their sustained support.

Antonia Albany, Nancy Allen, Lauren Alwan, Atlas Anderson, Robert Ayers, Andrea Barrett, Janet Berk, Shelley Blanton-Stroud, Cathy Borders, Mary Bonina, Vanessa Bramlett, Lawrence Brewster, Colleen Busch, Harriet Chessman, Melissa Cistaro, Mari Coates, Kathleen Collison, Martha Conway, Michael Croft, Janet S. Crossen, R. Cathay Daniels, Ed Davis, Katrina Denza, Carol Dines, Walt Doll, Ilze Duarte, Carolyn Duffy, DB Finnegan, Luke Fletcher, Joan Frank, Helen Fremont, Stephanie Fuelling, Nancy

Garruba, Michelle Georga, Ellen Geohegan, Rebecca Godwin, Stephanie Graham, Catherine Grossman, Christina Guillen, Teresa Burns Gunther, Annie Guthrie, Katie Hafner, Susan Hahn, Christine Hale, Daniel Handler and Lisa Brown, Jo Haraf, Adrianne Harun, Fran Hawthorne, Virginia Holst, Gretchen Horn, John Horton, Lillian Howan, Yang Huang, Janis Hubschman, Joanna Kalbus, Alice Kaltman, Karen Kates, Susan Keller, Caroline Kim-Brown, Scott Landers, Ksenija Lakovic, Evan Lavender-Smith, Della Leavitt, Jeffrey Leong, The Litt Family Foundation, Margot Livesey, Karen Llagas, Mardith Louisell, Jacqueline Luckett, Nancy Ludmerer, Neal Lulofs, Jean Mansen, Louise Marburg, John Masker, Sebastian Matthews, Grace Dane Mazur, Kate Milliken, Carolina Morales, Stewart and Barbara Klein Moss, Scott Nadelson, Betty Joyce Nash, Susan Neville, Mary Ann Newman, Miriam Ormae-Jarmer, Cynthia Phoel, John Philipp, Alison Powell, Lee Prusik, Gail Reitano, Dorothy Rice, David Ruekberg, Joan Silber, Michael Silva, Charles Smith, Michael C. Smith, Christy Stillwell, Marian Szczepanski, Kendra Tanacea, Karen Terrey, Renee Thompson, Martha Toll, Pete Turchi, Karen von Bismarck, Monona Wali, Genanne Walsh, Judy Walz, Sharon White, Meghan Williams, Tracy Winn, Rebecca Winterer, Heather Young, Rolf Yngve, Olga Zilberbourg

To find out more about our mission and publishing program, or to make a donation, please visit wtawpress.org.